"I don't understand!"

This was Torres, a little distant as her voice came through Tuvok's open combadge channel. *"This should be working . . . I'm running a system-wide diagnostic—"*

As if they had time for that. Janeway turned, and looked at Chakotay, letting the worry show. "We've got to hold on," she said. "Take all the power you need. Shut systems down anywhere you can."

His eyes widened with doubt. "I'll push the envelope."

The ship shuddered again, a violent punching sensation that came up through the deck under the captain's feet and drilled through her legs and up her spine.

"Hold on," she murmured.

"Captain!" Harry Kim shouted. "I'm reading phaser fire on deck nine! Crew quarters!"

"Security, seal off deck nine!" Ransom. Doing what Chakotay implied he might—what Janeway herself might do in this situation. But how?

STAR TREK VOYAGER®

EQUINOX

A novel by Diane Carey
Based on "Equinox, Part I and II"
Teleplay by Brannon Braga & Joe Menosky
Story by Rick Berman & Brannon Braga
& Joe Menosky

POCKET BOOKS
New York   London   Toronto   Sydney   Tokyo   Singapore

This book is a work of fiction. Names, characters, places and incidents are products of the author's imagination or are used fictitiously. Any resemblance to actual events or locales or persons living or dead is entirely coincidental.

An *Original* Publication of POCKET BOOKS

POCKET BOOKS, a division of Simon & Schuster Inc.
1230 Avenue of the Americas, New York, NY 10020

A VIACOM COMPANY

STAR TREK is a Registered Trademark of Paramount Pictures.

This book is published by Pocket Books, a division of Simon & Schuster Inc., under exclusive license from Paramount Pictures.

ISBN: 0-671-04295-5

First Pocket Books printing October 1999

10 9 8 7 6 5 4 3 2 1

Printed in the U.S.A.

EQUINOX

PROLOGUE

"Is it alive?"

"I don't care. I'm eating it anyway."

Sweat mixed with metal shavings grated against the captain's hand as he rubbed the back of his neck. Whatever it was, they were all going to eat it, down to the last dirty crew member still alive on his ship.

Funny how hunger could make the grotesque palatable.

He glanced at his first officer. The usually good-looking Max Burke, Casanova of the ship, lounge-lizard extraordinaire, was today a pathetic sight. His dark hair was dirty, black eyes sunken with fatigue and hunger, his face shadowed, unshaven. Attention fixed on his bowl, he plowed through the questionables handed him by their exotic Ankari hosts as if his captain's "I don't care" were a direct order to consume. Burke was the last to eat.

He'd been busy until now securing the ship from the last deadly encounter.

Behind them, Noah Lessing and Marla Gilmore checked a pile of cargo containers and other equipment for harmful emissions. The Ankari didn't have much to spare, but they were willing to offer.

And who in his right mind would turn down a dinner with big caterpillars who wore suits?

Across the campfire from the two officers, one of the Ankari waved its idea of a hand.

"Captain Ransom," the universal translator struggled, "we gift you ritual. You spirit like."

Accepting a glance from Burke, Ransom paused, then said, "We ritual . . . appreciate. We thank."

Burke muttered privately around his mouthful, "You sure we're not the ritual? Maybe they're . . . y'know, fattening the—"

"Shh. Hope not."

The two puff-faced Ankari who had the job of entertaining the visitors now revealed a device made of a dozen metallic tubes with their tops cut on the diagonal like organ pipes—or was it a device? It could've been a bottle of window cleaner. Inside was a gelatinous liquid that shifted from blue to green.

"Blast from the past, Rudy," Burke said, attempting a smile. "It's a lava lamp. I always wanted one."

Ransom also smiled and nodded at the two aliens. "Beautiful. Thank you for showing us."

The aliens paused, blinked at each other, then seemed—if he read segmented body language right—to shrug. Now they activated the device.

"Fortune spirit," the Ankari on their right buzzed. "Realm far, you travel bless."

"Oh, I get it," Burke grumbled, and went back to eating.

"Very generous of you," Ransom told the aliens.

The device was blinking now, its colors shifting.

"Ow!" Burke dropped his plate and covered his ears. An instant later Ransom heard it too—a head-splitting noise, a single tone, as if the highest note on a church organ were stuck on superworship.

Behind them, the rest of the crew flinched and tried not to react in a negative way despite the howling noise shearing their ears.

Ransom was about to wave the aliens to stop their "gift"—that it was lovely, more than generous, he and his crew just didn't deserve such a wonder—when a thread-thin black line appeared in midair over the campfire.

Beside him, Burke flinched. Ransom held him back with a trembling hand. *Wait.*

The black line parted as if a scalpel had cleaved it, giving presence to a fissure in the air above them and then to a bulb of phosphorescent blue light. From an inconceivable backstage curtain, a fluid form appeared; free moving and independent, it pierced through the fissure. Green—blue?—with some kind of face, two paws, and a short tail. Built for swimming?

In his biologist's mind, Ransom instantly analyzed the "spirit." Head at one end, tail at the other, floating upright, clutching hands—was that an opposable thumb? He couldn't tell.

The hands were knobby-knuckled and in repose. Average skull formation for gravity conditions, so it wasn't space-evolved . . . but it floated freely in spite of no visible antigrav hovering mechanism.

Back to the swimming hypothesis?

Otherworldly and translucent, the moving form slipped over the campfire and bansheed its way to an open place between two trees. There it floated, angelic and perplexing.

"Is it alive?" Ransom murmured.

Moving very slowly, Max Burke brought his tricorder around. "I dunno . . . but I'm going to eat it anyway . . ." The tricorder bleeped softly.

The alien form flittered with what might be electrical energy—might not.

"Not a spirit," the first officer finally concluded. "Nucleogenic matter . . . no—antimatter! High levels radiating right now."

"Now? In the same physical space with matter?" Ransom asked.

Burke shook his head at what he was reading. He had no answer. Here they were, and there it was.

"Life form?" he pressed. "Not an illusion?"

"Seems to be some kind of life," was all Burke would say.

Swirling merrily through the air around them now, the liquid animal danced like an ocean wave come inland for a visit, then lost dimension and slipped back into its scalpel cut.

The rift healed clean.

In his stomach Ransom's unidentified dinner crawled

around as if he'd forgotten to chew it. At his side Burke reviewed the graceful visitation on his tricorder screen, running analysis after analysis, his black brows flaring higher with every pass.

The Ankari hosts rocked with pleasure. They were proud of themselves for the show. Ritual, whatever.

Ransom cleared his throat. "You thank," he managed. "Pretty."

"Bless pretty voyage," one of them said. "Bless ship *Equinox*."

"You thank," he said again. When the two aliens got up and moved away, apparently satisfied that they'd been hospitable, Ransom kept an eye on them but spoke to Burke. "Max . . . what've you got? Brain-waves? Language? Anything?"

"It . . . I don't . . . does this make sense?" Burke showed him the tricorder readings. "If we could hang on to this for a few minutes . . . think of it! Look at the enhancement!"

"Shh," Ransom halted. "Let's do this by the book."

"We left the book in the Alpha Quadrant! Rudy, if we could contain this, the power flux—"

"Shh. Give me a chance to talk to our friends. Keep the crew working. Get that stuff loaded. Let me just talk to them . . ."

"It's inside!"

Over the single-toned whine made by the Ankari cylinder, Marla Gilmore's triumphant cry buzzed fiercely through the research lab aboard *U.S.S. Equinox*. Her thick blond hair fell forward over her shoulder as she leaned closer to the containment chamber's controls.

The lab was small, dim, and damaged, still stinking of fried electricals from the last time they'd had to fight their way out. Ransom worried that he was getting too used to that stink. If this worked, the cozy old ship would get a heck of a cleanup.

At first the fluid-creature was passive, exploring the multiphasic containment chamber Gilmore had built. It seemed curious, moving around it in a looping circle to every side, every corner.

Nearby, Max Burke furiously fed readings into the engineering link computer and the med link. The med link showed no change, but the engineering link flashed and its readings sped too fast to follow. That was one happy computer.

If Captain Ransom had entertained any doubt that the swimmer was indeed alive, that dissolved in a sudden screech. It realized it was trapped inside the containment chamber. Its green skin darkened to blue, and it began to thrash from side to side, up and down, screaming louder.

Burke's voice cracked as the containment field spiked. "Something's wrong."

"Rudy!" Marla Gilmore backed away from the chamber, horrified.

The creature's cranial membrane parted just as the fissure doorway had. Terrible features broke through the egg-yolk membrane, hideous features recognizable anywhere in the universe as threatening. As they watched, breathless, the creature imitated everything from horns to fangs to feathers as it splashed around the inside of the chamber.

"Get it out of there," Ransom ordered.

Burke's whitened hands worked on the controls. The alien cylinder's colors washed, but nothing happened to free the creature trapped inside the chamber.

Its screaming got louder, its thrashing more desperate.

"Send it back!" he shouted over the maddening whine.

"We can't . . ." But Burke worked faster, his desperation peaking with the creature's. Sweat sheeted his swarthy face, making him look old.

"Oh, God!" Gilmore's hands clamped over her mouth.

Inside the chamber, the creature went into some kind of convulsion, heaving its insides out all over the chamber walls until it finally slumped and its shrieking died to a low whine. As they watched, unable to activate the Ankari cylinder to take the creature back as easily as they had brought it here, the creature withered to half its size and began to desiccate before their eyes.

Nauseated, Marla Gilmore blinked at the chamber she had been so proud moments ago to have built. She clutched her arms to her chest, hands clenched, her expression pitiful.

Digesting the facts faster, Ransom stepped to the chamber wall and watched the last drying phase of the creature's death. "Max, is it dead?" he asked.

Burke indulged in a hopeless sigh. "Yeah. Something about the multiphasics. Those membranes can't take it.

If we could've held it here just a couple of minutes, the nucleogenics might . . . might . . ."

When his voice faded off, Ransom looked at him. Burke was peering into his screen.

"Max?" Ransom prodded. "Come on, give."

Parting his lips to speak, Burke was only able to offer a panting excitement that brought back the sweat beads on his forehead. "Rudy—it's still here!" He held a hand toward the monitor as if pointing out a window. "The enhancement properties are lingering!" Fiercely he swiveled to his captain. "Let me test the remains! Give me the authorization for autopsy!"

"What if it's sentient?" Gilmore protested.

"That doesn't matter now!" Burke reacted to an argument not yet made. "It's dead, Marla. Rudy, it's dead—"

"And there's no information so far that it's intelligent," Ransom agreed. "We tried everything. It was like trying to communicate with a cat."

Burke slipped from his chair and stood up. "There's a time limit here."

Effectively prodded, Ransom nodded.

"Do it."

As Burke rushed to his work on the bubbling corpse, Ransom turned to Marla Gilmore, quaking at his side.

"If you're lost at sea, you eat fish," he told her. "If this is what we think it is, then we've got a ticket out of the Delta Quadrant. Paroled . . . from a mighty long sentence."

CHAPTER

1

OR A SENTENCE TO BROIL IN HELL.

Science vessel, mouth of hell . . . explain the difference.

His vision blurred from a scalp wound on his forehead, Captain Ransom gripped the arms of his command chair and endured another shattering energy punch on his ship's shields. In his periphery he saw sparks blow forward from some unfortunate console behind him, but he didn't turn to look. Uncontainable free-roaming energy fractured the deflectors again.

He murmured an encouragement to the ship. Despite constant punishment, tough old *Equinox* was still standing up to the torture of unseen attack time after time. If only there were another ship to shoot at—a solid target would be so much easier for him and the crew to understand, to focus upon.

Red Alert flashed relentlessly. He kept meaning to turn it off. They were almost always at Red Alert these days. The flashing didn't help. They were beyond panic.

The ship, too, was in electrical panic, as if it actually knew. Racing along at high warp while under siege, the sturdy science vessel heaved itself forward on a spatial plane, spitting and clawing its way along while her shields sparkled in destruction's grip.

Rudy Ransom was dully aware of the crew members around him rushing from station to station, covered with grime, frayed to the last nerve ending, every one of them doing double duty every day—John Bowler, Dotty Chang, Ed Regis. There was Max Burke, of course, doing his best to fill the shoes of exec, even though his specialty was tactical, and he hadn't been ready for promotion. Some promotion . . .

Ransom winced in empathy as Burke tripped on a peeled-back piece of hull plating, his foot snagged in a dent. Chunks of debris swung on frayed cables from the ceiling, unrepaired, not even cut out of the way. Exposed circuitry sizzled brutishly. Scorched bulkheads smoked and smelled. Ransom sniffed, hoping for a molecule of fresh air. Dreams, dreams.

Staying in his chair, Ransom resisted the urge to help Burke to his feet. The crew didn't need to feel more helpless than they already were.

Burke staggered up and plunged to the nearest monitor. "Shields at twenty-nine percent!"

"Twenty-nine down, or down to twenty-nine percent left?" Ransom asked.

Burke's face was a blot of white against the dark bridge. "Down *to* twenty-nine percent! They're breaking through!"

The back of Ransom's hand swept a dribble of blood out of his eye. It was hot, gluey. "Let them."

Through a gush of brown smoke, Burke looked at him. "Sir?"

"Take the shields off line and recharge the emitters. That'll bring them back to full power."

Burke digested the idea, but hesitated. "The charging cycle takes forty-five seconds. We'll be vulnerable."

"We'll be dead if we don't get those shields back up." Ransom glanced around at the whole bridge crew, meeting eyes with as many as possible. "Arm yourselves."

Those two words, horrible and hated, doomed them to the next few minutes. He never said, "Red Alert" anymore. He said, "Arm yourselves."

Crew members stepped quickly around and over the blast-curled machinery and circuit guts spread across the deck, grabbing phaser rifles and hand phasers that hadn't seen the inside of a weapons locker in months. Burke struck a button on the console where he leaned. The "Arm yourselves" button for the lower decks.

Give them all a few seconds. Hold back. Hold on. Ransom himself stood up and shouldered his own rifle. So few people were on the bridge anymore . . . he worried about the crew down in engineering.

Only five people down there right now. When would they get a chance to sleep again?

His chest constricted at the responsibility. He was

batting about sixty:forty with this kind of order, wild chance, daring risk. Not too good. Bad odds.

When everyone he could see was ready, armed and alert, he counted off five more seconds on behalf of the lower decks, then sharply ordered, "Drop shields!"

Burke struck his controls.

Shields down. Ransom read that in Burke's stance as the first officer worked with his left hand while holding a phaser in his right. Everyone held still, except for heads swiveling, eyes flashing, chests heaving.

The dissonant otherworld frequency began as softly as a mosquito's whine, then speared up to an eye-popping squeal. Louder, louder! Invasion!

"Recharge cycle?" Ransom asked, keeping his eyes moving.

"Thirty seconds!"

Would they beat it?

What a way of life. This was like being caught in a spider's web, being able to rush from thread to thread, only to be caught on each one, to face breaking away again, to get caught again, *and* the spider didn't like them.

The crew swept their weapon muzzles in short arcs, trying to keep each other out of the lines of fire. The otherworldly whine screwed their feet to the deck, hammering their skulls from inside. From his position in the middle of the bridge, Captain Ransom was the first to see the hideous inevitability.

"There!" He swept his phaser rifle clear of Burke's head, aimed at an opening fissure in midair near the ceiling. The rip expanded as the captain aimed. Sweat squished between his hand and the phaser grip as he opened fire.

Burke ducked out of the way as half the remaining ceiling crashed to the deck where he'd been standing. While the fissure opened, Ransom kept firing at it, consumed with frustration as he saw another glowing ragged-edged fissure open behind Burke, and a third behind Chang.

The noise, louder now! Combined whining from three fissures, enough to drive a man to screaming. The phasers—more whining, howling added to the unnatural scream of the alien invaders—and bright, blinding heat rays demolishing everything they touched. Phasers on kill, scoring the interior of the bridge. They'd lost a crew member last week in sweeping friendly fire.

All around Ransom, the crew swung to fire again and again at the bulblike fissures opening above them. Not enough time. Burke, over there, still frantically working—

"Time!" Ransom demanded.

"Ten seconds!"

More screaming, but this time it was the panicked horror of human screams that rang with such poignance on the captain's human ears. This sound, by far, was more ghastly than the shriek of the alien invaders. Here they came!

Through the rifts, racing with demonic speed, the translucent, slug-tailed aliens batted around the bridge. Two, three—Ransom lost count almost instantly. The aliens entered a blindingly fast holding pattern for enough moments to notice, then split up.

Each one targeted a human. Wildly, Ransom squeezed the rifle's firing pad. The phasers squealed, harder and hotter. The overhead formation of wraiths broke. Green haze flashed around the bridge, distorting the crew's senses like strobe lights in a bar.

Attack!

CHAPTER

2

"WE'VE GOT A DISTRESS SIGNAL, CAPTAIN."

"Isolate."

"You're not going to believe this. I don't believe it—"

"Well, Chakotay, let me see it and we'll decide later to believe it or not."

Even through her own calm words, Kathryn Janeway caught a hint of nervousness. She knew what he saw, and she didn't believe it either. Federation distress frequency, here! Sixty thousand light-years from Federation space. Was someone baiting them?

The *Starship Voyager* had answered plenty of distress calls in the past five years, a tricky and haunting decision in itself for the captain of a powerful ship. Was it interfering to answer a call for help in a quadrant where the Federation had no authority? She didn't know. So she had made her own policy and always answered, sometimes to the good, other times . . . other results.

But this signal might as well be coming from her own ship—a Starfleet vessel where no Starfleet vessel should be, stranded impossibly far from home, on a constant quest to fulfill her duty to get home.

"Captain Ransom! . . . The Equinox! . . . *Under attack! . . . assistance!"*

Chilling. She hunched her shoulders. No—relax. The crew was watching.

Chakotay's shadow fell across her, warm and comforting as always, his wide shoulders bearing so much of her burden that Janeway sometimes enjoyed the temptation to shift it all to him, to have a captain again instead of always being one.

Around them the security of the starship provided a nest of safety in a hostile quadrant. The ship was in arguably good shape after a couple of lucky trades in the past month or so. As the screen struggled to focus before her, she became insecure in her privilege.

Before her an image crackled, its transmission damaged at the source.

A captain in trouble, rocking with violence in his command chair, begging for help in a quadrant without a heart.

"Captain Ransom! The Equinox! . . . *under attack! . . . assistance—"*

A Federation vessel? Not here, not a science ship, at this distance. It had to be a sensor echo or a malfunction. Janeway parted her lips, about to ask for a systems check, but Chakotay would already have done that. She held her tongue rather than insult him.

Instead she looked to her other side, to Seven of Nine. The lovely and terminally stoic young woman was coldly playing the message. Seven glanced at the captain, picked up a nuance, and muted the sound.

Together they watched the terror on the screen, saw the panicked crew rushing behind their desperate captain as he crumpled into his chair and pressed his shoulders into its backrest, his expression carved with rage as he fired his phaser rifle again and again.

"Ransom," she murmured. "He was in command of a science vessel. The *Equinox* . . ."

"The distress call was transmitted approximately fourteen hours ago," Seven reported.

Janeway narrowed her eyes, about to ask the most important question, but Chakotay spared her by answering it himself. "Three point two light-years."

That tied it. No echo.

Janeway's heart jumped, then pounded. Three light-years! She forced her breathing to remain normal. "Try to get a fix on their position."

Excitement—discovery! Friends! After five years of exile, of alien faces, confined to the halls of their own ship and no other, no equals, no comrades. Five years.

"What are they doing in the Delta Quadrant?" Again, Chakotay, with the operative question that Janeway preferred to have the answers for, yet did not.

In her elegant innocence, Seven posed a logical, if naive theory. "Perhaps they're searching for *Voyager*."

As her heart kept thundering, Janeway squeezed

one hand closed, tightly, and willed an outer calm. "The *Equinox* is a Nova-class ship. It was designed for planetary research, not long-range tactical missions."

She met Chakotay's eyes. There she read the concerns haunting her. Was this a trick? A lure?

Beneath his tribal tattoo, Chakotay's eyebrow crooked in silent understanding. He would check that too.

Without a word, he turned and hurried out of the room, heading for the auxiliary sensors to make a thorough defensive scan. He'd do a thorough job. Soon there would be answers.

She needed answers. The whole thing sounded wrong. *Equinox* was strictly an information-gathering ship, no assault capabilities other than basic shields and a few stern-chasers for defense. What was it doing so far away from charted space?

"Did you know this individual?" Seven asked, always probing, asking the kind of questions most of the crew knew better than to ask their captain at moments like this.

"Only by reputation," Janeway accommodated, never holding Seven's ignorance against her. "He was an exobiologist promoted to captain after he made first contact with the Yridians."

"Species six-two-nine-one," the girl said. "The Collective determined that they were extinct."

"So did the Federation. Ransom proved otherwise. I always wanted to meet him. Too bad it won't be under better circumstances."

"I look forward to meeting him as well. And his crew. I wish to expand my knowledge of humanity."

Glancing at her, Janeway tried not to make too big a deal out of Seven's lingering alienness. The girl was human, but had so long been infected by the cyborg horror that she still acted as much machine as alive.

"Let's hope you get the chance," the captain said simply.

Seven's large eyes flickered with a brief flash of life. "I've got their coordinates," she offered, taking refuge in data. "Heading two-five-eight, mark twelve."

A Federation ship broadcasting a distress call! Purpose surged through Janeway such as she hadn't felt in years. This was her real job, the thing she'd been charged to do, the duty for which her oath had been sworn—to protect and defend Federation assets, property, and personnel in space. For five years every decision had been troubling—should she go, should she ignore, should she contact. Always a trick to make the choice to respond.

But not today! For the first time since they'd been flung away from Federation space and trapped in the Delta Quadrant, there was no doubt about *Voyager*'s charge.

Her heart started bumping again. She touched the controls, freezing the redundant distress call.

"Set a course, maximum warp. Go to Red Alert."

Seven moved away immediately to carry out the order. That was all Janeway had to do—speak, and they would obey. A captain's privilege to offset the burden.

For the first time since she could remember, she worried not for her own crew but for another ship's leader lost in the Delta Quadrant. She peered at the frozen face of the man on the small screen.

"Hang on, Captain," she murmured.

Tense hours linked the frazzled distress call to the first glimpse of a troubled ship on the sensor horizon. All the first-watch officers were here, some who should have been asleep. Word had rocketed through the ship that another Federation vessel—even a Starfleet vessel—had called out in the vast empty night. They'd found a long-lost brother.

Everyone was here who had an excuse to be on the bridge. Janeway could've cleared the bridge, probably should have, but her own sentimentality stopped her. They deserved a moment like this.

Only her quietly roiling stomach warned of how quickly things could go sour. Chakotay sat at her side, his hands nervously gripping the chair. He hadn't been able to confirm the bona fides of the distress call or even to pick up definite emission signatures to confirm that this was a Federation ship. It could be a clever fake. He didn't like that. Chakotay wasn't one who really liked flying blind.

After five years of trouble and strife, Janeway was willing to take the chance of being trapped just to give her crew a taste of their old life—answering a friendly cry for help in the distance as they had all signed up to do. Even if things went wrong, they had had this momentary taste of their old cause.

Tom Paris had the helm—he'd pulled rank on the

watch officer. Harry Kim manned his own station. Tuvok on the sensors, B'Elanna Torres at tactical, Seven of Nine manning the science readouts, and Neelix here for no good reason except maybe to recognize his own quadrant's bad guys if this were a trick. Other crew, who were actually supposed to be on this watch, puttered around the bridge's upper deck, pretending they weren't bothered by the invasion from the other watch. Captain's prerogative, they knew, but still . . .

Even The Doctor was here, wearing the mobile emitter that allowed his holographic program to roam the ship instead of being confined to sickbay. Janeway had come to like having him around, as if he were a living physician rather than just a particularly quirkish learning hologram.

Janeway deliberately didn't glance around. That would've made them all self-conscious. Everyone else on the ship wanted to be here, too, she knew. Even joy had its limitations.

"We're approaching the coordinates." Tom Paris' voice had a forced control about it.

"Take us out of warp," she ordered.

"I've got them!" Kim let it all out. "Two thousand kilometers off the port bow! They're moving at low impulse."

Janeway frowned. Low impulse?

"Intercept," she said, then resisted the urge to tell Paris not to move too sharply or a ship *Voyager*'s size could plow over the other one like a bulldozer. "Tuvok, can you get a visual?"

The forward viewscreen showed only open space,

but in their minds they could already see the other ship. Everybody had checked the banks. They all knew what a Nova-class ship looked like: clamshell primary hull, simple engineering hull, two nacelles, a little squatty. Average.

Until today. On this particular day, at this hour, the little *Equinox* had her moment in the sun. She was the nearest handhold to home for the lonely *Voyager* crew, who almost never got to see their own ship from the outside. Now they could look out into unfriendly space and see a vision of themselves, brushstrokes of home in the form of a familiar design.

The first shape they saw with their naked eyes, though, wasn't the lines of Starfleet engineering. Instead it was an energy bulb fractured with blue and white demolition. Full shields, under assault.

Janeway leaned forward in her chair, squinting.

Now she could see the ship itself, veering toward *Voyager* on a Z-plane.

"They're heavily damaged," Tuvok reported, not nearly as Vulcan-stiff as usual. "Multiple hull breeches . . . warp drive is off-line—"

"What's happening to their shields?" Neelix interrupted.

"They're being disrupted," Torres answered, reading her engineering monitor, "by some kind of energy surges."

A simple statement, but to Janeway it said much more. Disruption meant assault. Surges of energy were different from shots or sabotage. It meant there was an unseen force acting upon the other ship. She was glad

Voyager had maintained Red Alert, all shields and precautions on-line. No visible enemy didn't mean no enemy.

"Weapons fire?" Paris asked.

Tuvok shook his head, even though Paris wasn't watching him. "There are no other ships in the vicinity."

"We're in hailing range," Kim reported tensely. Janeway could tell he was an instant from hailing them himself.

"Open a channel," she told him. He already had it open. All right, then. "This is Captain Kathryn Janeway of the Federation Starship *Voyager.* We're responding to your—"

"Voyager! *You've got to extend your shields around our ship! Match the emitter frequency!*"

Making one attempt at confirmation, Janeway asked, "Are you under attack?"

"Shields! Quickly!"

No hello, no formality, no nuthin. Save my ship.

She knew that tone.

"Do it."

Now the crew had something to do. Paris had to maneuver the starship directly above the science vessel to make full use of the shield dome. On the viewscreen they could see the shape of *Equinox,* about half the size of *Voyager,* engulfed in the fracturing bulb of her own shields. Tuvok had to gauge and calculate the assault in order to modulate the starship's shields to repel the level of attacking energy. Torres worked to reroute necessary power to the grid. Kim made sure the way before them was clear of meteoritic obstacles or gas clouds that would only make things harder.

Chakotay kept a close watch on the detail monitors at his chair's access, while Janeway watched the overall scene. Neelix sent his best good wishes across the gulf of space.

"We're in position," Paris reported.

Tuvok, at the same time, said, "I'm matching their shield frequency."

Janeway ticked off the seconds. She could order them to work faster, but why? Her ears were ringing. Anticipation? A midshipman's reaction. She tried to get control over it, but the whine only got worse.

Behind her, then, The Doctor's voice, talking to someone else on the upper deck—"Do you hear something?"

That was no ringing in the ears. Malfunction?

Janeway spun around, but Seven was already working the problem.

"Interspatial fissures are opening on decks ten, six . . . and one!"

Janeway turned again. "Tuvok!"

He didn't look up or respond at all. His large hands played on the controls with swift intensity. That was his way of responding.

The shields' activation lights blinked red, orange, then went to green. On the monitors around the bridge, schematics of the *Voyager*'s deflectors engulfing the *Equinox* as well as the starship made a big theoretical bulb in space. The attack was forced back by the starship's considerable power—whatever the attack was.

"Shields are holding," Tuvok told them.

"The fissures?" Chakotay asked, implying that he might be seeing something on the detail monitors that Janeway couldn't see on the large screen.

She was glad he was here.

"No sign of them," Seven answered.

After a moment of relief for all, Janeway pressed forward. *"Voyager* to Ransom. Captain?"

Her chest constricted. No response. Not a flicker. Had she failed before her rescue mission had even begun?

"Assemble rescue teams. Secure the *Equinox.* Tuvok, you're with me."

She spoke on the run toward the turbolift. If they thought she was worried, frightened, anxious—okay, so they knew her better than she liked.

The others followed her. Chakotay, Torres, Paris, Neelix, Seven, Kim, all rushing to collect tricorders, wrist beacons, hand phasers, and a medikit. The on-watch crew filtered back to their positions, allowing the primary crew to be the away team. Janeway was glad it happened to work out that way this time. She wanted her primary team to experience whatever was coming and to back her up if it went wrong.

A simple rescue mission, a Starfleet vessel. She hungered to be there.

The shields were holding. What could go wrong?

CHAPTER

3

COMMANDER CHAKOTAY LED THE AUXILIARY TEAM DOWN into the secondary hull of the science vessel, directly into the engine room. Somewhere above, the captain was picking her way through to the primary hull, heading for the bridge. They'd had to beam in down here, then split up. The *Equinox*'s primary hull had taken so much damage that they couldn't even find a beam-in point that wasn't so damaged that the sensors could't read the integrity of life support. Beam into a vacuum and you'll feel pretty silly at that last nanosecond before you die.

Beaming in—it seemed so ordinary in practice, yet today as Chakotay's body reintegrated and he could see again, there was only a hellish dimness to look upon and the whole beaming process made his skin crawl. A nightmarish tunnel laid out before him, overlaid with shadows and pulsed by the low thrum of drained power trying to come back on-line. It took him a moment to orient himself. The companionway to the warp core.

The shattered corridor might as well have been aboard *Voyager,* except that it was a little narrower. Chakotay found himself disconcerted to see this variant of his own ship so critically wrecked. This was the fate they had struggled against for five years, somehow keeping the starship through luck and pluck from looking like this.

All around him crushed and blasted electrical trunks lay open like forgotten surgery, several still snapping from their latest trial. The deck itself creaked under his feet, its structural bolts compromised by stress from the outer sections. Hull breaches hissed here and there. Not big ones, but troubling to see. This was a ship in trouble—Chakotay knew even instinctively—punctuated by the smell of leakage and burning circuits. The darkness itself cloyed at his shoulders, a cold cloak for a Starfleet officer to wear on a Starfleet ship. This was heavy damage, not just the damage of one assault. Sniggering guilt came over him that the *Equinox* crew had gone through this torment all alone out here. No, it didn't make any sense.

He led the way in. Behind him, Torres, Paris, Neelix, and Kim were tight-throated and silent. They too could see the plaintive echo of themselves and their own ship in this tunnel of horrors.

As he stepped carefully, tripping twice, shining his wrist beacon garishly through the wreckage, Chakotay raced through a sudden recollection of raiding a junkyard when he was twelve. He'd climbed the wrong pile and been trapped under a crushed runabout hulk. The yard's Rottweiler found him and barked until somebody came. Beating back images of losing a foot to a big dog, he picked his way forward. His beacon wobbled as he fielded a shiver through his arms and back.

It was cold! But only in the first corridor section. As he moved into the main engineering area, a curtain of cloying heat descended. The ship's atmospheric controls had gone wacky, completely confused.

Over there, the warp core throbbed at low ebb. Not enough power. At least it wasn't breached. Chakotay flinched inwardly as his beacon fell on something that wasn't crushed or crumpled machinery—a human body.

Dead. No life sign at all. Barely read as organic. Why?

He glanced behind him. "Split up. Neelix, the crew's quarters. Harry, Seven . . . check the tubes and conduits."

Nobody could even muster an aye, aye. He heard their careful footsteps angle off and tap away, occasionally encouraging something to crinkle or crash or clunk.

Behind him, Tom Paris pressed a little closer than necessary when Chakotay had to pause to move a wrecked insulator plate. "Sorry," Paris murmured, dry-throated. He didn't move back very much, though.

Chakotay found B'Elanna Torres in the dimness. "See if you can bring the main power on-line. Tom, stay with me."

Steeling herself in the spooky darkness, Torres headed through the ravagement to the warp core, seeming relieved to have something to do that didn't involve these bodies lying around. That was Chakotay's job.

He picked his way to the nearest fallen crew member. All his senses told him the effort was empty, but even in death he thought he'd want somebody to check, to touch him one more time, just as a futile gesture.

But this one—as the beacon fell across the face and shoulders, he didn't want to touch it. Beside him, Paris shivered.

"What happened?" Chakotay asked.

Struggling, Tom Paris raised his tricorder and worked it. "Some kind of thermolytic reaction. It desiccated every cell in his body."

What was left could rival Ramses for ugly. The eyes were gone, sunken back into the shriveled head. Darkened flesh had dried to a crust and peeled back from teeth bared in a grotesque smile. The throat was nothing more than paper skin stretched over cords, drawn drumhead tight and stretched so thin that the veins showed.

Paris turned toward the other unfortunates but paused to gather his innards. Chakotay paused with him, waiting, having a slightly easier time because he'd listened to his intuitive side and steeled himself for disaster. If the ship looked this bad, what must the crew look like?

Apparently, though, Paris had entertained higher hopes for a reunion with Starfleet brothers and sisters. Those were now crashing.

"You all right?" Chakotay asked him quietly.

Paris drew a ragged breath and pressed his lips against unconcealed nausea. "I thought we'd be able to . . ." He stopped himself, tempered down his reaction, and shook his head. "Maybe you better give me a little push."

"Only if you carry me." Rewarding him with a funereal grin, Chakotay took his elbow and accommodated with a nudge. Back to work, even if it was bad work.

"Commander!" Torres, kneeling at the warp drive's central core.

Chakotay moved to the core, then stopped to stare. What was that? Several exotic pieces of equipment had been added to the core itself—conduit, injector ports . . . almost old-fashioned, like someone had been building a core from scratch in a basement lab. Why would they refit their core?

"I can't make heads or tails of this injector manifold," B'Elanna Torres told him, frowning into her analytics. "And the dilithium matrix looks like it's been completely redesigned."

"We'll try to find one of their engineers to help us," Chakotay offered, a bigger promise than he could make good on, if the body to his left was any clue. "In the meantime, see if you can bypass the core."

She was already involved in dissecting, but managed to toss a late, "Aye, sir," his way after he'd already left.

Moving on through the lower hall, Chakotay kept his eyes swiveling over the twisted beams and plates and the cables spilled like intestines, his mind racing about what malevolence could have done so very much damage.

"Come on, Tom," he murmured as he stepped by Paris, who had found another unhappy body.

"This must've been some fight," Paris rasped, failing to find a more creative comment.

"Anything from outside that could've caused this would also have destroyed the hull," Chakotay mused. "Something invaded the ship and did this from inside."

"And I'll tell you what—look at these markings. Recognize this?"

Shining his wrist light to the point Paris indicated, Chakotay endured a moment of true denial.

"Phaser demarcations," Paris said aloud. "They were shooting full phasers in here. No holds barred. But I can't find markings of any alien weapons' discharges. Just Federation phasers."

"There's plenty of heat and radiation burns, though," Chakotay said. "Something caused it, and not phasers."

"Could be energy wash from the damage."

"It's targeted. Look at the corpses. High concentrations of burns and melting right near where they've each fallen."

Paris swung his light to the places Chakotay indicated. "That's a relief . . . at least the crew didn't go space crazy and shoot each other."

"We know that didn't happen. No phaser does . . . that . . . to a body."

"Guess I'm not thinking. Sorry again."

Offering only that funereal smile to encourage a very discouraged crewmate, Chakotay knew there was no real comfort to give and Paris didn't really expect any from him. He started to move again when Paris flinched so hard that he crashed sideways into a jumble of wreckage. Chakotay stepped toward him, but his concern was instantly wrenched away from Paris to a faint whimper deep in the pile.

He aimed his phaser there even before his wrist beacon made it. A flare panel, with its ports blown out, lay at an angle against an induction manifold readout panel. Several other strakes and twisted beams were pulled up into the same shape. Barricade.

The light sifted across the scorched metal and plastiform shapes that once had been part of a ship's inner fluidity, yet now were a bumble of salvage, cutting across shadows until it pierced the blown-out ports and ventured inside the barricade. There, the light touched a bruised cheek, a terrorized blue eye. Another eye, thankfully, and a scraggle of filthy blond hair. Uniform . . . good case of shell shock. He saw that even from out here.

"Ensign?" he encouraged.

The woman shuddered visibly, vulnerable and crushed back into a cove of anxiety. "Who . . . ?"

"I'm Commander Chakotay. *U.S.S. Voyager.*"

In very slow motion he moved the jagged-edged barricade aside and extended his hand, then waited for her to take it rather than grasping her before she was ready.

"But . . ." Her voice was shattered. "We're the only humans in the Delta Quadrant . . ."

Offering her a sad smile, Chakotay said, "That's what *we* used to think."

A comforting arm around her shoulders sent a chill

through her that Chakotay could physically feel running its course.

"What . . . what are you . . . doing . . ."

"Here? That's a big question. We have a lot of questions for each other," he said as he drew her gently to Paris.

"Well, what's this?" Paris began, trying to sound upbeat. "A stowaway?"

"I . . . I'm . . . Gilmore. Engineer's mate."

"Engineering. What luck." Paris gestured back toward the main core deck. "You can tell us something about that refit on your core—"

"That can wait a few minutes, I think, Tom," Chakotay told him. Paris looked surprised but got the message. Keeping his arm around the terrorized woman, he quietly asked, "How long have you been in the Delta Quadrant?"

"F-five years, seven months . . . two days."

Chakotay smiled again. "You sound like a Vulcan. Should I check your ears?"

His reward was a trembling grin. "I keep a diary." Her large eyes crimped sadly and a sob choked her back. "It's not . . . very nice reading."

"I'd like to read it anyway," Chakotay offered. "Let's get you to our sickbay."

Her shoulder suddenly hunched against his ribs. "This isn't real, is it? I'm hallucinating, aren't I? We're losing . . . They got in. The shields . . . we lost, didn't we? You're not here. I'm dying too. I'm dying! Poor Rudy . . . don't tell him I died . . . don't tell him."

Tears drained as her eyes crushed closed. Her arms

hung limp as she sobbed. Chakotay pulled her around to him and handed his phaser to Paris so he could get both arms around the girl. Paris' fair complexion grew russet with empathy as he met Chakotay's sad gaze. They wanted to have arrived a day earlier, to be more than just clean-up detail for this sorry and desperate crew of fellow Starfleeters. This should've been a better story.

Over the oily fluff of blond scraggle, he gave Paris a little nod. "Keep looking."

Unencouraged, Paris simply nodded back and moved past him.

Chakotay ushered the destroyed girl away from her prison barricade, which she had taken to be her tomb. No point letting her see this area until it was cleaned up. Later, much later. She had fought to her last straw, and even that had finally cracked.

They all had. He could see that, written in the phaser scorch lines all over the ship's pitiful interior.

Taking her out of the core salon into a passageway at the base of a Jefferies tube, where the bleeps of Torres' tricorder were softened by the sound-absorbing carpet, Chakotay paused and let the girl's racking sobs run their course. He didn't offer any comfort—it would've all been lies. She was destroyed, not stupid.

Voices? Where was his phaser! He almost called for Paris to come, then he realized that the voices were those of Harry Kim and Seven in the tube's secondary-level access conduit. They must be searching up there. Good idea. If he were going to hide, that's where he'd go.

Usually—but what was the *Equinox* crew hiding

from? That's what determined a good defense, and he saw no sign of the enemy here at all, except for the pure demolition of the ship's guts.

"Under here!" Harry Kim's sharp shout made Chakotay wish he were up there. He gripped the girl gently and listened.

Kim again. "Hang on . . . we're getting you out of here."

Good. They'd found somebody else alive.

"I don't . . . believe . . . we've met." A voice Chakotay didn't recognize. Sounded like the man was in pain.

"Ensign Harry Kim. This is Seven of Nine. I'm going to have to cut him out with a plasma torch. Talk to him. Keep him calm."

Then Seven's throaty voice, not really very calming, "State your name."

"Lessing . . . Noah. What are you doing on this side of the galaxy?"

"The answer is complicated."

"I don't care where you're from . . . I'm just glad you're here."

Through the tube Chakotay could hear a plasma torch sizzle to work. He resisted the urge to climb up there and help. They could handle it, he knew, and there was hardly enough room up there for another person to go banging around.

"Do me a favor," Lessing murmured. "See if my legs are still there . . . I haven't felt them in two days."

Chakotay winced and held his breath as the girl sniffed and began to recover against him. Please let the man's legs be there.

"Your limbs are intact," Seven said then, bluntly. At least it was the right answer.

"Thanks . . ."

"Seven, give me a hand over here," Kim asked then, and Chakotay got that feeling again that he should be up there.

"You will be alone for a moment," Seven's gravelly tone thrummed down the tube. "Do not be frightened."

Lessing's voice was weak but carried a thread of hope. "Too late for that."

There was a crash of fallen debris back in the main section. Paris rummaging around, probably. How many more crew were holed up in cubbies all over this pathetic ship? And the uglier question—how many were lying desiccated, mummified by whatever force had invaded the ship?

He wondered how the other search parties were doing. Neelix leading a security team to the crew's quarters. The captain . . . heading for the bridge. What would she find there? His chest constricted with concern. He knew what she dearly wanted to find and what it might mean to her to have come so close to rescuing another Starfleet ship, to finally be the big sister to other desperate Federation waifs, to do the job a starship is really meant to do rather than just race through space on a thinly veiled hope to get home.

Where was the rest of this ship's crew? There should be nearly a hundred people here. They couldn't all be hiding. They couldn't all be dead, could they? Stacked in coffinless indignity in the hold by their pitiful shipmates?

He rejected the hideous image. They were here somewhere. But where?

And where was the enemy?

Another dead one. Horribly disfigured. Teeth cracked, yellowed, offering a grotesque grin beneath dried eye sockets. Each one desiccated Kathryn Janeway's smoldering hopes a little more, and a little more.

Not all of the corpses were fully desiccated. Some bore the marks of partial mummification, others just flakes of destroyed skin tissue, as if they'd been sprayed with acid. Just as dead, though.

Her dreams of flying in like the avenging angel shriveled with each new discovery. She hadn't found a single living person yet. They weren't in the corridors or turbolifts.

Please, Chakotay, be having better luck.

And what a nightmare these corridors were. Whole door panels were blown completely off, lying smashed, cut in half, bent, crumpled, like the tons of other debris made of disembodied beams, ceiling panels, access hatches, trunk lids, and electrical guts. Much of it still hissed and fritzed, trying to keep doing whatever job it had done in life.

In life . . .

Behind her, Tuvok hadn't said a word, not a single word, since they'd left the secondary hull. That worried her. Stoicly he had followed as she led the way through the dark ship's neck, through the primary hull without the benefit of turbolifts, and finally up through the lift tube toward the bridge. Even when he stepped forward to help her pry open the lift doors that led to the bridge, Tuvok still spoke not at all.

Janeway's mind divided between the *Equinox*'s crew and her own. What were they all feeling? How awful was it to have the chance to rescue fellow Starfleet officers and have it turn out like this . . . and those like Tuvok, who left friends and family, even children, back home— for him this was a riveting slice of pure fact. He was the father of five. One child for each year he had been missing in action. Five years, and the Delta Quadrant was still unkind. Were they looking at their own fate?

She was glad Tuvok had the sense not to converse. She had nothing to say. Not yet.

The lift door squawked and actually cracked, its molecular structure somehow destabilized. Together, the captain and Tuvok stepped onto the bridge, weapons and lights first. Tuvok swept the bridge briefly with his naked eyes, then holstered his phaser and brought his tricorder up for a scan. When he cleared the area, he glanced at Janeway and gave her tacit permission to enter. At least he wasn't scanning any hostile life forms or deadly emissions. She didn't want to ask if he was picking up any life signs at all or if this was another killing field. She would see for herself. Some things were better found in person.

Someone coughed. Alive! She plowed forward, knocking her knees on wreckage, nearly stumbled, recovered, and forced herself on. Tuvok was so close behind as to come up to her side in a step. He went immediately toward the cough and got there first.

An officer . . . lieutenant, slumped over a console, just stirring back to consciousness. Sweat filmed the pasty face, but the dark eyes blinked with comprehension as the officer drew a hand across his face and stirred back to awareness of his surroundings. He blinked into Tuvok's light as if beyond shock, even at the sight of survival.

The captain . . .

Janeway lengthened her stride and vectored to the command chair. Captain Ransom—he looked dead. There was no pretty way to say it. His face was stony, frozen in a grimace, a clotted gash over his left eye, shoulders hunched, hands gripping his command chair's arms. A spent phaser rifle lay at his feet and a piece of ceiling brace had fallen across his legs. Might have been the thing that saved his life.

From what?

Anticipating the clammy chill of death as she touched his arm, Janeway flinched as the captain's eyes slitted open. He wasn't dead! Half alive, maybe, but this was something at least.

She touched his shoulder, then the side of his face as his head lolled. Alive . . . his eyes flickered at her touch.

"My crew?" Though ragged, his voice was strong with concern, even defiance. He actually wasn't done fighting.

"You took heavy casualties," Janeway reported, cloaking her own shattering spirit with protocol's cold efficiency. "We're treating the survivors."

Please don't ask about the dead ones.

"Who attacked you?" she asked, before he had the chance to think about the nonsurvivors.

"We don't know," he garbled. "We can't communicate with them. They've been attacking us for weeks . . ."

Pressing down on the chair's arms, he shoved himself to a better position, then instantly faltered and hardened with pain.

"Easy," Janeway said.

"I've got to secure the ship . . ."

"Leave that to us."

She attached a sedative marker to the side of his neck, but he roused more and swiped it off. "Treat me here," he protested. "I'm not leaving my bridge."

Warmly, Janeway smiled at his heartrending loyalty. She understood. What would she want someone to say to her?

"I can't pull rank on you, Captain," she said quietly, as if she'd known him for years. "But you're in no condition to put up a fight."

He blinked again, his eyes focusing briefly on the command pips at her collar. Four of them. Another captain. The sight seemed to ease him.

"So tell me," he managed, "how's Earth?"

Uh-oh.

Should she lie to him? Let him get a night's sleep before she told him the truth?

"I wish I could say," she admitted.

Ransom's eyes blinked and stayed open this time. Hope and faith and his estimation of what he was worth to the Federation all took a bad blow as he realized what she meant. "You weren't sent here . . . to find us?"

"I'm afraid not," Janeway said. Might as well get it over with. "We've been stranded in the Delta Quadrant for five years. We were pulled here against our will by an alien known as the Care—"

"Caretaker."

Captain Ransom sunk in his chair, comprehending the new weight upon them both.

Janeway's heart sank at his expression. She slipped her hands under his arms and got a grip on him to lift him to his feet. "We'll compare notes later. Let's get you to *Voyager.*"

"Rudy? Are you alive? It's not a dream?"

"Max . . . I thought they finally got you."

Captain Ransom slumped back in his diagnostic bed, but he reached across the short gap to the other bed and managed to catch Max Burke's wrist. Burke moved a little and found his captain's hand. Back from the dead. Suck blood now? Sleep in a coffin?

They already had been.

Ransom's legs were numb, but he could feel his toes through lingering mental and physical shock and the weakness of near starvation. Another slip through the noose just before it broke his neck. What about the others?

"How many alive?" he asked bluntly, raising his head with a struggle.

The *Voyager*'s doctor scanned him with perfunctory disinterest but seemed a little bothered by the question.

Strange—an Emergency Medical Hologram shouldn't be bothered by anything at all.

"Your crew suffered many injuries, Captain Ransom," The Doctor said. "We're treating them all." He paused, adjusted something on Ransom's treatment, then followed through on the question he couldn't avoid. "Captain Janeway will speak to you about your survivors."

His stomach cramping, Ransom squeezed Max Burke's hand, got a limited response, then let go of the grip. It would hurt only after another minute or two.

"Max, did they tell you how many?" he asked.

On the next bed, Burke closed his eyes a moment. "They only told me the captain wants to brief us when we're back to shape. I'd guess there's only a couple of handfuls of us left, Rudy. We know as well as they do what the last attack did."

A handful or two, out of a crew of eighty-seven. Four score and seven children ago . . .

He pressed his head back on the rest. "It's awful to survive," he murmured.

"Rudy," Burke groaned, "you kept us going. There wouldn't be even a handful of us left if you'd died first. Nobody would know what happened to the *Equinox*." He sighed and rubbed his thigh, apparently aching. "I'm glad we didn't end up a 'missing in action' note on some Starfleet blotter. The others deserve more than that."

The others. The dead, he meant.

Years beyond tears, Ransom let his hands tremble a moment before clenching them. He watched blankly as

The Doctor puttered around him and Burke. While this went on he tilted his head and looked past the hologram to the other beds, where he thought he could make out Noah Lessing, Marla Gilmore, and Mike Franco on other beds in the ward, unconscious or sedated. There were two more beds in his line of sight, both with bodies on them, but these were covered with thermal blankets all the way up over the faces. Hadn't made it through treatment.

He let his eyes drift shut again and tried to relax the twitching muscles in his neck. The shock of having lived when he'd given himself up for finished—he couldn't absorb it. This could all be the last-second dream before blackout.

Perhaps thinking this was prying, The Doctor administered an inoculation to Burke and said, "Excuse me, gentlemen," and disappeared into a lab, leaving them alone.

"Rudy," Burke began, lowering his voice, "do they know about . . ."

"I don't think so." Ransom lowered his voice to nearly inaudible. "The critical areas are fully contaminated. Nobody'll be able to get in there for days. That'll give us time. I have to probe out their captain's attitude."

"Look at this ship! It's so clean . . . and this bed! It's a *bed!*" Burke ran his hands down the blanket that covered his legs. His dark eyes were dull, shadowed, but hopeful. "No rips, no burns, the lights are on, smells good, heat, fresh air . . . I've never been on an Intrepid-class ship before. Have you?"

"Oh, yes." Ransom smiled. "Once, two weeks as a

science officer pro tem, and once just for a visit. At Starbase Eighty. We were receiving dignitaries from somewhere."

Burke pursed his lips, filled his lungs slowly, then indulged in a long audible sigh while gazing at the bright intact ceiling. "You know, when they found us and I started to come around," he mused, "I thought God was a Vulcan."

For the first time in months, Ransom laughed—right out loud. What a feeling! He'd completely forgotten. The muscles were so unused that laughing actually hurt. A good hurt, though, as hurts went.

A chance to live! Unbelievable! To have *help* . . . More Starfleet people—a powerful ship—assistance that meant it! Every time he closed his eyes he expected to open them to a smashed and smoldering bridge and suffocate as he watched his crew's bodies mummify in front of him, just before he started to dry up himself. But every time he opened them, this clean sickbay was still here. Max was lying beside him in the other bed. Marla, Noah, Mike still over there, resting, alive.

He couldn't believe Max made it. After the field promotion to first officer, Burke had always put himself in front of all the others when danger came. He hadn't balked once, never. He'd made himself a target to save others more times than Ransom had remembered.

Would Captain Janeway understand what they'd had to do to get this far?

As he made peace with the idea that he really was here, alive, with a handful of his brave and long-suffering crew, Captain Ransom began slowly to formulate his plans. They had to go through the motions, almost like being on shore leave with top secret information. There would be questions from *Voyager*'s captain and crew. He had to tell his own people what to say and not say, for now.

He had to think, to be ready. Just in case. *Voyager* was a paradise for them right now. He would have to prepare himself and the crew in case they had to return to hell.

CHAPTER

4

FOUR DAYS IN PARADISE. HOT MEALS, SHOWERS, CLEAN clothes, mending wounds. New people to talk to. Sympathetic eyes, encouraging smiles, hungry hearts. It really *was* paradise.

Rudy Ransom stood shoulder to shoulder with *Voyager*'s Captain Janeway and felt a camaraderie that had been lost for him. For five years he had been alone in an unlikely and unwanted command, something he hadn't trained for nor ever betted upon. It felt good to have another captain around, someone who knew what the burden was like, someone to make a few decisions for the next few days. For a few precious hours he hadn't been the one who had to do the hard thinking. His mind had actually shut down for a while, actually rested. *Voyager* was shore leave for himself and his cleaned-up crewmates over there.

They looked wonderful. He hadn't seen them clean and rested, in new uniforms . . . he couldn't remember the last time. The only thing that hadn't been erased by their days on the starship was the leftover gauntness of almost constant hunger. They were a thin crowd, the cheekbone brigade. He relished the looks of them, bunched up over there, all tidy, with their complexions coming back. Several of them were still in sickbay, still others were participating in this little ceremony by remote, from other places on the starship, in solemn privacy or with friends. He hadn't insisted they all attend. He didn't want to give them the order to be here for another good-bye.

On the other side of the mess hall lounge, Captain Janeway's primary crew stood in silent tribute. Each seemed a little proud, but a little troubled, too, as if they understood that this could easily be about them.

Ransom cleared his throat.

"We're here," he began, "to commemorate our honored dead. Lieutenant William Yates . . . Lieutenant John Bowler . . . Ensign Dorothy Chang . . . Ensign Edward Regis . . . and Crewman David Amantes served with distinction. Their bravery and sacrifice will not be forgotten. And they will be missed."

There it was—finally. The logging of commendation for all those killed in the line of duty on *Equinox.* Soon he and Captain Janeway would formally commit the posthumous medals and promotions for all those lost over the ship's long-term struggle. That would help.

The somber crews listened and controlled their nervous unease, which Ransom sensed rifling the air as he continued.

"Despite our recent difficulties, there is now cause for optimism. Thanks to Captain Janeway, and *Voyager.*" He turned to Janeway herself and added, "On behalf of my crew . . . thank you."

Janeway smiled sadly and stepped forward. "We'll have time to give the newest members of our family a proper welcome in the days ahead, but right now we've got our hands full. The *Equinox* is secure, but its primary systems are still badly damaged. B'Elanna, Harry, make it your priority. Captain Ransom has provided us with data regarding the alien attacks. Tuvok, Seven, you'll be working with First Officer Burke."

She paused, making sure they all knew which one was Burke. Then the pressing moment demanded just a little of the sentiment she had been obviously avoiding to spare them all an inevitable self-consciousness.

"To kindred spirits," she added somberly. "May our journey home together be swift. Dismissed."

Ransom met her gaze with gratitude for keeping it short, not dragging them through a diatribe about honor and duty and grandeur and goals. Those had been forgotten long ago aboard *Equinox.* Something much more fundamental had moved into the vacant house and haunted it since then.

Kindred spirits. Fellows in arms.

It was nice.

He looked across the mess hall at Max Burke, looking well fed and shaven, in fact looking younger than he ever had—or maybe they all just seemed young to Ransom now. Offering Burke a subdued smile and a— he hoped—subtle wink of warning, Ransom was careful to leave the crews alone without their captains. Janeway had already left. He did the same.

Max Burke watched his captain leave and wondered why Ransom had chosen to do that. He would rather have stayed together, take this big step with a bunch of little ones first rather than plunge headlong into . . . no way to finish that thought. No idea what was coming.

The moment was so pleasant that he hardly wanted to disturb it by moving, by talking. These angels around him would become human to him soon enough, and for a while he was enjoying thinking of the *Voyager* crew as supernatural wonders who had swooped in out of the silvery clouds to snatch him from the monster's grip.

Yes, of course, they were just doing the job they had trained for, but here, in the Delta Quadrant, for one Starfleet ship to find another Starfleet ship was way beyond routine mission. Both ships so deeply needed each other . . .

He clasped his hands and tried to appear cool, collected. He wanted to be some kind of legend to them, as much as they seemed legendary to him right now. Keep aloof, act calm, as if you damned near died every day.

Of course, on *Equinox*, they *had* damned near died every day. This still seemed like a dream.

"We should begin by familiarizing you with *Voyager*'s defenses."

"Hm?" Burke blinked. The Vulcan was standing next to him. Tumok. Trupok. Why hadn't he paid attention?

The Vulcan and Seven of Eleven were standing next to him. Now that wasn't her name, either, was it?

Start paying attention, Burke, or these people will get their guard up about you. So long since I've met anybody new—

He offered them what he hoped was a self-conscious shrug.

"Oh—can you give me a minute?" Burke responded. "There's someone I want to say hello to."

What a moment. Not only did he find himself surrounded by fellow Starfleeters, but one particular fellow . . . lady.

"We'll be in the astrometrics lab," Seven of Twelve said. "Deck eight, section twenty-nine."

"See y'there," Burke told them, but he was no longer interested in them. He hoped they understood. No, he really didn't care.

Summoning his best aplomb to cover up for nervousness and the sheer shock of being in this situation at all, he straightened his uniform, leaned forward, and managed to start walking with some kind of grace. There she was.

"BLT?" he asked. At least his voice didn't crack.

B'Elanna Torres had been eying him all this time, though the two of them had been trying to pretend, for the other's sake, that they had no more reason to call upon one another than upon anyone else. Burke, for himself, didn't want anyone to think he had some advantage here or had an old friendship to rekindle when everyone else here was starting new. What could he do? He *did* have more reason than they did.

"Max," B'Elanna responded, and she smiled.

Not an easy smile. She was glad to see him, but holding back. Why would she? She wasn't the type to hold back. Never had before.

Could it have something to do with these two other guys she was standing with?

"I tried to say hello in sickbay," she told him, "but you were sedated."

"I remember," he said. "I thought I was dreaming."

Awkward silence interrupted, finally broken when they managed a less-than-stirring embrace. Burke noticed the other two guys exchanging a glance that may or may not have been charitable.

"So where's my sweater?" Burke asked as he and B'Elanna looked at each other again. "The blue one? Class insignia on the back?"

"Oh . . ." She glanced at the other men. "Well, I'm sure it'll turn up. We went to the Academy together," she told the others in a tone that suggested she felt obligated to explain.

Burke stuck a hand toward the nearest guy. "Maxwell Burke."

"Tom Paris," the fellow said.

Then the other one seemed more willing to shake hands. "Harry Kim. Welcome aboard."

"First officer," B'Elanna commented, surveying him as if she'd never seen a uniform before. "Impressive.

The last time we talked, you were about to drop out of Starfleet."

What now? Tell her I wish I had?

"I heard you beat me to it," he said instead. "The Maquis?"

A flush of—was it embarrassment?—colored her cheeks. "For a while. Until I ran into these two."

Tom Paris got a funny expression. "It's been hell ever since."

They all smiled, but they didn't all mean it. Oh . . . now Burke started to get what was going on. This wasn't friendly banter. It was competition.

He'd have to talk to her later. Alone.

"Well, I told your resident Vulcan I'd be right there. Are you free later? I'd love to catch up."

How casual and flat the whole conversation seemed! Here he was, resurrected from certain and brutal death, and he was trying to act like a guy in a club with a bad pickup line.

"Sure!" B'Elanna said, not in the tone he'd hoped. "Why don't we all have dinner together?"

Burke might've been half dead and living in a dream world, but he wasn't a stupid corpse. Not yet, at least. She was avoiding what he was getting at. That meant the old communication was in there somewhere, and she didn't want it to come out in front of one or the other of these guys. Or both.

Nah . . . couldn't be both.

Better let her off the hook for now. There'd be time. For once, there really would be.

"Sounds great," he concluded. To Parry and Harris he said, "Thanks for having me."

"Our pleasure," the Asian guy said. Parry. Harris. Harry.

As Max Burke moved off in the direction Seven and Tuvok had gone, B'Elanna Torres folded her arms and tried to act casual under the searching glare from Tom Paris and the careful disinterest of Harry Kim.

"BLT?" Tom asked.

Hate this part. "Bacon, lettuce, and tomato," she explained, irritated. "It was a nickname. My initials."

"How romantic."

B'Elanna wanted to laugh, but this really wasn't funny, and it could be complicated. She wasn't hiding anything from Paris. He was getting it all. "We broke up over ten years ago. No need to go to Red Alert."

"How about Yellow?" he requested.

She shook her head. "You're cute when you're jealous."

"Who's jealous!"

Making a little sound in her throat, she turned to Harry and said, "I'll see you aboard the *Equinox*."

She strode off, and behind her heard Harry give Tom a clap on the back and say, "Well, 'Turkey Platter'? What do you say we get to work?"

Oh, this was going to be some experience.

"Commander!"

Chakotay turned at the call and found Ensign Gilmore trying to catch up to him without breaking into a jog. He'd noticed that about all the *Equinox* people—

they were all nervous, all holding back, trying to appear aloof and at ease while none of them really were. He couldn't blame them. They were trying to fit in, and it wasn't unusual for people to try too hard. This kind of thing would take time.

And tolerance from such as him, of course. Phasers on tolerate, full power.

"I've been assigned to one of the repair crews on the *Equinox*," Gilmore said as she came to his side in the bustling corridor.

She looked very different than the first time he'd seen her. She was one of those people who cleaned up well. Her blond hair seemed longer now that it was washed, and thicker. Her cheekbones showed more without dirt smearing her face, and her large doll-like eyes had traded in fear for worry.

There were crew moving everywhere lately, everybody busy with work about the newly discovered Starfleet ship, and the *Voyager* was more crowded with the *Equinox* crew on board. It was great.

"I was wondering," Gilmore went on, "if I could join a different team. On *Voyager*."

"Problem?" Chakotay asked. With that one word he was insisting she behave like a Starfleet crew member, giving him an analysis of her reasons for such a request—even though he knew.

She smiled nervously. "Oh . . . just a little posttraumatic stress . . ."

At least she admitted it.

"Bad memories," Chakotay understood.

"A few."

Now she was really pretending. Just a few?

"Actually," he offered, "I could use someone with your engineering abilities."

Genuinely relieved, Gilmore gave him an unencumbered smile. "Thanks."

They walked together in silence for a few paces, Chakotay hoping Gilmore would relax a little more, but maybe he was right the first time and that would be a longer process. They were all skittish. This was a big change.

"Clean ship," Gilmore seemed obliged to say.

"We do our best." He didn't pause to explain that keeping the ship clean was one of the ways they kept the crew busy during the long, long hours that composed the boring part of spacefaring, especially when the mission was just to go really far away. He didn't want her to feel as if her own existence until now had been too tragic to be worth anything—after all, she'd been somewhat busier on her own ship than just sweeping and polishing.

"I'm so used to dodging falling bulkheads," she said, "hopping over missing deck plates . . ."

Chakotay nodded, hoping to distract her from dwelling on the cloying past. "In a few weeks, you won't even recognize the *Equinox*. You'll be happy to go back."

She pressed her lips in a doubtful smile, but she was troubled by that. "Unless I decide to stay on *Voyager*."

Was she joking? No, he didn't read that at all. The veil of humor was too thin.

"You said you could use someone with my engineering abilities," she tossed off. Perhaps she realized her first comment was inappropriate.

"I don't think your captain would appreciate that," Chakotay said, and he turned the corner toward the turbolift. "He's got a skeleton crew as it is."

Ouch—shouldn't have mentioned that! Not with the condition those bodies were in when they were discovered. Slip of the tongue. He hoped she didn't notice.

They still didn't know how the "enemy" killed or even what they were. What kind of attack could cause that desiccation? Chakotay wanted to ask her, had the feeling she knew, yet had promised himself he wouldn't push these shaken-up people. They deserved a rest, not an interrogation.

Why would she want to stay? He could empathize with the way she felt about being comfortable and safe after what she'd been through, but leave her ship? Her captain?

Without exploring the questions in his mind, he let her off the temporary hook and tapped the lift controls. The door slid open instantly. One to a customer, no waiting.

He strode in, turned—Gilmore didn't follow him in. She was standing there at the vestibule but looking at the lift as if it were quicksand.

"Engineering's five decks down," Chakotay told her jovially. "It's a long crawl through the Jefferies tubes." When she mustered her will and stepped in after him, he ordered, "Deck eleven."

The lift doors closed and they were moving. He kept

watching her as she struggled to keep her anxiety under some kind of control.

She saw him watching her, saw the curiosity in his eyes, and ultimately explained, "I haven't set foot in a turbolift in over three months."

"Claustrophobia?"

She didn't seem to like the word, but didn't dispute it. "If one of those fissures opened up in here . . . where would we take cover?"

That had been her life, it seemed. Taking cover. He tried to imagine—hiding most of the time, slipping out to rebuild defenses, trying to snatch an hour of sleep, only to waken to that whining sound and an attack by something he still couldn't picture. The whole horror played in Gilmore's expressive eyes, though she was trying to hide it from him, trying to summon what was left of her shredded Starfleetness.

"We'll be out of here before you know it," he assured. Sounded empty, considering what she'd endured, though he had to try to stem her obviously mounting fear.

At the worst possible moment, just as the lift started to get a good hum under it and cruise toward deck eleven, a brief hydraulic whine disturbed the flow. Gilmore visibly flinched.

"It was only a graviton relay," Chakotay said quickly. "Nothing to worry about."

A tremulous grin disturbed the near-panic in her face. "Do I look worried?"

The sounds of the lift grew louder. Chakotay had never noticed them before. It actually did whine and hum as it got a stride. Gilmore's breath was coming in short sucks. Her hands were clenched. Just a few moments more—

"Emergency stop!"

The lift bumped to a halt. Luckily, it was almost at a deck and finished its seating before stopping. An instant later, Gilmore was out in the corridor on deck six.

When Chakotay got out there, she was trembling freely.

"If you don't mind," she shivered, "I think I'd rather take the Jefferies tube . . ."

And off she went, as if she knew where it was.

Chakotay indulged in an inward shrug and stepped after her. "I could use the exercise."

"I'm sorry if this is awkward for you, Captain Janeway, having both our crews on your ship, two captains, two first officers—"

Janeway smiled as she walked with Rudy Ransom through the tidy corridors of *Voyager* and counted her blessings. This was the fourth time he'd apologized for being a problem, getting in the way, stalling their forward progress, you name it.

"Captain, I keep telling you," Janeway said, "and one of these days you'll figure out that I'm not just being polite, it's nice to have a crowded ship for a change. Besides, it's not that crowded. New faces, new conversations, the reminder that Starfleet is really there and not just a figment of our imaginations—we're all enjoying ourselves. To do something positive for a change? I'd go out of my way for this anytime. We all would."

Ransom shook his head in reverie. "Every time we had an attack, I broadcast a distress signal on a Federation channel. I did it to make the crew feel better just for those last horrible seconds before we died. Every time we thought we'd die . . . I just wanted the last thing they heard to be their captain's voice calling for assistance from a friendly ship, even if the friendly ship never came. I wanted the last sounds to be words of hope, not just that awful whine and the screams of their shipmates dying in the corners. I never thought anybody would . . . actually answer. When *Voyager* responded," he added after a pause, "I thought I was hallucinating."

"You didn't act like that," Janeway comforted. "You responded sharply and got us over there. You told us what to do, we expanded our shields, and here you are. I'm amazed you could think so clearly after what you'd been through for so long."

"You think more clearly, not less." Ransom's voice was suddenly harsh. "Everything gets more clear."

"I'm impressed," Janeway said. "It took me most of my training to understand what a captain has to do under pressure. I trained for it, studied other captains, other situations . . . you never did that, yet you handled the situation when it faced you."

"I'm a scientist, not a battle captain," Ransom agreed. "Promotion was a surprise for me. When I discovered the Yridians, I was a science officer whose captain was in a coma. I wasn't even technically in charge of the mission. If the captain had come out of the coma instead of dying, he'd have gotten the mission credit. Instead, I got it and they gave me a ship of my own. I never expected that."

"You deserved it. You were the one who traced the Yridians and their living settlements, not your captain."

"Oh, I deserved that part," he said with a laugh. "But not a whole ship of my own. When they made me a captain, I thought they meant captain of research, not captain of a ship."

"What were you doing when the Caretaker . . ."

"Kidnapped us?"

He didn't seem as bothered by revisiting the event as Janeway thought he might be, as she sometimes was in the dark hours of off-watch.

"We were as close to safe space as we could be without sitting on top of a starbase. We were doing bio-scrapings of a comet-washed asteroid belt. Can you believe it? Simple as putting on your boots! It was a milk run. We were just learning how to fly the *Equinox*. None of us even knew the ship very well. We learned the hard way."

Janeway gestured him around a curve toward the astrometrics lab. "Science ships aren't really built to take the kind of pounding you've been enduring."

"She's a terrific ship," Ransom quickly defended. "I never knew she could take so much. She never broke down, not critically. Even with her trunks spilled and her electrical guts ripped out, she's still capable of warp speed and shields. Funny . . . when I first came on board her, I didn't really like her very much. I was used to the big Berengaria-class lab barges."

"Sometimes I think of *Voyager*," Janeway said, "as an island instead of a ship."

"Oh, not me. I'm all too aware of being on a ship in the middle of a big empty sea. *Equinox* has never seemed as secure as an island. That's where you're lucky."

"Well, now we're all lucky." Janeway offered one more smile before donning her captain-aplomb as they strode into the astrometrics lab.

Inside, Tuvok, Seven, and Maxwell Burke were at the console, studying graphics of both *Voyager* and *Equinox* on the large domescreen. The two ships were flying in formation, as indeed they were in real life, and the computer was duplicating their positions and energy emissions for purposes of analysis.

Janeway took two seconds to appreciate the loveliness of those graphics. Not only functional, they were beautiful to look upon.

Seven looked up. "I've run a thermographic analysis of our shields," she reported. Without Janeway's asking, she worked at the enhance controls, and the graphics above changed.

Dozens of hotpoints appeared and disappeared around the shield sphere that enveloped both ships, each point a crackle of violent energy as if something were trying to break through. Janeway realized with a spearing tension that they hadn't beaten off the assault—it was still going on.

"It revealed multiple stress points." Seven explained.

"We believe they're the result of alien attempts to infiltrate our vessels."

Now that that was confirmed, Janeway also noticed a certain orderliness about the flashes of hotspots. They appeared around the ship not in random order, but in a repeated sequence. As she watched, the sequence changed slightly, then repeated itself over and over again.

Tuvok stepped closer and indicated the screens. "Each time a fissure opens within a meter of our shields, it weakens them by point three percent."

Glancing now at the numbers and factors displayed by the lower consoles, Janeway looked up again at the graphic display and felt her whole nervous system go to Red Alert. "At the present rate, we have less than two days to mount a defense."

She wasn't just stating a fact. She was also throwing out a challenge. Someone would think of something, perhaps herself, perhaps one of the others. It was her job to prod them to think, throw the net out and see what jumped in. If she didn't, eventually the crew would get used to waiting around for her to come up with something. That was part of a captain's job too in a situation like this—stimulate and keep stimulating. Keep their minds on positive action.

Seven of Nine was the first to speak. She turned to Captain Ransom. "According to your bioscans, the aliens can only survive in our realm for several seconds."

Ransom nodded. "They're like fish out of water. But they can do a lot of damage in those seconds."

"Nevertheless," Tuvok picked up, "it is a tactical weakness. Perhaps we can exploit it."

"What've you got in mind?" Burke asked.

Janeway looked at him. Somehow the question sounded funny, the way he asked it.

Seven postulated, "If we can show them that we have the ability to hold them here," she said, "they'll think twice about launching another attack."

"The question is," Janeway probed, "how do we catch these fish?"

Would they have an answer? She hadn't gotten much out of Ransom about this problem. Of course, she hadn't pushed him. He was a captain, after all, and she expected him to be forthright with information that would help both their crews. He was, like the rest of his crew, still shell shocked, probably having trouble trusting even other Starfleet personnel. She'd seen plenty of illusions herself since being forced into the Delta Quadrant. It wouldn't be out of line for him to wait awhile, see if what he was experiencing was the real thing, not just an hallucination or an illusion, a trick or a trap. Janeway knew deep inside that she would hold back too, just to see, to be sure.

Yes, First Officer Burke was communing silently with his captain. They were looking at each other in the way that didn't need words.

Finally, with some kind of tacit permission from Ransom, Burke offered, "You build a trap."

So, they did know how to do it.

"Commander?" Janeway prodded. Keep them talking.

Burke looked again at Ransom and again received silent license.

"A multiphasic force field, to be exact," he said, still hesitating. Was he choosing his words carefully? "We wanted to see what we were up against. So we built a small chamber that could keep one of them trapped for several minutes."

Janeway waited a second to see if there was more, then said, "If we could expand on that technology, we might be able to create a latticework of multiphasic force fields around both ships."

Stiffening as if waiting for a blade to fall, Burke looked at Ransom. "Rudy?"

Another of those strange pauses, those wordless communications . . . Ransom's tight eyes worked. "If Captain Janeway agrees."

What an odd thing to say. He knew she wanted an answer, a course of action. Why was he so uncertain?

"We'll need to examine that stasis chamber," she told him. He knew that too, didn't he? This business of having to state the obvious . . .

This time Ransom didn't look at Burke or the other way around. Both men stared at Janeway and she got the idea they were holding their breath for a moment.

"I'm afraid that won't be possible," Ransom stated flatly. "It's in our research lab. That section was flooded with thermionic radiation during the last attack. It'll be days before anyone can go in there."

"The design schematics are in our auxiliary data-core," Burke quickly filled in, offering a fair but not great alternative.

"I'll see if I can download them," Ransom said before anyone else could speak. "Give me a hand?"

Janeway followed him out, giving him a chance to lead the way even on her ship. That was all right, he needed it. She was expecting the *Equinox* crew to have to be here longer than they thought they might, judging by the amount of damage turning up on that ship, and they should be allowed to feel as if *Voyager* had become their home away from hell.

He didn't need a hand, either. Nobody needed a hand downloading. What he needed, she supposed, was the company of a peer. Or perhaps it was only that he didn't want to go back to *Equinox* by himself quite yet. He'd been virtually alone as supreme leader of a team of young scientists, alone in the responsibility for their lives and their survival or witness to their grisly deaths. He'd stood that tide by himself, never breaking down. Max Burke wasn't really a first officer, but he had been shoved up to that position much as Ransom had been shoved into command. That wasn't the same as having a qualified captain as your first officer, which Janeway was privileged to have in Chakotay. She could sleep in confidence that her ship was in experienced hands. Ransom couldn't.

He and Burke obviously were very close, by nature and by needs, but even that kind of trust didn't replace years of experience running a ship in good times to be prepared for the bad times. The *Equinox* crew and their officers had been shoved headlong into the bad times. Janeway was happy to be able to give Ransom whatever moral support he needed.

And yet, he didn't trust her completely. She could sense that. Easily attributed to five years without being able to trust anybody other than his little crew, the lack of forthrightness and those glances of murmuring communication between Ransom and his crew somehow set off alarms in the back of her brain. They were holding back.

Frightened of commitment? Afraid that if they got too familiar with the *Voyager* crew they wouldn't be able to go back to their own ship, as regulations demanded?

No, that couldn't be it. They knew they'd have to go back. She thought she would want to go back if the situation were reversed and she had a miraculous chance to secure her damaged ship.

Was this fair? Fixing all her own reactions to other people? Maybe they felt something completely different. It had been so long since she'd been in a fleet . . . even a fleet of two. She hardly remembered how to feel.

Time, time. They all needed time to adjust. All these feelings and suspicions would even out. Janeway determined to make sure they evened out. Regulations would do that, protocol, routine, the command structure. Those forces would eventually take over and smooth out all the problems. Do things by the book, follow the rules, give and follow orders, report to superiors, improvise when necessary, but fall back on Starfleet motions and methods.

That would save them all. They were not just two isolated ships popping around deep space. They were

United Federation of Planets representatives on the far frontier, Starfleet officers and crew members to the last one, and they had a big book to fall back upon. That's what would save them, and would eventually bond them to each other.

Time. Time. Regulations, a sense of identity, a sense of purpose beyond just survival, and lots of time.

Did they have it?

CHAPTER

5

FUNNY HOW THINGS COULD BE. A GREAT CHANCE AT A CA-
reer, science, and get paid for it, a rank, and a captain
to take care of all the problems. One day, scraping as-
teroids, the next day fight for your life seventy thousand light-years from home. One day, dying in a
conduit, can't feel the legs anymore, and today . . .

Noah Lessing drew a sustaining lungful of air and
leaned on the *Voyager*'s doctor program, putting weight
on legs he was sure were gone for good.

"Try putting a little more of your weight on it," The
Doctor instructed.

Lessing realized he was holding back, afraid to believe that he could walk again. He thought he had been
putting weight on. Leaning forward more, he pressed
down on his newly fused right leg.

"Go ahead," The Doctor encouraged.

One step . . . two . . .

"Good. Any pain?"

"Just a little," Lessing said. It might have been a lot of pain, but he couldn't judge anymore between a little and a lot. He'd taught himself to ignore what he couldn't change, even if it killed him.

He was about to take another step when the sickbay door opened and that miracle of nature and mechanics strode in—Seven of Nine.

"My Angel of Mercy!" Lessing greeted.

"I came to check on your damage," she said emotionlessly. "It's less than I expected."

"Your doctor's something of a miracle worker—" Just as he said it, his left leg folded and he stumbled. He'd have fallen if The Doctor hadn't been holding him.

"That's enough for now," The Doctor said. "Seven?"

She stepped in and took Lessing's other side. She was far more firm and solid than the hologram, strangely.

"I had to rebuild the lower spine and both femurs," The Doctor went on. "With some rest and physical therapy, he'll be good as new."

Lessing resisted an urge to comment on how different The Doctor's attitude was than the same program on *Equinox*. Their ship's surgeon had died in the first week after they'd been hurled out of the Alpha Quadrant. They'd been treated by a notably cold hologram ever since. The counterpart on *Voyager* seemed happier, even satisfied that his treatments worked, and troubled when they didn't. He'd suffered over Lessing's pelvis and legs almost as much as Lessing had.

Has he let himself be steered back to the nearest biobed and found it a distinct delight to be able to sit instead of lying down. He gazed in mute appreciation at Seven and surveyed the landscape. The Doctor pressed a hypospray into Lessing's arm, distracting him for a moment, and when he turned again Seven was on her way out.

"Seven!" he called. "I didn't hear a Red Alert ... where are you going so fast?"

Seven looked at The Doctor, who said, "You may stay for a few minutes." To Lessing, he added, "Then, *rest.*"

Good. He was leaving them alone.

Lessing could think of plenty worse fates than being alone with an artist's dream like this.

"Beautiful ship you've got here," he said.

Oh ... what an opening line.

"It is sufficiently pleasing," she responded, perplexed. Seemed like she'd never looked at the ship that way.

She would if she'd spent the past five years on *Equinox.*

"After a week in the Jefferies tube," Lessing commented, "it's paradise. Did you know there are five thousand two hundred and eighteen plasma welds in a standard section of bulkhead?"

He thought he was making a sad joke, but Seven bluntly said, "Yes."

A laugh felt good. Lessing was the type who smiled

easily, and everybody always said he had a nice smile, so he never held back. Lately the smiles had been few, and it felt great to grin freely and mean it, not just make a hollow reassurance of something impossible to a desperate shipmate who needed a lift. He didn't have to do that here. He could laugh and smile, and mean it.

"I guess you *would* know," he chuckled. "The Borg are pretty thorough."

"And humans are . . . resilient," she replied.

He couldn't tell if she meant that as a compliment or not.

"Nothing to it," he joked. "Count a few plasma welds, calculate pi to a hundred places in my head . . . and imagine I was someplace else. Imagine I was home."

"Earth," she said. Was that reverie in her eyes? Or mystery?

"With Mom and Dad . . . all my sisters . . . Just talking about everything and nothing . . . being together with them again."

Briefly he left her, left the sickbay behind in his thoughts, wandered home again. When he'd first seen Seven's face over him, heard her voice and Harry Kim's telling him he was going to live after all, that he still had his legs and a chance to survive, and that they were Starfleet—he'd wallowed briefly in the idea of having been rescued. *Really* rescued. Somebody had come from the Alpha Quadrant to take them all the way home.

Then reeling in, finding out that the *Voyager* was

trapped here too, digesting the idea that they were alive, but not exactly on their way home . . . oh, well, small blessings. He'd learned to live with microscopic ones. He could live with this.

"Your method was successful," Seven congratulated. "You survived. Impressive, considering the circumstances."

Her sculpted face and body began to grow fuzzy as his eyes blurred. The hypo. Must've been a sedative. "Don't be too impressed," he muttered. "I don't deserve it."

How much did she know? He'd told her everything, hadn't he? All about the stasis chamber and the enemy aliens, the experiments, the captain's decision to keep going . . . she'd understood and been comforting about it. She'd even laughed that he was worried about how they'd all react to the story. Yes, he'd told her.

Or was it the sedative talking? Was Seven still here?

"You are to rest," she said. "Good-bye."

Lessing reached out with the last of his ability to focus and grasped her arm. "Seven . . . you saved my life. I hope . . . you never regret that . . ."

As he lowered himself to lie down on the biobed and Seven adjusted his newly healed legs into place so he wouldn't slip off, Lessing watched her beautiful blond hair in its tight twist and thought it looked like the swept tails of those animals they'd been experimenting on. Over and over in his mind he saw those creatures flying, fighting, screaming, their yellow tails sweeping and curled in fear and pain and anger.

He closed his eyes and dreamed of home, and knew he wasn't there yet.

Minimal power restored—good. A blip or two of encouraging light where an hour ago there had been dimness and collapse. A few consoles up and running, flashing eagerly, as if they were enjoying getting to do their jobs again, feeling the flush of unruptured energy through repair cables and coils.

Janeway reconnected two more fusion circuits and nodded with satisfaction. Beside her, Rudy Ransom picked at a station with greatly enhanced familiarity. Oh, a Starfleet engineering panel was a Starfleet panel, meet one, meet them all, but after a few years of personal treatment they started to act individually. Ships got personality just as babies did. They started out cut from the same die, only later to get the little bangs and bumps that set them apart, tiny repairs, stresses, quirks, strengths and weaknesses, each to its own. Ransom treated his ship's circuitry like errant puppies responding to his snap, and it worked. Everything he did happened ten seconds faster than anything Janeway did. He seemed proud of that, and she let him have it.

Behind them, several more of *Voyager*'s technical specialists were at work, resetting and repairing, replacing bent or smashed trunk sites and monitor screens, fingerpads, and crystal displays. There was a heightened sense of purpose even in the low-keyed banter as they spoke to each other.

Everyone seemed happy, except the *Equinox* crew.

They seemed self-conscious, distracted, close-mouthed. That was it . . . *they* were the ones who were supposed to be the happiest people around.

Oh, was that selfish! Janeway chided herself for these thoughts. Expecting others to act as she thought she might? Pretty unfair. She really didn't know what they'd been through. She and *Voyager* had experienced their logful of horrors, but few of them had sustained for the sheer months on end what *Equinox* had dealt with. What does that do to people crammed together on a small science ship with limited battle-readiness?

"I couldn't help but notice," she began, hoping to crinkle the ice a little more with Ransom, "that your crew calls you by your first name."

He tipped his head in either a nod or a shrug. "When you've spent as much time in the trenches as we have, rank and protocol are luxuries. Besides, we're a long way from Starfleet Command."

"I know the feeling," she said.

Did she? As much as he did?

"You seem to run a tight ship," he commented, attempting to hand back the problem to her. Maybe it was a compliment.

"We've been known to let our hair down from time to time, but I find that maintaining protocol reminds us of where we came from," she said, "and hopefully where we're going."

"I'd say it's worked quite well for you."

Janeway paused. Had he put an emphasis on "for you," or was she imagining it? Suddenly she felt a little self-conscious herself, a little class-guilty about having this powerful ship and enough crew to tend it. She'd always felt like the lost lamb, small in a big hostile quadrant, and now she'd stumbled upon a lost chick whom she could easily trample.

"We've overcome our share of obstacles," she attempted. That sounded wrong the instant she said it. Would he think she was trying to share, or compare? "Warp core breaches, ion storms, a few rounds with the Borg—"

"Borg? We haven't seen so much as a cube since the day we arrived."

"Consider yourself lucky." Her eyes crimped in disapproval. That was perfectly heartless. Why wouldn't this conversation go right?

Ransom didn't seem to take it the way she thought it sounded. "Have you ever run into the Krowtonan Guard?"

"Never heard of them."

The other captain paused for a moment, and his shoulders sank. "That's how we spent our first week in the Delta Quadrant. They claimed we'd violated their territory. It was either circumvent their borders and add another six years to our journey . . . or maintain course. I gave the order to keep going." His eyes tightened. "I lost thirty-nine. Half my crew."

Well, that was the end of the what-we've-been-through competition. Janeway's heart skipped as she gazed at him. She couldn't even come close to that one.

"I'm sorry," she offered warmly.

Neither the sympathy nor the memory was doing Ransom any good, unless it helped at all to talk to another captain about it, unburdening himself for the first time to an equal. "We never recovered from that loss," he said. "It changed everything . . ."

He looked at her, but only for a moment. He stopped talking.

"What do you mean?" Janeway encouraged, hoping he would keep talking, get it over with. Did she have to tell him it was off the record?

"When I first realized that we'd be traveling through the Delta Quadrant for the rest of our lives," he went on, struggling, "I told my crew we had a duty as Starfleet officers to expand our knowledge and uphold our principles. After a couple of years, we started to forget we were explorers. There were times when we nearly forgot we were human beings."

Offering silent solace for a few moments, Janeway reflected on how hard it must have been to uphold higher principles when just eating was a critical factor. Exploration was a pretty goal, but the starving explore for only one reason.

"This is a Nova-class science vessel," she comforted, beginning with the painfully obvious and working around to the rest, as if going up a ramp. "Designed for short-term research missions. Minimal weapons . . . you can't even go faster than warp eight. Frankly, I don't know how you've done it. You've obviously traveled as far as we have, with much fewer resources."

She held back from complimenting him that half his crew mostly survived, realizing how hollow that would sound and the counterpart of the favor was very, very sour. Half hadn't.

"I wish I could take all the credit," Ransom handed back. "But we stumbled across a wormhole. Made a few enhancements to our warp engines . . ."

He stopped with that. She sensed there was more, knew that B'Elanna was having some trouble with the warp core.

"May I ask you something, captain to captain?" Ransom began after a moment of hesitation. "The Prime Directive. How often have you broken it for the sake of protecting your crew?"

"Broken it?" The eternal haunting question. "Never," she said before really thinking. "Bent it . . . on occasion. And even then, it was a difficult choice."

Now who was holding back?

"What about you?" she reversed.

"Oh, I've walked that line once or twice. Nothing serious."

Somehow it seemed like the conversation was over. They weren't being open anymore. They weren't equals anymore. Something had changed and Janeway wasn't sure what that something was. They were the only two Starfleet captains in the Delta Quadrant. They had to make up new rules as they struck new situations, encountered civilizations that had never even heard of the Federation and had no idea or any care about its influence. The weight of that played hard upon captains who were used to having a certain reputation precede them and a formidable force back them up.

Ransom effectively changed the subject by a unique

trick—finishing his work. His familiarity with the quirkish reroutes and jury-rigging deep in the systems quickly untangled what otherwise would've been days of work for Janeway just to diagnose. As he straightened, he said, "There you are . . ."

For an instant she thought he was talking to her, until he stooped and brushed through the rubble, to come up with the ship's commission plaque.

U.S.S. Equinox. Commission date, officer manifest . . . a ship's ID tag.

Captain Ransom wiped the plaque with his bare hand, despite sharp metal shavings and a crackle of residual magnetic charge.

At the same moment as she was glad he found it, Janeway was crushed by the sadness of seeing that plaque driven to the deck, smeared with leakage and chips, in a situation that kept anyone from picking it up until now. If *Voyager* hadn't happened to be close enough to hear the distress signal and respond in the nick of time, that plaque would've been lying there as *Equinox*'s crew died around it. There was something pathetic about that. Somehow it bothered her, like a child's grave with no stone.

"It's a good omen," she offered meagerly. "Let's put it back where it belongs."

And let's get the rest of us back where we belong. Why does home seem so much farther away today than it did yesterday?

Two ships, flying together in space, as fleets from Earth had done for centuries, even millennia. *Equinox* and *Voyager* soared at warp speed—high for one ship, moderate for another—shrouded in the amniotic sac of the starship's shields, under assault the whole way.

Things were hectic. There was a time limit. People tried to walk and work quietly and calmly, compromised by an underlying sweat and knowledge that time was running out. Those aliens out there, operating on some other spatial plane, were systematically disrupting the starship's strong shields, shields that were already stretched thin by attempting to protect two ships.

Rudolph Ransom hurried through the guts of the bigger ship with his mind on the smaller one. The contamination in the critical areas of *Equinox* had staved off analysis of the area efficiently, giving him time to think of what to do. Either he would have a plan ready or time would run out and *Voyager* would be in the same position he and his crew were when the aliens started breaking through. Then, there wouldn't be any more opportunity for judgment making or room in the arena for challenges between Starfleet personnel. They'd have to work together to survive. He was counting on that.

He'd driven himself since coming aboard *Voyager* without having a full meal. Now the ship's EMH had ordered him to report to the mess hall or be fed intravenously. After months of surviving on handfuls here and there, the idea of a square meal was foreign. He would have to get reacclimated to some things gradually. Physical and otherwise.

But he still had to *report* to the mess hall. His combadge would log the entry, as keyed to do so by the EMH, and then he would be free to go.

The mess hall was not, and couldn't be expected to be, crowded. Not while the ships were under siege. People came and went, grabbing small meals to sustain them in their work to support the deflector system. Ransom wasn't surprised to see at least one of his crew here—but he was a little surprised that it was Max Burke. Probably under the same orders to eat.

Burke, though, was sitting down in front of a sailor's traditional square meal, though he did seem to be only picking. Ransom strode up behind him and pressed his shoulder. "I thought I'd find you here."

Burke glanced at him. "How could I resist? After two years on emergency rations . . ."

"Don't get too comfortable." Ransom didn't sit, leaning instead on the chair behind him. When Max's shoulders slumped in understanding, his hands suddenly clenched, Ransom lowered his voice and said, "If Janeway's any indication, these people will never understand."

"They're going to find out eventually."

"Not if we keep them out of the research lab. And away from the warp core injectors. Be careful what you say around their crew. And that includes old girlfriends."

A tacit warning, yes, yet very serious. For a captain to interfere in the relationships of his crew was one of the most delicate lines a commander could stride.

Janeway, he guessed, would agree. She seemed to run her ship with very little personal involvement among the crew members. Despite having been locked in the Delta Quadrant with virtually no hope of fanning out into more human society, it would've been normal and expected for people on the ship to start pairing up. Ransom hadn't seen much evidence of that so far. Maybe they were all holding back. Or Janeway had managed to lower a veil of deceptive hopes for them, convincing them they really could get back just by going fast.

They couldn't. Ransom knew that. Warp eight or warp twelve, it didn't matter. The distance between here and the Alpha Quadrant still swallowed an entire normal lifetime. If they did get back by just flying, the survivors would be old men and women—without families, without homes, with no stakes—whose relatives had all but forgotten them, whose children had grown up without them and gone off to build their own lives. Their ships would be out of date, obsolete, backward, relics. Only their information about the Delta Quadrant would be worth anything; and the fact was that if space couldn't be bent, then it didn't matter. The Alpha citizens couldn't come back and forth fast enough to make any bond between the quadrants. If distance could not be surmounted, then time would beat them. So what was the information worth? Nothing. Going home by going straight was useless, hopeless. Pointless. Janeway was fooling herself and her crew.

A sagging sensation cloyed Ransom as he moved away from Max before those thoughts popped out. He took a big chunk of food from his first officer's plate, popped it in his mouth, said, "Not bad," by means of a farewell, and headed out of the mess hall. He didn't like leaving Max with that posture, that defeated and fearful slump, worried that all this comfort would be critically temporary. But if they stayed and talked . . .

He didn't like the closeness of strangers. The crew was enjoying meeting new friends, but for a captain it was different. Janeway wasn't going to be the comrade he'd hoped for. He couldn't expect her to be. She ran a completely different kind of ship, one with different formative experiences over the past five years. Eventually she might be forced to understand, if things went the way Ransom expected. Too late, though. And he didn't have time to be her conditioner.

"Rudy!"

Halfway back down the corridor, Ransom discovered with some tension that Max had followed him out. Neither wanted to be seen talking secretly by any more others than absolutely necessary. Funny—though half the size, *Equinox* had provided more privacy. Of course, on *Equinox,* they hadn't had to talk much after a while. They only had two jobs. Defend and propel. No chitchat. No philosophy class.

"We can't talk here, Max," Ransom aborted as his first officer fell out of his jog.

"We have to talk somewhere." Burke lowered his voice. "I don't think they're the type to have security recordings all over the ship. They don't have any reason to. Please—I'm not sure what to do."

"All right, all right." Though he did not stop walking, Ransom slowed down.

Now that he had permission to speak, Burke fell disturbingly silent. Unable to leave his first officer with that question *What should I do?* pending, Ransom plunged into it.

"I've skimmed her logs. She's done more than bend the rules. She's openly and with deliberation participated in the Delta Quadrant. Answering a distress call is arguably against the rules. To hear some strict interpretations, even existing in somebody else's territory is against the rules! How can we deal with that in our situation? Nobody's ever been in our situation before. Starfleet didn't make any rules to cover this. The Federation Council never gave it a thought. The only other commander who has a clue what it's like to be this lost is Janeway. And she hasn't visited the edge yet."

"No . . . she hasn't. I always agreed with you, Rudy," Burke said, then held up a hand. "I still do, I still do . . . but how can we make them understand? Soon enough, I mean."

"We can't." Ransom lowered his voice more. "I know I've stepped over the line in their eyes. We don't have two years to examine the regulations and micromanage the morality. They don't have the capability yet to understand what we've had to do. How could they? Look at this ship! Clean, strong, supplied . . . they haven't even come close to the edge. We landed on it!"

"We sure did . . ."

"And I wanted to get home. I saw a way to get home. I used it."

"Don't isolate yourself," Burke protested. "We could've resisted. We wanted to get home too. It's all for one and one for all on *Equinox*."

An unexpected smile crimped Ransom's leathery face. "You know how I appreciate that. Especially here, where you're all—"

"Comfortable? Right . . . things always look different in a lounge than they do from down a well, that's for sure. But we'll never forget, Rudy. We're still with you."

"I'm glad, because we'll have to stick together. They're not going to understand. We have to forget about that. They won't get it. *She'll* never approve, that's for sure. She's never been to the Skeleton Coast."

Burke shook his head and laughed sadly. "I remember the first time you told us those survival stories from the Skeleton Coast. It made us feel so . . . possible! If those poor shipwrecked tourists could do it, so could we . . . heat, sandstorms, blindness, hundreds of miles of scorching sand and not even a snake to eat . . . I used to replay the scenes in my head while I was working. It kept my mind off how bad things were getting."

"You get inspiration wherever you can." Leading the way around a corner, Ransom found he'd made a wrong turn. Now they stood in a vestibule for a turbolift that was under repair. With a red caution tape across the open doorway, the lift stood in passive gawk, half its guts exposed, tools littering its deck.

Beside him, Burke stopped still. Together they stared at the electrical innards. Even dismantled, the lift was a hundred times more tidy than the shambled mess in any corner of *Equinox*. And this had no blood on it.

There they stood, not looking at each other. Ransom's voice moved as if veiled beneath the soft bleeps and whirs of the living ship.

"When you're dropped on the Skeleton Coast, the rules of civilization don't apply. It isn't a place for higher behavior. It gets down to finding enough water. Escaping the sun. Trapping a crab. How do you walk on burned feet? How do you keep from freezing at night? What do you use for toilet paper? It gets whittled farther and farther down . . . until all you're interested in is getting through the next few minutes. The lofty goals of humanity? They just don't matter. If you can't survive, then what difference does destiny make?"

The words all but echoed. The turbolift bleeped passively, flashing its little "Under Repair" light. Yes, lots of things were under repair in the Delta Quadrant.

Burke gazed at the red strip blocking the lift cavity. His voice was rough. "You *know* they'll hold us to that code."

"Because they've never had to live without it," Ransom quietly reminded. "We were trapped on the Coast. Nowhere, with nothing . . . dying . . . hopeless. We could never, ever get home. Nobody else welcomed us. We were completely alone."

"I know, Rudy, I know . . . if you hadn't been strong enough—"

Brushing off the compliment, Ransom sliced his hand between them. "Then something happened to change everything. We found ourselves inside a pack of wild animals. Even though it seemed worse at the time, it was really better because we suddenly had a fighting chance. If you're on a life raft, starving and scorching, it's better to just get in the water and fight the sharks. You might die, but at least you die fighting! And if you win, you've got a shark to eat. I like that better—the fighting chance. I want the fighting chance. You know, Max, I was never a fighting man. I never even handled a weapon after basic training. I never took any courses in tactics or strategy . . . but when you *have* to fight, when you're faced with that . . . by God, there's something about it that makes a man's soul cook!"

With an uneasy smile, Burke shook his head. "You're the something for us. You made us cook. You and your metaphors."

"That's right, me and my metaphors. If you're trapped in a pack of wild animals who can't understand your rights, what obligation do you have to respect theirs? It's down to pure survival. The rules of civilization say you still act civilized even on the Skeleton Coast," Ransom said, and paused. He gripped Burke's arm and made his first officer meet his eyes. "But you can't. We couldn't."

Stepping forward, troubled, Burke gripped the simple red strip between them and the torn-apart interior of the turbolift. Another barrier, pretending it could hold them. It couldn't.

The ship's circulation system came on in a vent over their heads, blowing adjusted cool air into the area where warm air had built up because of the open turbolift. The sound made Burke flinch.

"We swore an oath that even among savages we would be civilized," he said.

Ransom nodded. "We tried. It didn't work."

"What do we do?" Burke asked, not arguing because he knew that was true. They had tried, and failed. "What about the rest of the crew? They deserve a rest and it doesn't look like we're going to get one. Janeway and her crew are in for a miserable surprise."

"Then we'll fight again," Ransom told him stalwartly. "We've come too far to buckle now. We've got the fight in us. We're strong, we know that. Everybody thinks a science crew is just a bunch of geeks. We proved otherwise. I'll never quit. Our mission is to get home before we all really do turn to skeletons. That's my focus. It always will be. I'll never have kids of my own. I want to see your kids someday. Yours and Noah's, Mike's, and Marla's . . . I want two hundred grandkids. I mean to get 'em."

Burke laughed again, his black eyes more alive than they'd been in months. "Rudy, you're a work of art."

Ransom shrugged. "Since the first week," he went on, "I was determined that the rest of you would survive. I didn't care about the rules of civilization anymore. I still don't. No shower or full belly will ever make me forget again. When *Voyager* peeled out of space to save us, I swore a new oath to myself that I wouldn't slip. I'll destroy every savage I come upon, if necessary, to get all of you home. Once among civilized people, I'll gladly obey the rules of civilization again. But we're still among savages here. There are no laws."

Burke looked as if his dinner were coming back on him. Though there was doubt in his posture, there really was none in his gaze. They knew what they had to do. Unfortunately, that meant coming to grapples with the *Voyager* crew, who would not understand soon enough. It meant compromising friends before the friendship even had a chance in hell.

Ransom studied him silently for a few seconds. When he spoke, the words galvanized both of them.

"Do you want to be out here for the rest of your life?"

CHAPTER
6

Noah Lessing strode around on his newly fused femurs, appreciating as never before the minor miracle of possessing a pelvis. His wounds were gone. His uniform was clean. All by itself, just the clean uniform was something remarkable. No chafing! No smear of lubricant against his buttocks. No jagged rips with seared fibrous edges that had turned sharp. Add to that, fresh air and light . . .

"How's my Angel of Mercy?" he cheered as he strode into the astrometrics lab.

He knew she'd be here.

"Crewman Lessing," Seven of Nine greeted. "I did not expect you to recover so quickly."

"You've got an outstanding EMH," Lessing offered, not explaining that he'd been recovering fast by necessity for years now. On *Equinox* even the injured had to fight. Being able to actually rest—well, that was gravy. "Ours can barely hold a laser scalpel," he added, trying to be funny.

She didn't seem to get it. "The doctor is efficient," was her only comment.

Like trying to get a rise out of a sculpture.

Still hopeful, he moved closer. "I've been assigned to help you sort through the biodata. You saved my life . . . the least I can do is save you a little time."

He didn't tell her that his real motive was to stall her progress by a few hours. Rudy needed time. Max was right—these *Voyager* people, they didn't need to know everything too soon.

Seven looked at him, then turned down to her work again. No matter how he smiled, she didn't change. Same delivery, same response, low disinterested tone, faint curiosity, no real flame. Too bad all those looks were locked up in there. Apparently he'd misread those big pretty eyes. Lying trapped, half-dead, numb, and starved could do that to you.

Still, couldn't blame a fella for persistence.

He started to say something, some line he came up with that probably wouldn't work, when he was interrupted by a grisly familiar shriek. The alien tone!

He drew his phaser instantly, a reflex, without thinking. An instant later Seven drew hers. Braced for attack, they pointed at two different areas.

"Take cover!" Lessing rasped. "Get down! They always come from above!"

"What comes?" Seven asked, fielding her phaser toward the ceiling.

"The attacks! Contact your bridge! Tell them they have to fortify the shields! Tell them!"

"What kind of life form?"

"Nucleogenic! On a separate spatial plane! We don't know much about them! If a fissure opens, fire into it! Don't wait! Call them, call them!"

"Seven to bridge! We're under attack!"

"Chakotay here. We see it, lab, stand by. Tuvok, what's happening to us?"

"Checking," the Vulcan responded. Suddenly the question seemed silly—he'd tell as soon as he knew. Asking didn't hurry things up any.

Deafened by the ear-splitting screech of the alien invasion tone, Chakotay braced for action and waited. He held a phaser, as did every single member of the bridge crew. That was such a strange sight! This place was the brain center for attacks from outside, not inside.

"Lateral shields are off-line," Tuvok called over the noise.

"How's that possible?" Chakotay demanded.

Before he got an answer, Harry Kim shouted, "Fissures are opening on decks one, eight, and eleven!"

That accounted for the astrometrics lab. Unfortunately, it also accounted for sickbay, with injured and helpless crew still lying down there. Chakotay made a mental note to station security guards in sickbay. He'd never thought of such a thing before.

"Reroute power!" he called.

Too late—he should've reacted sooner. Tuvok needed authorization to do that. Though technically simple, rerouting a major power source was a command prerogative only.

Tuvok now worked freely and within five seconds the alien sound pinched to silence.

Squinting with leftover pain in his ears, Tom Paris asked, "What happened?"

Tuvok continued working with uncharacteristic ferocity to shore up the shield power. "Apparently," he explained, "the aliens began to focus their attacks on a single shield vector. It collapsed before the auxiliary emitters could respond."

A dim hopelessness gripped the bridge. They all knew what that meant.

Chakotay smoldered. "It looks like they've changed their tactics. We may have less time than we thought. Yellow Alert."

"Yellow Alert, aye," Paris responded. He looked glad to have something to do beside run from something they couldn't see and apparently couldn't outpace.

"Janeway to bridge. Report on that last incident."

Due to happen.

Chakotay glanced at Paris, then tapped the command chair comm. "Captain, Chakotay here. We think the aliens have learned to focus on weakened shield vectors. We closed the gap before they broke through, but I'm wondering how long we can keep that up."

"If they can learn one thing, they can learn another. They'll figure out what we do to stop them and they'll

either work faster or they'll just outguess us. It short-ens our time limit. Is everyone all right?"

"Everyone here is. We don't have any reports from the rest of the ship."

"Have security check on all personnel. Order the crew to work in teams of two or more. I don't want any-one left alone."

"Aye, Captain."

"Chakotay, meet me in the briefing room. Round up everybody who's been working on this. Have them get their data ready but tell them to keep the processing power levels low. We've got to start conserving now, before things get worse. If we don't get answers soon, we're going to start paying a price. And I don't like toll roads. Go to Red Alert."

"We've examined the schematics of your multiphasic chamber. It can be adapted."

Kathryn Janeway examined the cutaway as Seven of Nine described her analysis. She felt comfortable, but uneasy. Odd, the differentiation. She knew the comfort came from the presence of Chakotay, Tuvok, and Seven.

The unease—was that from Ransom, Burke, and Gilmore? Was she so unused to having strangers aboard, human strangers, that she couldn't relax about it?

The cutaway graphics of *Voyager* and *Equinox* showed every deck and section of the ships, high-lighted with a complex grid of force fields, under attack in what seemed a random pattern but apparently was not.

Tuvok picked up when Seven finished, to explain, "We intend to create an autoinitiating security grid. The moment an alien invades either ship, a force field will surround it."

Seven tapped another control while Janeway resisted asking obvious technical questions that they'd handle anyway.

"Once we modify our field generator," Seven said, "to emit multiphasic frequencies, it will power the security grids on both ships."

"How long will it take?" Janeway brass-tacked.

Tuvok shrugged with just his eyebrows. "Approximately fourteen hours."

Engineer Gilmore from the *Equinox* flitted her gaze nervously between Janeway and her own captain. "We don't know when they'll break through again. We may not last that long."

Chakotay, who had apparently become friends with Gilmore, came up with an option. "We could cut that time in half if we evacuate all personnel from the *Equinox* . . . focus our efforts here on *Voyager*."

Was it just a suggestion? Or had he already posed the unsavory idea to his new friend?

Janeway watched—no, they all looked surprised, taken aback by the idea of abandoning a ship they had so long fought to keep flying. Another feeling she found hauntingly familiar.

Max Burke looked at Rudy Ransom. In fact, everybody was now looking at Ransom. Conflict began to brew softly beneath the surface of cooperation.

"I don't mean to force the issue," Ransom slowly began, "but I am prepared to return to the *Equinox* with my crew."

The next moment passed awkwardly. Suddenly they had a big problem on their hands.

Janeway stewed as she waited. She really shouldn't order another captain to abandon his own ship. Regulations might back her up, but there was a tacit understanding, generations old, that the captain himself would have to make that decision—and it usually involved a ship that couldn't limp another inch. *Equinox* wasn't to that point yet. She was still salvageable and moving under her own power.

But the time . . . there wasn't time . . .

Lose one ship and perhaps prevail, or keep both ships and weaken the shields irrecoverably?

She had her own ship to protect. Standing poised on the brink of sacrificing another captain's ship for her own, she hated her command.

"What's the protocol for this situation, anyway?" Ransom asked. "Two ships, two captains . . . who gets the last word?"

As a scientist rushed to command, it wasn't unusual that he didn't know. Troubling, though. Janeway held her breath at the idea of having to tell him.

"Starfleet Regulation One Hundred Ninety-one, Article Fourteen," she said, rather mournfully. " 'In a combat situation involving more than one ship, command falls to the vessel of tactical superiority.' "

Horrible—that seemed to take away all judgment in a situation that desperately needed humanizing. She wasn't quoting the whole regulation, the part about a captain's autonomy and how 'tactical superiority' didn't include ordering another captain to abandon his own functional ship. Someday he would find out, and he would hate her almost as much as she hated herself right now.

She hoped he didn't know. What was that look in his eyes?

"I looked it up this morning," she added, softening the idea that even the straitlaced Janeway didn't lie around in the late of night memorizing regulations.

"Good thinking," was all Ransom said.

Max Burke glared with undisguised bitterness at Janeway, though he didn't speak up.

While she could, she played her last card. "In this case, protocol recognizes my authority."

She held her breath again. They could just as easily look it up, find the fine line between tactical authority and ordering another captain to sacrifice his command. Later, though. For now, she needed an edge.

Ransom eyed her, suddenly cold. "Are you ordering me to abandon my ship?"

He was going to make her say it. She couldn't blame him.

Trying to ease the bad feelings quickly rising, she gave him the only offer she could under the circumstances. "I'd rather not have to."

Give the order yourself. Take the last step.

His crew watched him. Her crew watched him too. All their immediate futures were in Ransom's hand.

This, though, was nothing new for him and he was still up to it.

"That protocol was written in the Alpha Quadrant," he told her. "I'm not sure it makes much sense here."

He said he wasn't sure, but that was his way of putting it nicely. By that, Janeway could tell he was absolutely sure and had been acting upon that certainty. How could she blame him? At a maximum of warp eight, *Equinox* was in the Delta Quadrant for the rest of their lives and then some. How could she condemn him for not letting go?

The moments were ticking away. The shields weakened even as she entertained her sympathy for him while also playing this unfriendly game of poker, whittling him down with half a regulation to nobody and nothing, the worse thing that could happen to his kind of person, and her.

A captain without a ship.

"The regulation stands," she said, trying to make the forceful sound gentle.

Ransom could see, as all could, that Janeway wasn't about to budge with that clock ticking. There would be no discussion. If they were to save themselves, she had to make sharp turns.

He opted for a strategical retreat.

"Who am I to dispute protocol?" he began. Turning to his crew members, he added, "Give Captain Janeway your full cooperation."

Burke stiffened. "Rudy . . ."

"That's an order, Max."

By this, Ransom spared Janeway from having to start ordering his crew around—just yet. That would come, they both knew. There could only be one captain.

"We'll get through this," he added.

Burke mentally retreated, eyes still hot.

"If that's all, Captain," Ransom said, "I'd like to go back to my quarters and collect a few mementos."

Janeway wanted to feel relieved. Something held her back. "By all means," she accepted.

Something was wrong with that. He had agreed too quickly.

Not fair—could it be just barely possible that he'd had enough of that torture chamber they'd called a ship and saw the logic of taking a stand in a single fortress? No sense underestimating him until he gave her a reason. After all, captaincy hadn't ever been his dream. Command was something forced upon him by a vectoring off from his real skills. He might very well not be so sorry to see it go.

She tried to give him the benefit of her doubt and the credit he deserved for setting his ego aside for the good of all. It took a big ego to be a captain, and the thing was heavy to move.

They had their plans. Rudy knew what he was doing.

So did Max Burke as he slipped into the *Voyager*'s roomy engineering area. So big, and quiet. *Equinox*'s long-suffering engine room was a hellhole, crackling and shorting almost constantly. The noise had nearly driven him crazy before he finally learned to tune it out. Now that he didn't have to hear it anymore, the lonely thrum of a healthy warp core nearly made him cry.

Cry? Didn't have time.

That's an order, Max.

Crew moved about, way over there. Burke nodded to them, but said nothing. He didn't want their attention. This would go better if they just stayed busy trying to supplement the shields. They were getting ready for the transference, the abandonment of *Equinox*. Problems . . . how to get the *Equinox* ditched, let it drift out of the shield sphere, then close the shields without a rift that those aliens could slip through. There had to be some kind of break. Shield energy wasn't exactly an egg yolk.

He poked around, pretending to be busy too, so no one would talk to him. They didn't know him, and their sympathy would keep them away. No one knew what to say. "So, abandoning your ship, huh? Tough luck. Glad it ain't mine."

The isolated monitors on the lower deck's command station were silently prodding through the mathematics of the problems they were anticipating for the upcoming maneuver and what would be needed after that to secure the shields, perhaps eventually even throw off the siege. He stepped down to them and knelt at the access displays.

Burke didn't even try to correct the assumption that those aliens could be thrown off. They couldn't. They weren't going away. They had to be fought. Janeway and her crew were spitting over a canyon even though they couldn't see the other side.

Was that crewman leaving? Yes!

And there went the other one! What luck—he was alone. All of engineering to himself, while the crews worked on deflector problems. This wouldn't last.

The command station's force-field generator was in full operation, a direct tie-in to the systems he had to sabotage. He brought his tricorder around and secured the remote to the junction bolt. Button, button, pressure pad . . . work fast.

Searching . . . searching . . .

DOWNLOAD IN PROGRESS.

Perfect. Hurry up, hurry . . .

How long would Marla's shutdown of the security alarms hold up?

"Intruder alert."

Burke flinched and looked up. Oh, not now.

B'Elanna Torres. Fancy meeting her here . . .

She was just coming out from the companion-way, luckily in front of him, where the casing of the computer console blocked her view of the operating download. Burke stepped around in front of the console so B'Elanna wouldn't come around here.

He had to distract her or get her out of here. Somehow he had to get the remote off the bolt.

"Same old Max . . ." She approached with that old swagger. Still had it. "Going through my things without permission. That's a command station. It's off limits without my direct authorization."

"I didn't realize," he told her fluidly, pretending to be

interested in something else entirely. "You going to throw me in the brig?"

She smiled. Also still had it. "Oh, I think I can overlook this infraction. Can I help you with something?"

Offering a schoolboy shrug, Burke tried to look teasingly guilty. It was a great cover.

"Just doing some homework . . . studying your propulsion system. If there's a chance I'm going to be stuck on *Voyager,* I thought I should learn my way around."

Hoping that "stuck on" didn't come out with too much of an emphasis, he closed the space between them. Would the old sensations sizzle? Distract her? They were already distracting him from his own purpose.

"Maybe you could tutor me . . . over dinner."

What an idiotic thing to say. They were in a killing situation. Dinner? Sure, between deadly attacks and desperate defenses. Had life come to seem so leisurely here compared to on *Equinox?* Rudy was right— Burke was getting too comfortable. Dinner. Of all the—

"Problem is," B'Elanna began, "you were never really interested in the work. Or the meal. Something tells me you haven't changed."

Another step brought them too close for just friends. A flicker of hope—she didn't back away.

"You'd be surprised," he commented. *How I've changed.* "I'm not the . . . what did you once call me?"

Her eyes flickered with questions, then she remembered. "P'tak."

He grinned. "I'm not the p'tak I used to be. Let me prove it to you."

Reverie brought an uneasy smile to her shapely mouth and guilt to her eyes. "Don't get me wrong. It's good to see you again . . . but ten years . . ."

Burke let his expression tell his thoughts. "Tom Paris?"

She seemed relieved, but not happy. "Tom Paris."

Oh, well. "You could do worse."

With B'Elanna thoroughly involved in that old triangle, Burke slipped back to the command station, knelt, and recovered his tricorder, using a little sleight of hand to also retrieve the remote off the bolt. He slipped it into his hand and clenched it, tapped the schematic, which now read, *"DOWNLOAD COMPLETE."* He stood up again, thanking his stars that he'd waited long enough. There wouldn't have been a second chance.

Holstering his tricorder and hiding his deception, he turned to her. "So . . . we're on for dinner? Just you and me?"

"Get going!" she said. "Or I *will* throw you in the brig."

As he left, he felt her eyes on him.

Better there, than other places.

The soft lights and controlled atmosphere of *Voyager* created a falsely reassuring environment for both crews. Although the crew members were hurrying about in preparation for a defense against the unknown, concentrating on the shields even before the problem of getting out of this altogether, Chakotay had expected the *Equinox* people to take the abandonment of their ship worse than they had. He had to give them credit. To the last, they were accepting Captain Janeway's questionable order to release a functional ship that was legally under the authority of its captain.

"Before we abandon the *Equinox*," he continued, "we should try to salvage any useful components."

Around him in the mess hall, a place that had become the clubhouse for the stressed crew and a meeting place for decisions—somehow more accommodating right now than the briefing room—Harry Kim, Marla Gilmore, and several others huddled around PADDs and coffee. Chakotay liked this—even in adversity, they were starting to feel like shipmates.

"Let us start with your dilithium crystals," he suggested, looking at Gilmore.

"What's left of them," she conditioned. "I'm afraid we're down to a few isograms."

Kim tried to make a joke. "That's barely enough to power the sonic showers."

It wasn't funny, or very encouraging.

Gilmore shifted uneasily. "Can I make a suggestion?"

Chakotay gestured. "Please."

"Forget about primary systems. They're too badly damaged. Let's focus on supplies. We've picked up a few items that might come in handy." Showing him the information on one of the PADDs, she clarified, "We've got a dozen canisters of mercurium . . . and two kilotons of kemacite ore."

Chakotay turned to Kim. "Tell Neelix to make room in cargo bay one."

"Right."

"Could you use a synaptic stimulator?" Gilmore asked.

"Depends," Chakotay said. "What is it?"

"A neural interface you wear behind your ear. It taps into your visual cortex and shows you different alien vistas. Think of it as a poor man's holodeck."

Kim smiled. "So that's how you kept yourself entertained."

"Beats checkers . . . the Ponea gave it to us."

"Never heard of them," Chakotay encouraged.

She smiled, this time more genuinely. "We called them 'the life of the Delta Quadrant.' They see every first contact as an excuse to throw a party."

Another clue about life aboard *Equinox*. Every first contact *was* an excuse to throw a party. At least it was to everyone else. Chakotay divined from this that life aboard the other ship had been no party when new life forms and civilizations were discovered. It must've taken a horrible lot of bad encounters to drive a Starfleet crew to shun first contacts.

Gilmore gazed at the table. "I wish we'd encountered more species like that . . ."

Neither Chakotay nor Kim said anything, though they glanced at each other.

"You're the first friendly faces we've seen in months," Gilmore unburdened. "I'm glad we found you."

"The feeling's mutual," Chakotay said right away,

then determined to change the subject. "Those modified plasma injectors look elaborate. What were you trying to do?"

Her hands lost some of their color. "Oh . . . we were experimenting with ways to enhance our warp drive. But it didn't work."

Of course it didn't. They were a shipload of scientists with maintenance engineers on board. There was nothing innovative, not mechanically, about *Equinox* or her crew. Gilmore wasn't up to the task of modifying the warp drive. Chakotay doubted they'd have had the power to increase by more than one step in speed, and that wouldn't do much good this far out. He also knew she must understand that. Perhaps this was another result of utter desperation. Of course it was.

"Maybe we should let B'Elanna take a look," Kim suggested, not thinking of the facts the way Chakotay did.

"It won't work," Gilmore admitted. "We tried for months."

They paused as Naomi Wildman marched in through the port-side door and stalked right up to the table with the clarity of a six-year-old's determination. She offered a rehearsed stage smile and came to a mockery of attention, looking at Marla Gilmore.

"Hello there!" Gilmore greeted, obviously taken aback at the sudden appearance of a child.

"Commander, permission to interrupt?" the little girl asked Chakotay.

"Granted."

"Ensign Gilmore?"

Gilmore grinned. "That's right."

The child held out her hand. "Naomi Wilman. Captain's assistant."

"Is that so?"

"I wanted to officially welcome you aboard the *Starship Voyager.*"

"Glad to be here."

"If you need anything," the little girl pressed on, "replicator rations, a tour of the lower decks, I'm your man!"

Gilmore smiled, and Chakotay tolerated the aberration of adult behavior, wondering if it wouldn't be nicer to see a child acting like a child instead of training to ape adult ways as if that were normal or even healthy for her. A kid should be a kid, not a crewman.

"Thank you, Miss Wildman," Gilmore accommodated. "I'll keep that in mind."

"As you were!" Naomi beamed into that stage smile again, about-faced, and left.

Gilmore watched her go, both touched and confused. "I didn't realize you had children on board," she said, without commenting on the weirdness.

"Only one," Kim said. "She was born here."

"I have a nephew," the unfortunate woman said, giving in a little. "Back on Earth . . . about the same age. Well, not anymore . . . I guess he's a teenager by now. I probably wouldn't even recognize him."

Chakotay regretted that he hadn't managed to stave off the emotion even by cloaking it in engineering prattle. "You'll see him again," was all he could think to say.

It rang hollow and inadequate.

Before the moment could sour further, Gilmore's combadge buzzed with Captain Ransom's voice. *"Ransom to Gilmore."*

She touched the badge. "Yes, Captain?"

"Report to the Equinox *bridge."*

"On my way. Duty calls." She seemed relieved to get out of this.

Chakotay nodded his permission, even though she didn't need it when her captain was calling.

How much longer was he officially her captain? Chakotay had never been in this particular situation before. Would the shiftover take place when *Equinox* was cast adrift? That would be a hard moment for all of them, and it would create problems he didn't want to explore yet.

He would have to talk to Captain Janeway. Things would come up that they would have to iron out.

"Assemble a salvage team," Chakotay told Kim, trying to angle back to hard work rather than this haunting anguish that cloyed the decks.

"Aye, sir. She's nervous," Kim observed sadly as he watched Gilmore slip through the port door. "I think she's worried about letting their ship go. I guess it'd be hard to abandon a ship you'd fought so hard to save."

"Must've been like that for Shackleton," Chakotay mused.

Kim's boyish face crumpled. "Who?"

"Oh . . . a terrible tragedy on Earth. I forget the year. Nineteen twenties, I think. Exploration vessel, sailing ship, got caught in the Antarctic ice floes. Its crew tried to survive there, tried to save the ship, but the hull was screwed into place as the ice closed tighter and tighter. You know glacial ice is different from water ice, don't you?"

"Never really gave it a thought, sir."

"Packed snow is harder and denser than frozen water. It inexorably crushed the ship while the crew watched. The *Endurance*."

"Did they live?"

"I think most of them did. It's been a long time since I read the account . . . they certainly were survivors in the most heroic sense. They made a transantarctic trek. On foot."

"On foot—whew."

"But they had to watch their perfectly functional ship be slowly crushed. They just couldn't get her out of there." This must be something like that for the *Equinox* crew. Their ship is still functional, but it was time for the icy trek.

"Seems a shame," Kim went on, "to cut loose a whole Starfleet ship when we're so alone ourselves. I don't think our crew likes it any better than their crew does."

"Mmm," Chakotay uttered distractedly. "I wonder if we could fool the aliens into thinking the *Equinox* is still their target. Get them to follow the derelict while *Voyager* gets away."

Kim looked up. "Sir, we're still not sure what makes them attack us at all, never mind whether or not they'll follow *Equinox* instead of us."

"I know. But there's a certain logic in their attack, that's what bothers me. They didn't come after us when we first veered in. They didn't split up and come to meet us as we approached. They stayed with *Equinox*. I can't imagine why they would . . . as ships go, two Starfleet ships are basically similar. The same emissions, the same construction materials, the same pulsations . . ."

"Are you saying they're intelligent?"

Chakotay shrugged, unwilling to go that far. "No evidence of that yet. If we had time, we could explore it. We've only got a few hours, barely enough to support our shield network, never mind try to communicate with something on another astral plane. There's obviously some higher evolution going on, after all, because they have heads and tails and some kind of hand. But so does a lizard."

Kim leaned forward and lowered his voice. "Do you agree with the captain? Is it right to order another captain to ditch his ship even though it's still under power? If it were derelict, that'd be different. What do you think?"

Hoping the rest of the crew would just opt not to think about this, Chakotay found himself caught, as first officers often do, between his captain and those who were looking up to him as the senior officer who represented the crew when he wasn't on command watch. There were subtle shifts of consultation in a ship's complement. The captain was on duty now; that made Chakotay the voice of the crew for a few hours. Kim felt able to bring a serious and troubling question to his first officer.

The fact that Chakotay didn't answer right away betrayed his doubts.

"It's complex, Harry," he began inadequately. "We haven't been faced with anything like this. The captain's winging it."

"But can she *do* this?"

"She's doing it. Captain Ransom is going along without protest."

"Would you do it?"

The question, so innocently and honestly posed, raised the hairs on the back of Chakotay's neck. Back up the captain? He would. Do the same thing?

"I don't know," he said. "There's a certain damnable flexibility built into Starfleet. There had to be. Look at us, after all. The regulations and laws were developed for a fleet that could contact each other in a dependable network all the way back to Starfleet Command. Nobody ever anticipated *Voyager* and *Equinox*. Would I do what Captain Janeway's doing? I can tell you that everything looks different when you change chairs. Captains aren't cut from the same mold. Ransom's got his own methods, his own tricks that got them this far. He's got his own timing, his own judgments, his own criteria for deciding what's more important—the crew, the mission, the ship. . . . That's why some regulations are confoundingly vague, or even contradict each other. And as a Starfleet captain, Ransom is privileged with a certain latitude in interpreting regulations. Especially so far out here, without anyone to consult."

"Or anyone to back him up," Kim pointed out,

empathizing. "What does it do to a captain to be *that* alone? Oh, I know—we're alone, too, but I've never felt like we were really all that much alone. Maybe Captain Janeway and Captain Ransom have felt differently. I've got the luxury of having a captain and a first officer to support me. Who've the captains got?"

Chakotay slumped back and slugged the last of his coffee, now cold and bitter.

"Just us," he said.

"Let me get this straight. You lived on a Borg Cube for nineteen years?"

Noah Lessing absorbed the idea with a shiver. Seven of Nine was aloof, cold, mechanical, gorgeous—but somehow he'd convinced himself she'd been Borgified for only a year or two. Nineteen . . . That was almost her whole life. And almost his.

"A series of cubes," Seven explained as they hurried through the corridor. "Twelve, in all. The Collective re-designates drones to optimize efficiency."

"Guess that makes you an army brat," he teased. "Me too. My father was a terraforming engineer. I lived on a dozen different colonies before I went to the Academy. It's a disorienting way to grow up."

"Drones adapt. I was never 'disoriented.' "

"This may sound like a strange question . . . do you ever get homesick?"

She did something shockingly human—bobbed her brows. "This may sound like a strange answer. But yes."

Lessing smiled his easygoing smile. " 'Cube, Sweet Cube.' I can understand. Surrounded by like-minded people—"

"One mind, to be exact."

Oh, that was another shiver. One mind? To be only a cell in a body, without control or thought? He couldn't empathize with that one.

"Noah!" Marla Gilmore hurried to catch up with them. As Lessing turned to greet her, she asked, "Did you get a call from the captain?"

He nodded. "I'm heading there now."

He turned to Seven, knowing he shouldn't be fraternizing in a way from which he might not be able to cleanly extricate himself. He shouldn't get to like her too much.

"We'll continue our Q and A later," he said, then added to Gilmore, "She wants to learn more about humanity. But I'm afraid I've been asking all the questions. I'll keep my mouth shut next time."

Seven glanced at him and simply moved off down another corridor. He wasn't sure what that meant.

"If there *is* a next time," Gilmore muttered when they were alone.

"What do you mean?" he asked.

"I have a feeling the captain isn't calling us to a social gathering," she told him, keeping her eyes moving. "When Janeway ordered him to abandon the *Equinox,* I saw the look on his face. He's got something on his mind."

"Rudy's face," Lessing said, only half jokingly, "isn't

that easy to 'read.' You don't think he's going to defy her, do you?"

"Wouldn't you? Our ship's still viable. His command hasn't been legally abrogated. I don't know about you, but this doesn't feel right."

"Leaving *Equinox?* Not fighting to keep our ship?"

"None of it feels right. Leaving, staying, fighting, not fighting. . . . I've been concentrating on the aliens for so long, I don't remember how to think any other way. I can't tell right from wrong anymore."

"That's not our job. Our job is to support our captain. *Our* captain."

Gilmore's expressive eyes worked in a troubled way. "Our captain . . . aye."

They moved together through *Voyager* to the transporter room without saying anything more. Lessing experienced a surge of raw fear as the beam gripped him and he knew he was going back to the box in which he had almost died.

Yet, the pull of their own ship was almost tangible. They had fought for it so many times that they possessed it completely, in a thoroughly whole-souled way. He'd known in the back of his mind that he would come back. They all would. This was the platform of their reason to exist. They hadn't ever expected to find another friendly ship, so *Equinox* was their world.

When he rematerialized on board *Equinox,* sure enough the sensation of uncertainty flowed completely away and that old possessiveness replaced it, as if he were suddenly filled with purpose. This was their ship, the ship they had fought for and which had fought for them, holding up beyond anyone's guess that she could. Even her designers had set limits and said she couldn't be stressed beyond them. Those limits had been broken the first year. She'd gotten them through. Now she was hanging here, being good, waiting for someone to take her reins again.

Minimal power pulsed, but in more places than before. Repairs had been going on continually. Most of the *Voyager* crew was gone now, no longer trying to save, repair, or clean up the *Equinox*. Lessing and Gilmore changed places on the transporter pad with the last of the other ship's crew as they left with cases of supplies. Salvage . . .

Without speaking another word, Lessing led the way to the bridge, Marla following. That was all right. She was uncertain. Lessing tried not to think about this. The captain was waiting.

On the bridge, Rudy and Max were already there, looking at a monitor that displayed the schematic of the force-field generator. Others in the crew lingered around. Lessing nodded to them. It was good to see them again, without the peppering of somebody else's crew.

"Are we alone?" Rudy asked, looking up at his crew.

"Only *Equinox* crew on board now," Max confirmed, checking the bioscans from encrypted combadges all over the ship. "We've managed to clear out the others without their realizing it. Most of the *Voyager* crew assigned here thinks some of their own are still here.

Oh . . . wait a minute. Somebody just beamed, down in engineering."

"Never mind that for now," Rudy said. "It's probably just a salvage team or that Borg girl finishing her capacitor transfers. Just make sure we're comm-insulated."

"We are," Marla assured. "What happens to *Voyager?*"

Rudy Ransom gazed at his last engineer with insecure sympathy. She hadn't said, "What happens to them when we leave, when we abandon them, when we betray them, when we split up the only Federation unity in the Delta Quadrant?" He knew all those things were running in her mind, and in all their minds. They'd found friends, discovered they couldn't trust those friends as much as they wanted to, and now would have to be bad friends themselves. Such was life here. They would handle it, as always. He could never do this if he didn't believe that.

"They've got weapons," Max answered so the captain didn't have to. "Shields, a full crew . . . they'll survive."

Rudy avoided grinning in approval at him, but he was proud. What that word *survive* had come to mean to them—a virtue and a victory all in one word.

"Maybe we *should* abandon ship," Lessing said with hesitation. "Try to forget everything that's happened here . . ."

"A shower and a hot meal," Ransom bristled. "That's all it took to make some of us forget what's at stake here." He turned to face them, noting Lessing's clear shame. "We're proceeding as planned. Any further objections?"

He knew Lessing hadn't been making an objection, exactly, only posing a last-ditch chance to think about this, but Ransom was done thinking. He'd been done for hours.

"I need every one of you to give me your best," the captain challenged. "As you always have."

They were already all with him. He could tell. Even Gilmore, in her typical cloak of doubts, sadly and warmly nodded.

"This won't be easy," Burke said, consulting a wall monitor's display. "The generator's located on deck eleven, next to the warp plasma manifold. We can't get a clean lock without boosting the signal." He looked to his right. "Marla, we need you to set aside your claustrophobia and crawl through the access port to set up the Transport Enhancers."

If there was anything to overcome, she was already handling it. "Understood."

"We'll have to take the internal sensors off-line," Burke added. "Noah, you're elected."

"You can count on me, sir," Lessing said, as if making up for his brief lapse.

"I'll disengage the power couplings from engineering."

Ransom gave them his best confident posture. He was telling them they had to leave the comfort and safety of salvation to go back into the trenches, but soldiers had been doing that for centuries uncounted. From the Roman marches to the Battle of the Bulge, from Tarkus to Cardassia, troopers had returned to the pit of hell for the sake of duty. At least they were going together, shoulder to shoulder, without contamination from a bunch of people who wore the same uniform but who would never understand how that uniform looks when it's soaked in bloody mud.

"You'll have time for one more shower," he told them. "Make the most of it."

CHAPTER

7

Kathryn Janeway sat still and scratched her hand, disturbed. If only Ransom had fought a little, argued some, defended his command, just for a few minutes. She'd quoted half a regulation, and he'd folded to it without even checking.

Somehow she felt worse than if he'd argued.

Now Seven and Tuvok were reporting a power fluctuation in the security grid, within tolerance, but still troubling. It shouldn't have happened. Everything was on-line, being monitored, being tended. This was Red Alert, not a coffee klatsch.

Seven, standing before the captain in her ready room as Janeway sat at her desk, explained that she had tried to correct the flux, illustrating her efforts on a cutaway graphic. It zoomed into a single deck section as Seven explained.

"The discrepancy is in the research lab on *Equinox.* I could tune our field generator to match it, if we can determine the frequency of that multiphasic chamber. The lab, however, is still permeated with thermionic radiation."

"I thought it would have dissipated by now, Captain," Tuvok said, almost apologetically. "We discovered that three EPS conduits have been rerouted to the lab. They are emitting the radiation."

Janeway looked at the PADD he handed her. "Any theories?"

"Only one," Tuvok said bluntly. "Ransom doesn't want us to enter the research lab."

"He *has* been adamant about protecting his ship. I thought it was simply a captain's pride . . ."

But maybe I'm being a sympathetic jerk and he's outthinking me.

"I want to take a closer look at that lab," she decided. "If we can close off those EPS conduits, how long will it take to vent the radiation?"

"Several hours," Seven said.

Janeway frowned. She was getting to hate that word *several.* How many? Two? Ten?

"I don't want to wait that long. Send The Doctor. He'll be immune to its effects. Tell him to look for anything out of the ordinary."

"Shall I notify Captain Ransom?" Tuvok asked. He was right to ask.

"Not yet." Janeway lowered her voice despite the privacy here. Perhaps it was the distaste in her mouth that made her quieter. "Let's wait until we test your theory.

Have The Doctor maintain an open comlink and give us continuous reports while he looks around. Tell me when he's in."

"Captain?"

"Oh—Chakotay." Janeway sighed, greeting him wearily as Tuvok and Seven turned to leave the ready room. Like most of the crew they were uncomfortable here and usually tried to leave quickly. This, unlike the bridge or the briefing room, was the captain's private domain, on the edge of action. Through that door was public land. Here, not so. This was the think tank, but only the captain's. More private even than her quarters, she actually spent much more time here than there.

"Am I disturbing you?" Chakotay asked when they were alone.

"No, not at all. You look tired. Sit down for a minute."

"Only a minute," he accepted. "We've shored up the shield power by tapping into the impulse pellet containment system, gained maybe another hour and some minutes. Time to breathe, at least."

"Any information about these life forms attacking us? That's what I really want."

"Nothing substantial. Well, nothing helpful."

"No communication. Language."

"None. Not even nonrandom impulses. We've had a team working on it, but I had to take them off it for a while and have them help the deflector crew. Everyone's stretched thin either salvaging *Equinox* or trying to keep our shields up and our propulsion units on-line in case we might be able to outrun them."

Janeway tried to keep a leash on her dividing thoughts. "If they exist on an astral plane that parallels ours with some kind of folding effect, outrunning them may not be an option. They might be on a permanent wormhole that could stretch one mile for them and ten thousand light-years for us."

"That means we fight." His words were steady, though significant with perception of how very long a fight that could be.

"Yes," Janeway uttered, "or we communicate. That's an imperative."

"Not everything communicates," he pointed out in a slightly warning tone. With one elbow pressed to the chair, he tried to be casual. "There's a big range between swarming and sentient."

She held out a hand. "They're intelligent. They changed their tactics. They learned that by concentrating their efforts on one shield, they could get it to fold. They *learned*. They aren't just attacking anything they see. Not only learning, but learning something technical."

"Technical to us," Chakotay focused. "Maybe to them, shield energy is as natural as silk to a spider. They do have that natural nucleogenic base, and it would take us tremendous technology to duplicate it."

Sniggering doubts entered her star system. "True, I suppose . . . or they might actually be smart and it just looks natural to us."

"Does this mean," Chakotay began, "you're questioning Ransom's interpretation of the Prime Directive?"

Unwilling to say that straight out, Janeway hesitated. "They might be a nasty civilization, but if they *are* a civilization, then the directive applies."

His eyes swept the lovely vista out the viewport behind her. "We can say that when we're standing behind intact shields and we can go have a hot dinner in a clean mess hall."

"I don't know, Chakotay." Tense, Janeway sank back into her chair, feeling as if she were shrinking. "Something's wrong."

Purposefully he leaned back too, but in a more relaxed way, probably hoping to telepathically get her to do the same. "Is there something I don't know?" he asked. "What kind of 'something' are we discussing?"

Janeway inhaled a choppy breath of the fresh air, noting that there was a slight rise in temperature. The air in here wasn't as crisp and cool as usual. The ship was stressed, selectively preferring some systems over others.

"I wish I were sure of things," she vented. "Is there an animal spirit guide to walk me through a relationship with another captain who might end up living in my house for the rest of my life?"

"Doesn't seem like you'd need advice. Not *you.*"

She laughed. "What does that mean, not *me?* Oh, don't answer. Have I been so far removed from dealing with other Starfleet officers that Ransom's reactions strike me as too accommodating?"

"You mean giving up his ship?"

"Of course," she said. Instantly she wanted to bite back her tone, but too late. Narrowing her eyes, she sought his dark gaze and the pool-quiet passiveness that always underpinned his attitude. "Wouldn't you have struggled a little?"

"I'd have struggled a lot," he offered. "There's no measuring what he's been through or what it does to a man to lose half his crew. Maybe he kept fighting because he had to, without the passion for command. We've relieved him of having to carry the load anymore."

"Mmm," she responded dully. "I'm afraid I'm being too hard on him."

Chakotay paused and thought. "I don't think he sees it that way."

Shifting her aching back, Janeway felt her stomach tense. "I've never usurped another captain's command before. Oh, it's one thing to have the authority or even the tactical advantage. It's something else to tell a captain with a viable ship that it's time to dump it. How long before someone has to tell me that?"

"There's another problem, too." Chakotay stretched his shoulders against the chair back and, despite the time crunch, actually crossed his legs. "Ransom is senior to me by twenty-two months. By the book, the minute we cut loose the *Equinox,* you have a new first officer."

Was there something wrong with the atmospheric pressure in here? Janeway groaned and palmed back a straggle of her brown hair. "Why do you have to be so damned thorough! Do I have to think about that?"

He raised one shoulder and lowered it. "If regulations are going to rule the roost, we both have to think about it."

In the quiet room, under soft lighting, she pressed all ten fingers to her forehead, closed her eyes, and indulged in a gale-force grimace. How could something so positive and hopeful turn so tricky in a matter of hours?

"Space travel is for the birds . . ." Lowering her hands to the desk with a thump, she eyed him critically. "Are you ready to give up your post?"

Raising his chin with cursed nobility, he quite seriously said, "Captain, I'm ready to do whatever makes the ship run better in your eyes."

"I may have to shoot you."

"Depriving Ransom of his command *and* his seniority is unwarranted in my estimation. I'd be lying to say I didn't think he deserves the posting. Not only that, but he'll have a significant portion of the crew who still regard him as their commanding officer. You can't ignore them. Crew attitude is critical. That's how we blended the first two crews," he reminded. "Yours, mine—"

"Ours." Janeway pressed her wrists to the edge of her desk. "It's possible he doesn't care one way or the other. He's not a battle captain, not by training. He's a scientist. His promotion was a reward. A science crew doesn't expect to fight for its life. By the time they arrive at a duty location, all the battles are supposed to have been fought already."

"By captains like us."

"Yes . . . us."

"But he's *been* a captain now for a long time," Chakotay flatly said. "His command wasn't pro tem.

And he's done the job, he's brought them through. You can't wish that away just for my sake."

"It's not just for your sake," she said, suddenly shrill. Almost immediately she deflated and grinned miserably at herself. "Sorry. It's for my sake too. I don't want him as my first officer. I want you."

He grinned too, flattered. "That may not remain as your prerogative. By the book, you can't erase an officer's seniority because you want to play favorites."

Ah, the nasty ring of truth. Janeway frowned. "I'm spoiled. I've been away from other Starfleet influences so long that I've gotten too used to having my way. We've been together now longer than most crews. We haven't had people transferring in and out as a ship usually does. We've all gotten ironed into our positions. You and I have gotten used to our privileges, and the lower officers have gotten used to having us as a buffer between them and the big decisions. Now, all that might be turned upside down."

"I don't like Ransom very much," Chakotay admitted, "not that it matters. He's a little hard-bitten for me, but who can blame him? Considering that he never trained for a long-term crisis, or to be a captain at all, it's to his credit that they're alive at all, never mind actually making distance progress."

"Oh, well, that's another thing!" Janeway leaned forward, elbows on her desk. "How have they made that much progress? One wormhole? Have you ever heard of a wormhole that covered that much distance?"

"Nobody has that answer, Kathryn. Are you saying he's lying?"

"No . . . maybe . . . no, but only that he seems to have his answers too quickly."

Chakotay fell silent a moment, a brief mutuality of suspicion and doubt. "Captain," he ultimately suggested, "you could be misreading all of this. Don't get me wrong—so could I."

"All right," she challenged. "How would you read it differently?"

Janeway watched him as he sat there and thought about it for another moment, appreciating him.

"When you're drowning," he began, "all you want is one more breath of air. It comes down to that. You don't care that you're freezing, that your clothing is in shreds, you haven't eaten in a month, or that you look silly with your hair wet. All you want is that breath. Then, all at once, you're rescued! You're lying on the raft, starved, freezing, but you don't care because you can breathe. Then, after you've been breathing awhile, you start to think maybe it'd be nice just to have a blanket. When you're starving, you don't care that you have no shelter and you stink."

"All that is short-term," Janeway said. "You're either done drowning pretty soon, or you're dead. Ransom's experience lasted years. What does that do?"

"Like slow starvation, then," Chakotay altered his analysis. "All you know is that you're in a ditch with a load of bread and what people think doesn't matter. The world is great because you have the bread. It doesn't matter that people are looking down at you because you're a bum. A while later, you've eaten and hunger isn't your motivator anymore, and you start thinking about how nice a real bed might feel. You start to notice the people staring at you because you're smelly. Well, maybe I want a little more than to sit here and eat bread. Your other priorities are coming back online. Motivations rebuild like a computer reloading. Eventually you start to realize what you were trying to do before you were starving and drowning. Maybe you still want to try that."

"Starving, drowning . . . when you empathize, you don't beat around the bush, do you?" Janeway blinked, overwhelmed by the clarity of his perceptions, hoping she was interpreting them right. "You're saying Ransom might be satisfied, even happy, to be a researcher again? He might not want the first officer's posting?"

He began now to doubt his own logic. "I'd still want it, but that's me. I'm just saying that the *Equinox* crew is acting too cool to be normal. They gave themselves up for dead, made their peace, and suddenly they were resurrected."

"And the near-death experience has driven more than one person to instability."

"They'll come back, is what I'm saying," Chakotay tried to explain. "They haven't had enough time to settle down, remember what they really want, who they are, or even decide who to trust or what their mission should be. But they will. They'll slowly 'reload their programming.' "

"Yes, it's what's so unique about humans," Janeway added. "We're never satisfied for long. If we were, we'd never advance. We'd just settle down with the bread and the bed and eat and sleep ourselves into atrophy."

"What are you going to do? Tell him regulations give you authority to order him to abandon his ship, but you're going to ignore regulations when it comes to his seniority?"

His reissuing of the critical question, this time, couldn't be brushed off or turned philosophical. It was real, tangible, and problematic. Soon it would gain a sharp reality, and things would have to change.

Janeway entertained a brief, insane moment of handing command over to him and Ransom and retiring to some nice pink planet somewhere.

"Starfleet regulations represent solidity for us," she told him. Her voice was a cold rasp, deep in her throat. "Regulations are civilization. They're my anchorage. If we're going to be saved, regulations will be what saves us."

He nodded, flexed his legs and placed both feet on the carpet, and leaned forward. For a second or two he gazed at the carpet, then looked up, then stood up.

"Understood," he said, unreadable. "Whatever you wish, Captain. I'll back you up."

"I'm in."

Voyager's Emergency Medical Hologram had known since the beginning that something very special was going on. Discovery of a totally new Starfleet ship, so far-flung from Federation space, had raised the heart rates and metabolism, not to mention the spirits, of everyone on board. Even Tuvok and Seven, two separate interpretations of Vulcanness, were reacting with heightened senses. Now the EMH had another group of physiologies to track, to log, to care for. There was something pleasant about that, even for a hologram.

This area was still very dark. No one had been working here because of the contamination. The research lab of a strictly science-oriented vessel was a complex place. Every wall was stocked with storage, incubators, computer analysis equipment, scrapings, chemicals, slides, and everything that could be pressed into service on a floating science platform.

Unlike the utilitarian tidiness of *Voyager*'s labs, this area was cluttered and mangled, its deck almost hidden under wreckage.

Once his ocular program adjusted, he began to move through the wreckage, surveying the lab, his goal the multiphasic chamber only ten steps away. Instantly he saw the chamber and its unexpected contents. Inside the stasis compartment was a twisted, petrified mass, obviously organic, but crystallized. Its football-shaped skull was eyeless, its mouth gaping, frozen.

No one had reported this. As the ship's only doctor, he would have been the one to be consulted.

"I've found the multiphasic chamber," he reported as he opened his tricorder to analyze the corpse. "There's some kind of organic mass inside. It appears to be a member of the alien species, but its cell structures have vitrified."

Moving the tricorder, he shifted analysis from organic to mechanical.

"This is more than just a stasis chamber," he reported. "It's some kind of matter-conversion technology. Stand by . . . there's a control port here. Hmmm . . ."

From *Voyager,* Tuvok was monitoring and recording the analysis. *"Doctor?"*

Strange. The Vulcan sounded impatient. Vulcans shouldn't get impatient. That was against their programming.

"The chamber," The Doctor continued, "contains a polaron grid and a submolecular sequencer. It looks like it was designed to convert the alien cell structures into some kind of crystalline compound."

Then Seven's voice, *"That function was not specified in their schematics."*

"I have a feeling there's a lot here they didn't 'specify.' " Moving to a work station, he enabled the monitor and read the alphanumeric data scrolling anxiously on the screen. "I've accessed their research log. They're encrypted . . . but judging by the file headings, they've performed this procedure dozens of times."

Informed now, he crossed to a specimen stand that held a vial filled with a dark granular fluid.

"More of the alien compound," he reported, "but it's been biochemically altered. They've extracted the base proteins. Its molecular structure is most unusual . . ."

"Can you be more specific?" Tuvok asked.

"It appears to store a great deal of nucleogenic energy. I'm not an engineer, but I'd say they were trying to convert this material into a source of power."

Once activated, a nearby wall monitor provided an unexpected correlation for a research lab, a schematic of the exotically modified warp core. Why would that have anything to do with . . .

"Doctor," Tuvok asked, *"can you discern whether*

the specimens were alive or dead at the time of their . . ."

"Their 'use'? I can't tell that yet. I understand the gravity of your question. Tuvok . . . you'd better notify the captain."

"I'm going to miss this ship."

Though Max Burke openly appreciated the talents of a passing female *Voyager* crew member striding past him and Rudy Ransom, Ransom wished his first officer would keep his eyes to himself and his mind on their problem. The ship was almost ready—their own ship.

"Once we're back on Earth," Ransom told him sternly, "there'll be plenty of pretty girls. Status?"

"Ready on all fronts," Burke reported, virtually whispering, "the transport enhancers are in place. And Noah's created the subroutine to mask *Voyager's* internal sensors."

"Power couplings?"

"Bypass controls have been routed to our bridge. All you need to do is say, 'Energize.' "

Ransom paused as someone else walked by and disappeared. "Janeway wants to bring the security grid online at nineteen hundred hours. We'll have to act before then. Tell the others to—"

As they rounded a T-sect, two security guards strode toward them with undisguised purpose, one with his hand on his phaser.

"Max—" Ransom calmly nodded toward another corridor, then steered Burke down that way. A few more paces . . . step lively. "The transporter room's not far from here. Keep moving."

Janeway was smarter than he thought. Or he hadn't fooled her at all. He couldn't tell which. He hoped he'd fooled her some because, if so, there might still be a way out of this.

Would the guards chase them? Would they open fire? Even phaser stun was questionable against a post captain. Did Janeway possess the nerve to have given that order already? To fire on another ship's officers without due process? She couldn't be that sure of her standing, regulations or not.

Twenty more steps. The transporter room. He could lock the door once he was inside. Most of his crew was already on *Equinox,* still working. He bet Janeway wouldn't already have slammed them in the brig before consulting their captain about the circumstances. He and Burke were the last—if he could have those twenty steps—

"Captain Janeway wishes to speak with you."

The Vulcan appeared in front of them, heading them off, phaser drawn. Another security guard was with him.

No mistake. They'd figured out some of it. Part of it.

Beside Ransom, Burke's hand slipped to his own phaser.

No—

Ransom put out his own hand, stopping the challenge before it turned sour. Behind him, the footfalls of the other two guards converged. He braced himself, willing Burke to take the cue.

"All right, Mr. Tuvok," Ransom said strictly. "That's enough. We won't draw on you. You're holding weapons on Starfleet officers, do you realize that?"

"Of course, Captain," the Vulcan said. "We determined that your passions might compromise us all. This is a precaution. Captain Janeway is waiting for you. Mr. Burke will accompany us to a holding area until the captain makes her decision."

"Until *she* makes her decision," Ransom echoed bitterly. "She hasn't even been to the gate yet, Mr. Tuvok. Why don't you stand aside and let me lead the way. Because we both know you won't fire on me."

Janeway sat at the head of the table in the briefing room. Her unhappy task lay before her, in the form of a mute witness to war crimes—a lab palette with a couple of handfuls of alien matter reduced to crystals. Her anger fused the room. It felt hot in here. Confirmation of bottom-feeding suspicions was a bitter thing.

Two armed guards stood at the door. At the opposite end of the table, by himself, was Captain Ransom.

Or was he a captain now? His ship about to be abandoned, a maneuver to which he had acquiesced . . . through the broiling rage, Janeway could see no clear answer. Fuming with the sourness of the moment, she lay unchecked tension upon the funereal room.

"Ten isograms," she said harshly, accusing. Picking up the PADD with the operative data, she scanned it for the twentieth time. "If I understand your calculations, that's enough to increase your warp factor by . . . what? Point zero three percent for one month?"

Ransom was silent. Apparently she had the numbers right.

"Unfortunately," Janeway went on, "that boost wouldn't get you very far. So you'd need to replenish the supply. And that means killing another life form. And another. How many lives would it take to get you back to the Alpha Quadrant?"

The question hung, boiling, in open air. Hot in here now.

The other captain's eyes were cold and unapologetic. Janeway put the PADD down. No point hashing percentages.

"I think you know the reason we're under attack," she said. "These aliens are trying to protect themselves from *you*."

Ransom shifted in his chair, losing some of the defiance. "Sixty-three," he bluntly said. "That's how many more it'll take. And every time I sacrifice one of those lives, part of me is lost as well."

"I might believe that," Janeway snapped, "if I hadn't examined your 'research.' These experiments were meticulous. And they were brutal. If you felt any remorse, you'd never have continued."

"Starfleet Regulation Three, paragraph twelve," Ransom shot back with utter confidence. " 'In the event of imminent destruction, a captain is authorized to preserve the lives of his crew by any justifiable means.' "

A can of worms. She determined not to get into a wrangle with him over the definition of "justifiable."

That was the trick word, the one they both knew was meant to offer captains interpretive flexibility. She'd lose that argument.

The only answer was not to budge, and not to argue.

"I doubt that protocol covers mass murder," she accused.

Ransom ground his teeth. "In my judgment it does."

"Unacceptable."

His small eyes flared coldly. "We had nothing! My ship was in pieces!"

Taken aback by his intensity, Janeway said nothing. There was no good way to handle this.

Without her prodding he got a grip on his meltdown. "Our dilithium was gone," he suffered. "We were running on thrusters. We hadn't eaten in sixteen days! We had just enough power left to enter orbit of an M-class planet. Lucky for us, the inhabitants were generous . . . The Ankari . . . they provided us with a few supplies. They even performed one of their 'sacred rituals' to invoke 'spirits of good fortune from another realm.' To bless our journey."

Bitterness tainted his words, but Janeway could still see no true regret, no bending toward the idea that he had broken a moral code and a legal one.

"But these weren't spirits," Ransom went on. "They were nucleogenic life forms. Our scans revealed that they were emitting high levels of antimatter. So we managed to obtain one of the devices and constructed a containment chamber that would prevent the life form from vanishing so quickly. But something went wrong. It thrashed around and started to vitrify. We tried to send it back, but we couldn't reverse the flow through the device's fissure." For the first time, his eyes grew shaded with sorrow. "We examined the remains and discovered that the enhancement properties were still present."

Now he looked up at her, and the challenge returned, now glazed with harsh reality.

"It was already dead! What would you have done!"

A perfectly legitimate challenge. Janeway sat with her chin tucked, fuming, and would not answer. She dared not sympathize or she would be condoning his interpretation. There were things she would have to keep on her side. Right now, silence was the tool. She had a new role to play that did not include simply being another captain.

"We traveled over ten thousand light-years in less than two weeks." Ransom sounded more defeated now, defiance and surrender flashing back and forth. "We'd found our salvation! How could we ignore it!"

"By adhering to the oath you took as Starfleet officers," she told him icily. "To seek out life. Not destroy it."

"It's easy to cling to 'principles' when you're standing on a vessel with its bulkheads intact, manned by a crew that's not starving!"

"It's never easy," Janeway countered, suddenly thinking of Chakotay. Her voice was firm, rough, like a recording. "But if we turn our backs on those principles we stop being human. I'm putting an end to your experiments. And you are hereby relieved of your command. You and your crew will be confined to quarters."

She nodded to her guards, who approached to escort Ransom out.

"Please," Ransom begged, "show them leniency. They were only following my orders."

"Their mistake."

Another hot potato. How far should a crew go? She expected orders to be followed too.

Bitter and trembling, obviously angry at either her or himself, Ransom let the guards usher him toward the door. As the corridor panel opened, he turned back to her.

"It's a long way home, Captain," he warned.

Lips pressed tight, jaw aching, Janeway watched the door sweep shut, separating her from the ghastly duty she now found dumped in her lap. What was it like when your feet were on fire?

Had that last sentence been a threat? Or was he warning her that she was looking at a future fractal of herself, her own command?

Stiff as an old woman, she pushed up from her chair. Every bone in her legs clicked as if carrying on the argument by themselves.

The bridge turned cold as she entered. She sensed it, but as if she were walking into an hallucination. Chakotay, Tuvok, Seven, Paris, Kim, The Doctor, others . . . she sensed the eyes of each one, and met none.

"Doctor," she said, looking at the main screen until she could muster what it took to look at him, "return to their research lab and retrieve all the data you can locate on the aliens. I want to find a way to communicate with them."

The normally bellicose hologram simply said, "Aye, Captain," and mobilized.

To Seven, Janeway gritted her teeth and stiffly said, "Go to their engine room. Take those warp core modifications off-line."

Seven didn't even muster the "aye" The Doctor had managed. She simply left. Even she, apparently, could feel the gravity change now that their grim captain was here, dragging her baggage.

Only Chakotay dared approach her as she lowered into her command chair.

"Captain?" he urged.

She dug her fingernails into the fake leather on the chair's arms. She didn't look at him, or anyone.

"Let's try," she said, "to make first contact the *right* way."

CHAPTER

8

"WHAT'S GOING TO HAPPEN TO US?"

Marla Gilmore's question didn't exactly take Commander Chakotay by surprise, though he hadn't come up with an answer for something he expected to be asked.

"That's up to Captain Janeway," he said, shoving the responsibility over the wall. "You'll be confined to quarters until we find a way to make peace with these life forms you've been killing. If it's not too late."

Gilmore was anxious as they hurried down the corridor, with a security guard, fully armed with a phaser rifle, clomping behind them. Knowing she was technically in custody, her mood was tense and troubled, yet carried a certain flow of relief. For Chakotay, the guard was just added protection, but not against Gilmore.

"To be honest," she said, "I'm glad you stopped us. Living the rest of our lives knowing what we'd done . . ."

"You could've stopped yourself. Why didn't you?"

"I don't know . . . when the captain ordered me to modify the warp core, I concentrated on the work. I tried not to think about how it was going to be used."

"Well, think about it now. Because we need your help."

He stopped at the door of the astrometrics lab—not her quarters, and not the brig.

"Commander?" She blinked, perplexed.

"After you."

In the lab, Seven of Nine was working at a console, and even her posture of aplomb was suffering from the frustration. On the domescreen, a graphic display showed the *Equinox* warp core and the weird modifications that had been made to it.

"We're having trouble making sense of all this," Chakotay told Gilmore.

"The schematics are encrypted," Seven pushed in. "I can't access them."

Chakotay kept looking at Gilmore. "Do you know the encryption codes?"

She hesitated. Her hands pressed to her thighs in a kind of resistance.

"Your captain's been relieved of command," Chakotay clarified. "You take orders from me now. Do you have the codes?"

With a blink as if awakening, she said, "Yes."

Seven stepped back from the console. "Proceed."

Gilmore did as ordered, though obviously she was uncertain and torn, her loyalties, training, and instincts all clashing.

Moving to her, Chakotay shifted from commanding officer to shipmate for a moment. "Think of it this way, Ensign. You might live with yourself a little easier."

While she worked, Gilmore's breathing was hollow and ragged as she fed the codes into the computer, then cleared the double-secured access authorization, using both her personal identification and Ransom's. That was a deep encryption, to need two IDs.

The guard was waiting for her at the door. As she turned, she flinched at the sight of him.

Turning to Seven one last time before incarceration, Gilmore sadly told her, "You said you wanted to learn more about humanity. But I guess we're not exactly prized examples. I'm sorry . . ."

"On the contrary," Seven returned edgily, "you've taught me a great deal."

Unsettled by that, Gilmore simply went out in front of Chakotay and the guard.

Feeling guilty that none of these major and haunting decisions were his, Chakotay caught up with her and set the pace a little slower. As he watched Gilmore at his side, he was thinking of Kathryn.

"Did you try to communicate with the aliens?"

"Of course we did," she said defensively. "Our universal translator only picked up random signals. We think it might've taken some damage."

"Did you try to repair it?"

"When we had time." She gazed at the carpet as they walked. "You think we're horrible, don't you?"

"What I think doesn't matter. It's Captain Janeway's interpretation of the law that matters now. We've never had a law enforcement role in the Delta Quadrant until now," he went on. "There was no one else who had sworn to live under our laws."

"Until now." Gilmore slowed down even more, to an uneasy stroll. She didn't have to hurry anymore, after all. "Please don't judge Rudy too harshly. I know this seems to you like a giant step, but for us it was a lot of little steps. An inch at a time. At first we tried to keep the nucleogenics alive and just borrow the power. If only that had worked! We tried for weeks to modify our containment chamber just to hold them for a few minutes and let them go back. When we tried a second time, a third—every time we really expected them to live. We *really* did. Every time we failed, there was just enough difference that we tried again. We kept getting little bits of hope that we could keep them alive and ourselves too. There were a few variations on a theme, but every time . . . they ended up dead."

"And each time, since they were dead anyway—"

"Yes, we used the nucleogenic matter. Of course! Why not? You would too, if you were in our shoes. Rudy kept trying to communicate with them and kept failing. We would've happily traded for their natural dead, like an organ donation. We didn't want to kill. But they wouldn't talk, or just plain couldn't. All they did was attack and attack. When the aliens kept breaking through, we defended ourselves. That means more of them died. And, yes, we used the corpses. So would you."

Chakotay felt his chest constrict with the truth of it. She was right—this was different from indiscriminate slaughter. And she was also right that he might've done the same thing, given the same circumstances. They hadn't just shot into the water.

"We're scientists," she quietly reminded. "Science was our way to survive. We couldn't make it with speed and brute force and tactical advantages and sheer power like a starship could. After two years of trying to communicate, we gave up trying. Wouldn't you? They'd been viciously attacking us without ever pausing to learn signals or even try to talk to us. They were just killer bees, animals with some sense of organization who attacked us every chance they got. We defended ourselves, and some of them got killed. When they died during attacks, we used the matter. Then on Christmas Day three years ago, we got caught in a nova wash. We were completely stuck, trapped. We struggled for days to get out. Do you understand? We were dying by centimeters. We gave ourselves up for dead. It wasn't the way the story was supposed to end. I saw Rudy during that time . . . he'd failed. Suddenly he hadn't just lost half his crew—he'd lost all of it. On New Year's Day he ordered us to summon one of the creatures with the Ankari device and use the matter for a boost. It worked. The creature died, and we lived. After a while, it wasn't so hard to summon them when we needed to move ahead again. In Rudy's mind, he's hunting animals, not murdering people. He never jumped happily over that line. He zigzagged over it an inch at a time, until we were finally all the way over it."

"Captain Janeway's not going to see it that way," Chakotay warned. "Things are pretty cut and dried for her where regulations are concerned. In her mind, that's what has saved us."

"And what saved us was suspending the regulations," Gilmore said. "Captain Janeway hasn't lost half her crew. I scanned your logs . . . you've been a lot luckier than we have. She hasn't paid that high a price for decisions in the Delta Quadrant."

"Not like that," he confirmed.

"Maybe you could talk to her," Gilmore suggested nervously. "Help her understand us. If you were on the Skeleton Coast and the natives wouldn't trade with you, would you kill them to get your supplies? Well? Would you?"

Chakotay thumped his hands on his thighs by way of a shrug. "I really can't say. I've actually been there, but only after they put the resort there. As I understand, it was a savage place. They had to virtually terraform it."

He was trying to change the subject, but she didn't go for it. With more force than he gave her credit for, Gilmore challenged, "Would you hold on to your nobility and just die? Or would you fight?"

"I might fight," he said. "But I'd be wrong."

"Then up the ante. What if your crew was with

you. Sit and watch them die because the natives won't trade? Or would you go and steal and kill to live?"

"The theory goes," Chakotay said, "that Starfleet officers swear an oath that they'll die first."

"What if you had your children with you? How tight does the noose get before you *do* cross the line and you think you're right to cross it? After a while, the question becomes 'Will I kill somebody else's child so mine can live?' That's wrong too, but you start to think it. You convince yourself it's fair because the other guy is keeping water from you and he knows you need it."

"We have to be bigger than our needs," Chakotay attempted halfheartedly.

"You might let yourself die," Gilmore responded, "but would you be so noble if that little girl Naomi were the one dying? How far would you go to save her? To gain one more day? Or a thousand more lightyears?" She laughed without a bit of mirth. "We talk about rules and regulations and commandments as if we're androids programmed for yes or no. These aren't yes-or-no problems. I never thought it'd come to this . . . to be honest with you, I thought we'd die before we had to be accountable."

Chakotay offered a sympathetic glance. "You're very loyal to him. He must deserve it in your eyes."

"He saved all the rest of us," she said. "It's only in the past few weeks that our shipmates started dying again. He kept all of us alive all those months. When we were starving, somehow he found food. When we were out of power, somehow he traded or bought power. When we needed medical supplies, he beamed down to a swamp planet by himself and collected botanical substitutes. He was sick for months after that. But he smiled all the time because he knew he'd done it for us. Loyal? You bet I am, Mr. Chakotay. I didn't like what we were doing, but I'd do it again for him."

The weight of these problems, the intensity of them, made Chakotay feel physically heavier. This wasn't going to get better any time soon. If the aliens broke through, the same firefight that ravaged *Equinox* would be here in these bright corridors, scorching them into dark and fearful tunnels.

"He might still be right, you know," Gilmore pointed out. "They could still turn out to be just animals."

"They attacked in an organized manner," he countered. "They changed tactics. Then they changed them again."

"So do the Borg. But didn't you kill them when you had to?"

"If you all feel this way," Chakotay asked, "why didn't Captain Ransom make this argument to Captain Janeway?"

"Why should he? He's a captain in his own right. He doesn't have to answer to a peer. She's not really his superior. Besides, we've already been through all this for ourselves. Rudy shouldn't have to justify himself again."

She stopped walking and put her hand out suddenly, catching him by the arm. Behind them, the security guard came to a defensive stance and lowered his rifle to her.

"Stand easy, crewman," Chakotay ordered, meeting the guard's confused gaze.

"Aye, sir," the guard said, and relaxed.

Gilmore seemed bothered by the rifle, but she focused on Chakotay.

"Will you talk to Captain Janeway?" she asked. "Explain to her that we weren't celebrating every night because we got a chance to be mean and nobody was around to stop us? It's your job to help her understand, isn't it? Isn't that what a first officer does?"

For the first time in years, Chakotay found himself torn between two crews, two philosophies, and two relatively successful methods of command that clashed with each other. Both had worked in isolation, yet only one could prevail in unity.

He took her elbow in a reassuring way. "I'll try," he promised.

Dark and damaged, the *Equinox* research lab was a troubling place for a hologram with a conscience. *Voyager*'s doctor worked with deliberation at the consoles, but he was getting absolutely nowhere. The captain was anxious, he knew, to find a way to communicate with the nucleogenics, if they could indeed communicate at all.

"Computer," he began, irritated, "I decrypted this data file. Why can't I access it?"

"EMH authorization is required."

"Your EMH is still functional?"

"*Affirmative.*"

"Activate him."

Across the bay, the *Equinox* doctor fritzed into solidity, a perfect duplicate of the *Voyager* physician. The vision was somehow comforting, at least supportive.

"Please state the nature of your medical emergency," the *Equinox* EMH introduced, only now noticing that his counterpart was here instead of a patient. "Who are you?"

"Your counterpart from the *Starship Voyager.*"

"Where's Captain Ransom? My crew?"

"In custody."

The *Equinox* EMH eyed him curiously, indeed with a certain hostility. "How were you able to leave your sickbay?"

The *Voyager* EMH waggled his arm, where the little gift from past encounters was the only item setting him apart from the other hologram. "This device allows me to go anywhere I please. In case you weren't aware, your crew has been running criminal experiments here."

Picking up a PADD on the end of a diagnostic bed, the *Equinox* EMH crossed the deck to him. "I know. I designed them."

"You? That's a violation of your programming!"

"They deleted my ethical subroutines."

The *Equinox* EMH made his statement casually while eyeing the mobile emitter with understandable curiosity. Perhaps envy, if a machine could dream.

Evidently a machine could plot. The *Equinox* EMH

made a single sweeping motion, using the PADD as a
weapon.

Too late, the *Voyager*'s EMH calculated the results of
the swift move. He felt the PADD strike his arm, felt
the impact drive the mobile emitter against his arm, and
felt the frazzle of panicked electrical impulses surge
through his body.

Abruptly, he felt nothing.

"Captain? A moment?"

"Come in, Chakotay. Be aware, though, I won't pretend to be in a good mood. What are you doing here?
We're at Red Alert."

Feeling their relationship make a not so subtle shift
from friends to officers, with Janeway holding the
higher cards, Chakotay amended his idea about sitting
down and remained standing before the captain's desk
in the ready room.

He'd been asked a question, and his commanding
officer was standing by for an answer. Not exactly
what he'd had in mind when he came in here. Chakotay was a statuesque man, accustomed to having a
slight edge of intimidation, just by virtue of physical
presence. It worked on most people. It never had on
Kathryn Janeway. Her sense of purpose was as big as
he was.

"I had a talk with Gilmore. There are some things I
agree with. Since I'm her first officer now, it's part of
my duty to bring her concerns to the appropriate level.
In this case, there's no—"

"Forget it. I'm not letting them out of confinement.

When we extricate ourselves from this mess, I intend to convene a court-martial."

Chakotay shifted his feet. "Well, that's more or less the message. Captain—would you mind if I sit?"

"Yes, but go ahead anyway."

Now he didn't want to. He did anyway. Once seated, though, the equality failed to buffer the ferocity in his captain's face. She was completely hardened to her cause, still furious, daunted by the failure to communicate with the life forms now putting siege to her ship.

She waited, no longer prodding him to speak as she might have in better times. If he had something to say, he would have to get to it himself or she would dismiss him and that would be that.

"I've been speaking to Gilmore," he began, as awkwardly as that, "and I have to admit some of her perceptions shook me up a little. She made me realize that Captain Ransom isn't taking care of himself. He's looking out for his crew. He's eaten up with guilt over losing half his crew because of one judgment call. Now the chance of getting the others home is consuming him, whatever the cost."

"I can't forgive him, if that's what you want, Chakotay," Janeway aborted. "He stepped over the line."

Adjusting his tone to mollify her, Chakotay tipped his head as if in thought. "All due respect, Captain, but that depends on where it's drawn."

Her brown eyes were cold, bitter, and lay upon him with acrimony. "Are we going to have a seminar on ethics, you and I?"

"You have to admit," he attempted, "the directives are deliberately elastic. They have to be. If not, we can't even defend ourselves. And we will, if they break in. We'll kill them to preserve our own lives. We've done it before. We draw and redraw the line every day. We draw it in one place to defend ourselves, in another to . . . answer a distress call, for instance. Ransom drew it where he drew it. If the galaxy had been as hostile to *Voyager* as it was to *Equinox,* what might we have done if we were handed a chance to get home? Do we sacrifice ourselves to an evolution that might or might not happen?"

"We don't know they haven't evolved to intelligence already," Janeway rasped. Her voice was strained. "We have to assume they do, and find out later that they don't."

"If you're in the woods and hungry, you hunt the moose. You take the bees' honey. And you don't worry that a million years from now they might evolve into a society."

In the shadow across the desk, Janeway's jaw hardened. "Are you challenging my order to relieve him of command?"

"I'm questioning it," he said, trying to keep from matching her level of frustration and steely resolve. "He's a post captain. His ship is still functional and could still be mended, and if he wants to kill the bees and take the honey, I believe there's precedent for his point of view."

"They're not bees," she insisted.

He leaned forward. "That's all they are so far.

There's no evidence of superiority. So far they're just flying around and screaming and showing their teeth. Are we never going to step on a bug because a billion years from now it might have a sentient granddaughter? What do we do when we reach the cats and dogs and dolphins? Never hurt one because they squeal and play together and attack in an organized fashion?"

Janeway slammed both palms down on her desk. "There's going to be a court-martial on this ship, Chakotay. You'll be one of the presiding judges. You'd better divide your empathy from your sense of law and order long enough to remember where you come from. Or have you retreated to your Maquis sensibilities and forgotten about the laws that give us everything we have?"

"Ransom knows he's up for a court-martial, Captain." Chakotay let his tone ignite. "He knew that all along. When he gets back to Federation space, if he ever does, he faces ruin and disgrace and trial. He knows there's a whole command of officers with your opinion waiting for him, but he was willing to subjugate his own future so his crew could get home. If we make it back, Ransom's ruined. The same fate might be awaiting us—have you thought of that?"

The captain turned to frozen rock before him, and indeed it seemed she'd never thought of that. Could it be that she had always dug her decisions so deeply into her sense of regulation and directive that she thought she was justified every single time? Was that how she saved her sanity?

"He's wrong," she insisted. "You can kill the moose, but you can't kill the natives."

"Marla says they couldn't tell the difference between the moose and the natives." Seizing his opportunity, Chakotay came to the edge of his chair. "We've bent the Prime Directive. Others might just as easily say we've broken it. From eating grubs to storming strongholds, we've participated in the Delta Quadrant as if we're alive and we're here. Others who haven't been through the same might make the call on us—say we should've destroyed ourselves before we contacted anybody and altered their futures, or that we should've stranded ourselves on some planet and lived out our lives with no chance of influencing anybody else."

He knew he had something there. As Starfleet officers, they knew about the line in theory, a little in practice, but never to this level. Chakotay struggled, too, as he watched his captain struggle. This was a fire he might himself have to jump into someday, if anything happened to her, and he found himself cruelly intrigued by her not-so-interior battle.

The ship pulsed around them as if waiting for her answer. Suddenly the hums and thrums of energy that constantly burbled around them rose to a symphonic pitch, matching their heartbeats as if kettledrums were hammering.

As Janeway stared at him in hurtful challenge, Chakotay pushed on with these thoughts, defending a man he didn't like, explaining actions he found questionable, for the sake of his captain's ability to make a decision he found daunting.

"When the time came for Ransom to let the other half of his crew die, Ransom couldn't do it. How do we know we'll be strong enough? What do we do, Captain, when it's *really* 'us or them'? Would you die for a whale? Some people would say yes. Fine. Would you let your child die so a whale could live? Five children? Thirty-nine?"

"These aren't children, Chakotay. These are Starfleet officers. Every one of them understood what they were getting—"

"So we're all expendable?" he interrupted. "Why are we fighting, then? Are we expendable first? Or last? When do you start fighting, Captain? When do you kill? The ante keeps ratcheting up. We draw the line, and the line moves."

She stared at him. The words were crushing.

He was ready to continue, to force her to examine herself and find that answer, but they were cruelly interrupted by Tom Paris' desperate cry from beyond the entrance panels. *"Bridge to captain! Defenses are breaking down!"*

"Later," Janeway snapped to him, and plunged for the door. In that instant, everything between them changed. They took refuge in necessity.

They charged onto the bridge to the punctuation of Harry Kim's panicked report back to Tuvok and Seven, at the defense grid—"I'm picking up spatial fissures! Hundreds of them!"

Kathryn Janeway was grateful when Chakotay ran immediately to tactical and shoved aside the terrified crewman manning the post. She didn't really want him in the middle of the bridge at the command station right now, and she sensed he didn't want to be there. This was one of those moments—after such an altercation between commanding officers—when it was altogether better to have one person in indisputable charge.

"Looks like they stepped up their attacks," Paris gasped from the helm.

Janeway slid into her command chair as the ship trembled noticeably. "Reroute all available power to the shields."

At the tactical station, Chakotay was now authorized to do that drastic measure. She could hear the clicks and appropriate answering buzzes as he worked and silently thanked him for his efficiency and the support he was giving her now that hadn't been present only seconds ago.

"They're holding," he said, "but at this rate, it won't be long before the aliens break through."

"Bridge to Tuvok." Janeway almost didn't hit the comm in time. "We need that security grid!"

"We're preparing to bring it on-line. Charge the emitters."

Janeway almost told him they couldn't do that from here, when she realized he had been talking to someone else, Seven or Torres, down there in astrometrics. No, not Seven—she was still on board *Equinox*, trying to work on that warp core's dilithium matrix.

Leaving them to their work, she struck the comm again. "Bridge to The Doctor."

"Sickbay here."

"Did you find anything?"

Irritated to a breaking point, she grew instantly impatient when he hesitated with what should've been a yes or no answer.

"Could you . . . be more specific?" he asked.

Could a computer lose its memory?

Blistering from her encounter with Chakotay and now this new surge of assault, Janeway leaned closer. "Neural patterns, cortical scans—anything that could help us program the universal translator!"

What a swollen boil it was to state the bloody obvious under these conditions.

What was taking him so long!

"Negative," he finally reported. *"I couldn't access the* Equinox *data files. They were encrypted."*

"Keep studying the information we have," she said. "See what you can come up with."

She stopped short of demanding answers he didn't have yet.

"Acknowledged," The Doctor responded, almost musically.

Why did he sound so satisfied? He had no reason to sound as if he liked his job right now.

"We're going to have to try something drastic," Janeway said, half to herself.

At tactical, Chakotay looked down at her as if his prediction were already coming true. Generously, though, he didn't point that out in front of the crew. "Ready when you are, Captain," he said. "What do you have in mind?"

"I don't know yet, but I can't do it dragging another ship like this. Prepare to cut loose the *Equinox*. Get Seven off as soon as possible."

"Whether she's finished or not?"

"No . . . let's let her finish if possible—why don't you see how much more time she needs?"

"Aye, aye. Chakotay to Seven of Nine. What's your status?"

"I've dismantled the antimatter injectors. But I'll need several minutes to neutralize the dilithium matrix."

"We don't have much time."

"Understood."

As the comm clicked off, echoing that rotten word "several" again, Janeway looked up at Chakotay as another heavy assault shuddered through the ship. "Is she alone over there?"

"Yes," he said, his feet spread apart for balance as he worked. "She's the last. Would you like me to send a support team to help her?"

"No, I just wanted to know if there was anyone else to evacuate. This might have to be fast."

"She's the last of our crew," he clarified. "Most of the *Equinox* crew is still over there. They were leading the salvage teams when we arrested Ransom. We just confined them to their quarters."

As much as it made sense, Janeway disparaged the idea. "We'll have to get them over here pronto. Bridge to Tuvok, I need that grid!"

"Aye, Captain, nearly ready."

"Keep the line open. I want to hear what's going on."

"Aye, aye. Activate the grid."

As Janeway listened, and watched the auxiliary monitoring console across the bridge, she heard a surge of energy that gave her a moment's hope. An instant later, though, the energy peaked, whined, and fell off audibly to a buckling rumble.

"What happened?" Tuvok's voice.

"I don't understand." This was Torres, a little distant as her voice came through Tuvok's open combadge channel. *"This should be working . . . I'm running a system-wide diagnostic—"*

As if they had time for that. Janeway silently smoldered. Shouting at them wouldn't speed things up. She turned, and looked at Chakotay, letting the worry show in her eyes which before had been nothing but cold rocks to him.

"We've got to hold on," she said. "Take all the power you need. Shut systems down anywhere you can."

His eyes widened with doubt. "I'll push the envelope."

The ship shuddered again, a violent punching sensation that came up through the deck under the captain's feet and drilled through her legs and up her spine.

"Hold on," she murmured.

"Captain!" Harry Kim shouted. "I'm reading phaser fire on deck nine! Crew quarters!"

"Security, seal off deck nine!" Ghastly awareness rushed through Janeway's guts. Ransom. Doing what Chakotay implied he might—anything Janeway herself might do in this situation. But how?

On the upper deck, Chakotay called over the thrum of attack. "Shields are weakening! Eighty-four percent!"

"Tuvok to bridge. The field generator is off-line. Its power couplings were disengaged."

Torres' voice sounded in the deep background. *"Someone reconfigured the internal sensors so we couldn't detect it!"*

Janeway leaned forward and shouted at the monsters in the mirror.

"Whatever it takes, get that grid on-line!"

CHAPTER
9

ARMED AND DANGEROUS. GRIPPING THE PHASER RIFLE he'd taken from one of the unconscious security guards outside the crew quarters, Rudy Ransom led his handful of crew down the *Voyager*'s corridor, pleased at their skill with ignoring the rumbling and shaking that ravaged the ship.

Unlike the *Voyager* crew, who were disoriented every time the ship wracked, his own team rushed right through it. This had become their normal habitat.

Luckily they were all here, held in the same astoundingly comfortable and clean crew's quarters—Burke, Gilmore, Lessing, Morrow, Nash, Tassoni, and Sofin.

"You broke us out just in time," he said over his shoulder to their doctor. "How are you moving around outside of sickbay?"

"This device on my arm is a mobile emitter," the

doctor explained as he jogged. "Evidently they acquired it from someone they encountered in the Delta Quadrant."

"It figures," Ransom complained. "They've had a lot more luck than we have. Lessing, keep up, kid!"

"Right behind you, sir!"

"It'll take them days to untangle that field generator. Now Miss Janeway will be getting a taste of what we've been through. I hope she chokes on it. Max, where's the rest of the crew?"

"They're all being held on *Equinox*, Rudy. At least, they were last I heard."

"We've got to get off the ship."

From behind, the doctor called, "I re-routed transporter control to a panel in the next junction. We can—"

Phaser fire threw a grid of blistering light bands across their path. Security guards!

Ransom shoved Gilmore down an adjoining corridor, then lay down a blanket of covering fire. "Doctor! Lead them off! Meet us back on *Equinox!*"

"Aye, aye. I'll ditch the emitter and meet you on board."

"Go!"

As the doctor rushed down the corridor, the two security guards took the bait and followed him, apparently not recognizing him in the flash and dust of phaser fire. Good. Ransom had bet on that.

Continuing to lay down fire, he gestured the others around the corner.

"They've sealed off the deck!" Burke said.

161

"Don't worry."

Ransom stopped at the wall junction panel and worked it.

"We're getting out of here. When we beam on board, Max and I will go straight to the bridge. Marla, you'll have to go to engineering and stun that Borg girl before she gets a report that we've escaped. How fast can you move?"

"You can beam me directly there, Rudy. Just divide the transporter focus."

"You set the beam."

"Aye, sir."

"Let's go."

They rushed into the transporter room, a little adjunct chamber that wasn't the main transporter room. Luckily, Starfleet had standardized long ago and the minimum number of pads for any secondary transporter room was now eight—to handle large emergencies, under the assumption that adjunct transporters had to be used only in times of crisis.

Just enough.

"Set the controls, Marla."

Ransom motioned the others to take position on the pads while he turned back to the door panel and used his phaser rifle to fry the locking mechanism.

Now it'd take a torch to get in. Perfect.

"I've set it to automatic, split beam." Marla worked the panel and spoke over the next thrum of attack. "Their shields are down—forty percent!"

"Doesn't give us much time," Max commented. An old story for them.

"Everybody stay where you are," Marla said. "There's no second chance. They've detected the unauthorized transport . . . they're trying to block it. I'm bypassing the Ops controls! Now or never!"

She jumped up onto the only empty pad and drew her phaser.

Ransom shouldered his rifle. "Next stop, the *Equinox!*"

"Janeway to Seven of Nine! Seven! Respond!"

"Just ignore them. What've we got, Max?"

"Marla must've knocked out that girl," Max Burke said as he and Ransom plunged onto their bridge. Burke took tactical immediately. "I'm getting ignition on the warp core, just like we need . . ."

"The rest of you, take any post you can run," Ransom ordered, distributing his crew. "Lessing, unlock all the crew quarters and get everyone else to posts, then take the helm. Let's man our ship, boys."

"Aye, aye, Rudy!"

"Damn!" Burke acted as if he'd burned his fingers on the tactical board.

Ransom cranked around. "What is it?"

The ship shook violently, stress points actually cracking. Automatic sealant hissed furiously between the inner and outer strakes of the bulkheads.

"B'Elanna's erected a security matrix. I can't get a lock on the field generator!"

"Try overriding the command codes," Ransom told him. "Consider yourself authorized."

"I know what to do," Burke said with a crow of victory. "It's a triquadric algorithm. A trick I learned from an old friend."

"Just do it, don't explain it."

"The shields are falling," Michaelson called from the science monitors. "Roughly eighty seconds left."

Like all of them, he was dulled to the frantic nature of these events.

Ransom considered that an advantage. Janeway's crew would still be shaken, frightened, freaked. His wasn't.

"Janeway's hailing us, Rudy," Lessing informed with ironic cheer.

"Put her through, what the hell."

In a loud blast of alarms, klaxons, and shouts, Janeway's tight features appeared on the main screen. Ransom dropped deeper into his command chair to square off with her.

No greeting, no nothing.

"If you don't stop what you're doing, we'll both be destroyed!"

"What's my alternative? Thirty years in your brig?"

Another shake bolted through the ships bonded by a single set of shields.

"I'll open fire if I have to," Janeway threatened predictably.

"We've been through worse." Ransom knuckled his chair controls, cutting off the comm system.

There was no point arguing further, no good way to defend himself. She couldn't understand, he knew that. She was doing what she thought she had to do, and so was he. That argument could never resolve itself.

Scholars and admirals had already spent decades trying to hammer out that particular piece of ore. He and Janeway would not today form it into anything useful.

"She's firing on us!" Lessing shouted.

Ransom turned sharply. "Max!"

"Stand by!" Burke stayed admirably calm and tapped his controls one at a time, not like playing a piano with all fingers. He had to get it right the first try. "Okay, BLT. Remember this trick?"

He tapped a final button.

"Where is it?" Ransom asked, swiveling.

"Up there," Burke answered, pointing to a graphic monitor on the upper bridge. It scrolled to show a schematic of the *Voyager*'s astrometrics lab. As they watched, the graphic of the field generator flashed and blinked out.

"Transport complete." Burke's voice was loaded with quiet satisfaction. "We've got it."

To Lessing, Ransom ordered, "Get us out of here."

"I can't! Warp drive is down!"

"Bridge to Marla, report!"

"One of their crew tried to dismantle the antimatter injectors! Repairs are underway!"

"What about the field generator?" he asked Max.

"I'm integrating it now. The generator's in place . . . I'm bringing the grid on-line!"

To Ransom, his crew sounded excited, but somehow controlled. Purpose could do that. They now had their purpose back, crisp and focused.

This was good. They needed this. They had been accepted but not understood on *Voyager.* This was better.

Their own ship, their own shipmates, and souls that had come to terms with what they had to do to survive.

The alien tone invaded his ears, familiar now and supercharged with challenge. They were breaking through.

Ransom picked up his phaser and glanced around to be sure the others were armed.

To Burke, he made the critical call of the moment. "It's now or never!"

The tone grew louder, louder still.

"Hold your fire!" Ransom ordered as a spatial fissure opened like some grotesque birth going on near the ceiling. The crew was braced but did as he ordered them.

Two seconds . . . three . . . there it was!

A tailed alien, dinosaurian and mythical, surged through the fissure and flew like a fruit bat around the bridge. It rushed at Burke, but then was jolted back by the force field they kept permanently erected on the bridge. Caught, the alien instantly reversed itself like a high diver making a flip, but it hit the other side of the force field that had instantly snapped up.

Trapped!

In midair the alien whipped up and down, back and forth, as if its tail were a flag, its extended clawed arms the pole. Screaming hideously, shrieking so high-pitched a sound that it matched its own breakthrough tone.

Ransom and the others watched together as it thrashed itself to death, striking the force-field grid and electrocuting itself at every hit. Only a few more seconds . . .

When the alien finally suffered a final attack and slithered in a heap to the deck, Ransom felt less for it than he ever had. Finally, the damned slimy things had taken the last bit of humanity from him. Or Janeway had.

To Michaelson he snapped, "Get that to the lab."

He swung around as Lessing's console bleeped and the now-helmsman said, "Sir, the engines are up and running!"

"Set a course for the Alpha Quadrant, maximum warp. Engage."

"Keep firing!"

Captain Janeway clung to her chair and focused on a dozen places about the bridge in sequence. The ship was firing freely now on *Equinox*, whose crew was aboard and had stolen the deflector field generator. If Ransom hadn't been a criminal before, he was one now.

The alien tone squealed in her ears, deafening her to the rote responses of the crew around her.

She pushed out of her chair. "Arm yourselves!"

At his station, Harry Kim was sheeted with sweat. "Fissures are opening, all decks!"

All—

Dividing her attention between the bridge and every other deck, Janeway felt her brain boil with determination to defend her ship and crew at any cost. Above her, ragged and glowing bulbs formed and scarlike fissures opened within them, expanding as quickly as an envelope opening. She took aim and fired.

Then another one opened—and another! Four! Six!

With her single action, she gave permission for all the others to fire at will.

Rifts cracked the bridge's atmospheric fabric with alarming randomness now. Phasers fired and aliens shrieked in their rage and murderousness.

At the center of the bridge, Janeway was the pivot of all the action. She spun and fired, spun and fired, fighting for control to keep from shearing off someone's head in the instantaneous reflex of shooting again and again at targets that just opened up here, there—

She heard the scream from behind her an instant too late. As she tried to spin, she tripped on the command chair's mounting. She fumbled.

The alien shriek was millimeters away when she recovered. Before her rushed a demonic face, stretched into the grimace of an unmistakably animalistic predator. As it struck her, she heard a thousand sounds—the alien tone, their shrieking voices, the screams of her crew, the whine of phasers, the pummeling of her own heartbeat, and Chakotay's anguished cry as the alien dive-bomber struck her at full strafing speed.

"Captain!"

CHAPTER
10

"THE SHIELD-GRID IS BACK IN PLACE. THE ALIENS ARE staying clear."

The victory in Max Burke's voice was unadulterated. They'd survived again, but again at a cost. Before, it was always a cost in lives. Today it was a spiritual cost.

Rudy Ransom kicked aside a bump plate among the litter on his bridge. "Are sensors picking up *Voyager?*"

Off his console, Noah Lessing reported, "It looks like they're under attack."

The report carried a loaded question: *Should we go back and help?*

Disturbed to the bottom of his guts, Ransom added up his options. They'd come this far. Janeway had pushed him farther over the line.

"Maintain course," he said.

Sweating and working to control an inward shudder,

Max Burke stepped down to his captain's side. "It's too bad we have to leave them."

"There's not much we can do," Ransom agreed. "We'd be back in the same boat, literally. The shields from one ship can't protect both. We saw that. Janeway had her chance to make a united front. She decided to flash her feathers instead."

Burke nodded. "It's all right, Rudy. You did the right thing. They wouldn't back us up. At the first disagreement, they took us into custody."

"If they don't get killed, she might understand us a little more."

On the port-side monitor, a clear view of *Voyager* surging along with her nominal shields crackling and compromised bored to the guts of both men. They knew what that felt like. There was a strange and unsatisfying win in seeing Captain Janeway finally having to see what it had been for the *Equinox* crew.

Ransom felt his jaw stiffen. "She's only scratched the surface of the Delta Quadrant. Five years seems like a long time, but we're all still fifty years from home. Who's she kidding? This *is* home. Without the nucleogenics, that ship is the end of their dreams. How long before her crew starts wanting real lives? Family lives? Futures with a chance for a home instead of crew quarters? A wife or husband instead of a department chief? They're young now, but that won't last."

"You're always thinking of us, aren't you?" Burke commented. "That's why we'd do anything for you. You're nothing like Janeway."

A tinge of guilt rammed through Ransom's chest. He

held up a hand. "No, Max, you're wrong. She's just like me. You saw the way she resists. She just hasn't been to the edge yet. She hasn't figured out that she won't last either. There's no magic youth potion, and she's ten or twenty years older than most of her crew. When will she start wishing for a peaceful retirement and a life of her own?" Ransom grasped the bridge rail and watched the monitor as *Voyager*'s shields flashed in a Halloween display of color and light.

"I hope she lives," he said. "She's got a lot to learn."

A locomotive made of rubber and gel and teeth and claws drove Janeway to the deck. She felt her pelvis, then her shoulder blades slam to the hard carpet as the side of her head scraped the rail's support stanchion. Energy crackled around her body from the contact. Phaser fire grazed her cheek, forcing her to roll to the right. Mocking her on the main screen was a clear view of the *Equinox* soaring off from under *Voyager*, rushing away to pursue her own captain's vision of survival.

As the single instant of attack telescoped and stretched out, she fell off the command chair's platform and down to the lower deck. It saved her life. The alien scraped by, an inch over her, driven off by Chakotay's phaser.

A burning sensation seared her left cheekbone, leaving her half blind and disoriented. Her skin crimped, her mouth tugged to the left as if stretched. Her neck felt as if it were cracking like scorched plastic. As she constricted her stomach muscles and forced herself up,

Janeway was faced with the horrid tableau of Chakotay firing again at another alien. The creature who had scraped Janeway now veered into the highest edge of the bridge ceiling, jackknifed, and struck Chakotay in the back. This time, it didn't miss.

Paris launched from his helm and fired at it, but too late. Chakotay was already down. The alien skimmed over Chakotay into Janeway's line of fire and Kim's crossfire. It screamed, withered, and sizzled out of existence.

Chakotay—if it ended this way, without a kind word—

Now her cheek and neck began to shrivel and turn cold. The burning sensation dried to a crisp ice as she dragged herself to her command chair and pummeled the arm console.

"Tuvok! Give me tactical control!"

She did the craziest thing she could think of. Authorize the ship's self-destruct sequence, which shut down all the safeties and allowed her to send a single surge of blinding power to the deflector pulse, giving the shields extra strength. With her head swimming, she forced herself to remember to disengage the self-destruct when the alien tone began to die down and the fissures sealed.

Two fissures in her periphery collapsed almost instantly. The attack had been beaten back, for the moment at least.

"Won't hold for long," she murmured. Had she been talking? Saying something else? A faint echo of her own voice implied that she'd been thinking aloud. Now that her head began to clear, she stopped doing that and looked around to assess her crew.

Tousled and sweat-sheeted, Harry Kim pulled toward his station. So did the others.

Except Paris . . . he was kneeling beside Chakotay, his face a plaster of worry and crawling revulsion.

Janeway pushed up a little to see Chakotay's face. Like crumpled paper, one whole side of his skull was vitrified, dark and sunken. *Oh, no.*

Empathizing with him, she touched her own wounds. Felt like broken cardboard. Beneath it there was a sizzle of desiccating tissue and fluids. But she was alive. Was he?

"Bridge to sickbay," Paris choked. "Medical emergency."

Nothing happened. No answer.

"Doctor, respond."

Janeway's hands shook. Why wasn't The Doctor answering? Had the aliens shut down the comm system somehow?

Aware of Janeway's eyes upon them, Tom Paris glanced at her, then motioned to Ensign Rogers on the lower deck. "Ensign . . ."

Clutched by grief and guilt, Janeway couldn't voice her gratitude at his effort to get help for Chakotay. All she could focus upon was her first officer, lying there after saving her life, still distant after saving her soul.

As Paris and Rogers carried Chakotay to the lift, out of her line of sight, the captain gripped the arms of her command chair, struggling to steady herself. Until now she hadn't realized fully what Chakotay was talking about before.

He was right. Deep in her heart she had always known that Ransom's level of desperation could come to *Voyager* if they got a little less lucky. She'd heard too many Donner Party stories to think it could never happen to her. Some turned to cannibalism, and some let themselves die first. She knew, in this epiphanic moment, that she might have the cannibal in her.

Cannibals eat the dead. How long before she would be willing to make somebody dead?

Around her in the air hung the stink of blowtorched aliens, the drifted leavings of their fluids and skin incinerated by phaser fire. Her phaser, her crew's. She'd made the aliens dead so she and hers could live.

So many things could yet go wrong—when would she be forced over the line? She had to stop him, stop Ransom, before she got to the line.

"Casualty reports are coming in," Harry Kim struggled. "Two dead . . . thirteen wounded . . . and we took heavy damage to the engines."

Janeway forced her rattled brain to process his words. "The *Equinox?*"

"They have gone to warp," Tuvok reported from somewhere.

"Any sign of nucleogenic particles?"

"No."

"Then they haven't engaged their 'enhanced' warp drive yet. Keep looking for—"

The universe parted again and the tonal shriek returned. The crew braced again, drew weapons again, the worst was here again.

"Stabilize the shields! Double shield the bridge, Tuvok. If we don't have a command center, we don't have a ship. Phasers!"

Two more bulbous fissures opened overhead. She braced her legs and started shooting, firing directly into the globes as if going after a tumor with a scalpel laser.

Tuvok worked furiously, nursing the shields until the whine of invasion fell away again.

"Captain," Harry Kim began, his black hair flopped into his eyes, "that sound . . . it's registering as patterned."

As he squinted at the analysis screens, Janeway asked, "That shriek? You think it's something more than just a shriek?"

"I'm slowing it down on the sonograph. It's got a definite pattern about it."

"Does it repeat?"

"Yes, parts of it repeat. It's got inflections, though. Could it be a language? Should I run it through the linguistics banks?"

"Ransom said he tried that. Why don't you try running it through all the other banks. Maybe something in the system will recognize it on a free search."

"Aye, Captain."

Janeway crossed the bridge on shuddering legs, grasping anything she could hold with her free hand, to support herself. "We can't go on like this. We'll cut up our own ship with these phasers if we have to keep firing inside. Can you reinforce the shields with a plasma transfer?"

"You must go to sickbay, Captain," Tuvok told her strictly. "Your injuries are severe."

"No, I'm staying here."

For a surreal moment, he actually stopped working and faced her, offering a body-language ultimatum. "Report to sickbay, Captain. You must survive those wounds for all our sakes. Commander Chakotay may be dead by now. The loss of both our commanding officers would be a critical blow in this situation. Go to sickbay. I will take the bridge."

Janeway backed off a step. "Damned Vulcan. Looking out for me by pretending you're looking out for yourself. Do you think I'll fall for that?"

He nodded once. "I could knock you to the deck as a head start."

A hurtful smile cracked her vitrified facial muscles. "Make sure everyone keeps a hand weapon that's fully charged at all times."

"Aye, aye."

"I'll be back."

"Of course."

"Thank you."

"My pleasure."

Commander Chakotay may be dead by now.

It was a long way to sickbay at Red Alert and under attack. All around her, crew members rushed through the corridors, armed with weapons, carrying repair kits, med kits, rifle-charge packets, and wounded shipmates. They all met Janeway's eyes, and she felt bad about the terror in their faces at the sight of her. She knew she should be on the bridge with a whole face. Instead, she was wraithing about the lower decks, half desiccated, hauling her phaser rifle with both hands, looking like some kind of shredded monster from the bowels of mythology. She was giving them one of those nightmares that keeps coming back.

Then she stumbled on her own nightmare—a dead alien lying in her ship's companionway vestibule, decimated, gray, mottled. Not a phaser kill ... someone had been desperate enough to spray coolant on this one to kill it. A hideous way to go. She wondered if her poor crew member had lived after inhaling the coolant spray.

So much horror. Anger rose in her for the ghastliness of the open universe and for Rudy Ransom, who had brought it down upon them all.

"Captain!"

Neelix rushed to her, in his usual state of overreacting. This time it was a notable freakish concern. He was holding The Doctor's mobile emitter. How did he get that?

"I found this in the corridor on deck nine! You might want to take it to sickbay."

Though she took the emitter from him, she said nothing. Her eyes were still fixed on the dead creature. All she could do was hold it and stare. She watched its bizarre journey to the meat locker, her mind barely registering how crazy things had to be for Neelix to be giving her comments that closely resembled orders. He didn't even wait to see if she were indeed headed to sickbay or somewhere more important. In fact, he was already gone.

Sickbay was the other end of the nightmare. The deck was littered with wounded, lying on blankets, crumpled in corners, waiting for biobeds. Tom Paris was hovering over Chakotay, who had the privilege of a biobed, naturally. Paris seemed shaken, fighting for control, irritated and drawn out.

"Any sign of The Doc?" he asked her without formality.

"I've got him right here," Janeway said. Crossing immediately to a console, she placed the emitter on an activation pad and keyed the controls. *Zip*—instant physician.

"Please state the nature of your medical emergency." The Doctor blinked, looked around at the nature of the wounds and the sheer numbers of wounded, and added, "Don't bother."

"Start with Chakotay," Paris ordered harshly.

Janeway watched, noting the oddest thing—for just an instant, The Doctor didn't seem to know which one of the wounded was Chakotay. Only when Paris said, "I've stabilized him, but he's got internal injuries," did the holo-doc focus on the man Paris was standing beside.

The captain followed him to Chakotay's side, her stomach turning at the sight of her half-withered first officer—her friend, her confidant and life support. "We found your emitter on deck nine," she told The Doctor, implying that she wanted an explanation.

He worked on Chakotay swiftly, with the efficiency of a computer, of course, pressing a hypo to the first officer's neck, then his chest. "I was taken hostage by the

Equinox crew," he said. "I deactivated myself to escape." He paused, then asked, "Did you stop them?"

"No," Janeway blistered.

Chakotay moaned, drawing all their attention. Janeway and Paris leaned in with concern.

"I'd ask for a status report," he groaned, "but I'm not sure I want to hear it . . ."

His voice—to Janeway it sounded like church bells.

"You sound terrible," Paris uttered, his relief unshielded.

"Harry's analyzing the sound we've been hearing," Janeway told him, bluntly implying that near-mummification was no excuse for lying down on the job. "He thinks it's some form of communication."

Chakotay tried to raise his head, but instantly weakened. "As soon as I get out of sickbay, I'll . . . lend him a hand . . . I once figured out how to speak with a Terrellian Seapod . . . this couldn't be that much harder . . ."

At the idea of distractions from her new purpose in life, Janeway stiffened. "We should all be focusing our efforts on finding the *Equinox.*"

Through the hollow gourd of his partly destroyed face, Chakotay's eyes searched for reason in that goal. "First things first . . . we've got to stop these attacks."

There was more, but he didn't speak it. *Don't we? Captain?*

"Our enemies aren't the aliens," Janeway coldly said. "They're the humans on board the *Equinox.* It's crucial that you don't—"

The alien tone interrupted her as if it were following

her around the ship. She drew her weapon, Paris grabbed for his, and even the wounded on the deck huddled and raised their phasers. Chakotay managed to put his hand on his own phaser at his belt.

By then, the sound had faded.

"Tuvok's working the grid," Janeway said with quiet gratitude. "Shields are holding, but they won't forever. Chakotay—"

"One moment, please," The Doctor interrupted. They had to wait while he sprayed a lubricating compound on Chakotay's wounds. Chakotay gritted his teeth and grimaced, but managed to keep from flinching. Immediately The Doctor applied a synthetic poultice of gel and grown skin. "Allow me a moment to fuse this, Commander."

"I can't see now . . ."

"Is that supposed to happen?" Paris asked.

"Your eyes will be fine in a few minutes. I've just anesthetized them until the tissues and blood vessels fuse."

As his wounds quickly healed, Chakotay attempted to sit up, failing until Paris stepped in to hoist him to a sitting position. He swung his legs over the edge of the bed and sat, breathing deeply, while the synthetic poultice worked to regenerate the cells of his face and skull.

"Don't stand up yet," The Doctor ordered. "The regeneration will disorient you for a few seconds."

Janeway looked at The Doctor. He seemed uninterested. He didn't call any of them by name or rank, as he usually did. The captain decided this was probably just her own injuries working on her. All her senses were heightened, her emotions hot-wired. She was expecting him to be that way, too, and he never would be.

"Let the *Equinox* go for now," Chakotay advised, looking at her with his one restored eye. "We can track them later, if you want. We're all heading in the same dir—"

"If they keep killing nucleogenics," Janeway snapped, "they'll pull ahead and we'll never catch up. He'll be loose in the Delta Quadrant. He's a serial killer and I'm not letting him get away with this," she vowed.

Chakotay hung his injured head briefly, pressing both hands to the edge of the mattress. "He's not a serial killer, Captain. That's an unfair characterization."

Bristling, she lowered her chin and glared. "It's my job to hold all Federation citizens to a standard of behavior and that's what I mean to do."

"Only Federation citizens?" he prodded. "Is right only right for us?"

As Paris and The Doctor both backed off a step, noticing the gravity of this conversation, Janeway hardened inwardly and leered at Chakotay's healing face. "Don't push me," she warned sternly.

"Let me help Harry," he compromised. "You and I can concentrate on different work for a while."

She hated that he was being wiser than she was. Still, sense was sense. "All right. I'll go that far. Report to the bridge as soon as you're finished cooking. Then we'll see what we each have to do to quiet our demons."

Miles of sand, rocks . . . waves gently rolled and broke on a crystal white shoreline. The water was not exactly blue, the clouds not exactly silver, and still the similarity to Earth was enough to set a heart stirring.

A seabird, something like a pelican without the bucket, flew across the vista, crying its airy song, proving that a high sound could summon wind, sun, and spray and not only the whine of demolition.

As the breeze rose from the sea's arms and rushed across the ivory sand, causing pebbles to whistle and reeds to sing, a faint metallic chime invaded the *pax botanica.*

"Who is it?"

"Max. I've brought you a visitor."

"Hold on."

The wide-winged bird swept low into a wave trough, skimming the surface with easy precision even as the wave rolled along. *Crash*—it stabbed its beak into the water. Without even a flap of its huge wings, it speared an eel and soared on with its prize.

Survival. What a beautiful thing.

BBBzzzap.

The vista disappeared. Once again Rudy Ransom was sitting in his quarters, a destroyed place but somehow comforting after the episode on board *Voyager.* He took the virtual reality device from behind his ear and reluctantly turned it over and over in his hand. He would go back later and watch the bird swallow the eel.

"Come in," he invited.

Max Burke came in first, leading a somewhat mussed-up guest with a laceration on her forehead.

"Glad you're okay," Ransom offered.

Devoid of any need to be sociable or even civil, Seven of Nine looked at the device in his hand.

"Synaptic stimulator," Ransom explained. "I was just taking a stroll along the Tenkaran Coast. You're welcome to try it."

"State your intentions," the girl told him bluntly.

"Once we get our enhanced warp drive back online, we'll be on our way home. But it'll still take us a few months. You can spend that time in the brig or you can become part of this crew. I'd prefer the latter."

"I'd prefer the brig."

Ransom shrugged a little. "You know, Janeway's not the only captain who can help you explore your humanity."

She raised her chin. "You would be an inferior role model."

So Janeway had convinced this breathing machine that all situations were cast in stone. Too bad.

"One day," he told her, "you'll realize that not every situation is black or white. Janeway clung to her morality at the expense of her crew. Maybe you should try to learn from her mistake."

"Her only mistake was trusting you."

With disappointment, Ransom forced down another shrug. He'd come to peace with himself and wasn't about to let a Borg, of all life forms, stir up any regrets about moral absolutes. How many people had she killed during her time plugged into a cube?

To Burke he simply said, "Take care of her wound."

If only things could be different.

But nothing was.

"First-degree phaser burns . . . minor lacerations . . . looks like we'll have to amputate."

In the sickbay, Max Burke ran the med-scanner over Seven's scalp wound. She didn't respond to his attempt to at least humanize the situation a little.

"That was a joke," he encouraged. "You're supposed to smile, make a witty retort—"

"I'm familiar with human banter. Yours is crude and predictable."

"An insult! Better than nothing. You know, Seven— can I call you Seven? There aren't a lot of luxuries around here. All we've really got is each other. You might try letting your shields down or else it's going to be a lonely trip . . . well, I'll be damned! We've got a stowaway!"

As Seven frowned in confusion, Burke tapped the controls for the EMH.

The Doctor appeared, but he looked perplexed and out of place, almost dizzy. Burke knew instantly what had happened.

"Seven?" The Doctor began.

"We are captives," the Borg girl explained immediately.

"I was attacked by their EMH."

Burke scanned the controls. "Looks like he downloaded you into our database. Good. Go treat your friend." He handed The Doctor a tricorder and gestured toward Seven.

When the hologram hesitated, Burke encouraged, "Are you refusing to treat one of your own shipmates?"

Eying him bitterly, The Doctor relented. "No. I will treat any of you, assuming you live long enough to come down to sickbay. Captain Janeway will be firing on you soon, and you won't have a chance."

"She won't kill us," Burke said. "Rudy's right. She's not to that point yet. Arresting us is one thing. Executing us without trial is something else."

"Ransom to Burke. We're ready to try the warp drive. Let's have Red Alert, Max."

"Acknowledged. I'm on my way. Or, shall I say, 'we're' on our way. See you later, Doc. Unless you decide to misbehave, that is. Seven, come with me or I'll stun you. Doctor, you're authorized to use the research lab, aren't you?"

"Well . . . yes."

"Meet us there and you can keep treating her. If you don't, I'll shut you down and she can get infected or whatever happens. Right now we don't much care about you. Seven, this way."

"Marla to Ransom."

Ransom glanced up as Burke appeared at the door of the research lab, with Seven of Nine behind him. As soon as they appeared, The Doctor frazzled into solidity nearby. No—this couldn't be their doctor. This one looked angry, even put off. Maybe his program had been compromised somehow.

"I thought you were on the bridge," Burke told him as he came to Ransom's side.

"Lessing's manning it. I wanted to be here for the power shift, in case you need an extra hand."

"Thanks."

"Marla, go ahead," Ransom said into the comm.

"We're ready."

"Acknowledged. Infuse the enhanced warp drive with twenty isograms of the compound."

"Aye, sir."

"Ransom to bridge. Lessing . . . engage."

They held their breaths—certainly he held his. Beside him, Burke was poised, silent.

The ship hummed, gathered strength, began to tremble and whine in a mechanical way. That sounded right, most of it . . . there was still damage, yet the ship struggled valiantly to reach warp. Almost there . . . almost . . .

*KRRRRCHUNK*CHHHH—

"What happened!" he gasped. Loss of power!

From the engine room, Gilmore called, *"The power relays are off-line! They've been encoded!"*

Both Ransom and Burke turned to Seven of Nine. Ransom warned, "Give us the codes."

"No."

Coldly Burke shook his head. "I scanned her before. There's Borg technology throughout her cranium. If she won't give us the codes, maybe we could extract them ourselves."

The Doctor said, "Seven's cranial infrastructure is highly complex. You'd need months just to figure out what she had for breakfast."

Well, that was unexpected—defiance? Ransom

watched Burke, who seemed to know what was going on.

"That's why you're going to help us," the first officer told the hologram.

The Doctor came to something like attention. "I refuse."

Since Burke seemed to know what was happening, Ransom stood by and let him handle it.

"Do it," Burke said, "or I'll erase your program."

"Be my guest."

"Doctor," Seven protested.

"Don't worry," The Doctor said. "They need me. They'll be cutting off their holographic nose to spite their face. Now, I suggest you—"

Without waiting, Ransom reached over to the sickbay auxiliary connection and hit a final control, setting into motion a series of bleeps. The Doctor's demeanor suddenly changed. He was no longer defiant, but rather cold and remote.

"Get to work," Ransom ordered him. "You know what we're looking for."

"Very well." The Doctor turned to Seven. "Have a seat."

"Doctor?"

"I deleted his ethical subroutines," Ransom explained. She might as well know she had no more comrade here. "He'll be a little more cooperative now. Doctor, keep me posted. Max, let's go help Marla. If we don't have warp speed soon, *Voyager* will catch up to us and we'll be singing to her tune again."

CHAPTER

11

MUSSED CLOTHING, TORN HAIR, SMEARED WITH LUBRICANT and leakage, smelling and scratched, Kathryn Janeway sat on her darkened bridge in a shadow cast by a particularly ill-placed work light that was trying to illuminate an area on the lower deck where two crewmen were lying in a trunk up to their armpits. Tuvok, Paris, Kim, none of them looked any better. The haunting image was remarkably reminiscent of her first glimpse of the *Equinox*'s bridge—how welcome and how pathetic it had seemed to her. A Starfleet ship, in the grip of turmoil, its crew struggling valiantly to keep going one more minute at a time, the bulkheads and ceilings in midcollapse, scored by phaser etchings, cables hanging like veins from gaping wounds . . .

Too familiar now. Too close. No more nice clean ship

with tidy corridors and a healthy crew. No more safe haven.

Her face and neck were back to normal at least, though still stinging from the reintegration treatment. She was too aware of Chakotay and kept glancing at him as he worked up there on the circle deck.

Had Rudy Ransom's crystal ball just been clearer than her own? Sharpened to a focus by the crushing loss of thirty-nine shipmates who had entrusted their lives to him? Had he seen the ugliness of reality because he had been forced to stand toe to toe with it, whereas Janeway had been buffered by a clean ship and a full belly?

No. I won't cross. I don't care how close I get to the line. No matter how easy it is to understand you, I won't let you drag me over it.

When Chakotay approached her, somewhat fishily, and handed her a PADD without a word, she took it with more willingness than she might've an hour ago. Alternatives were turning thin and going extinct. Any glimmer would do.

"It's not exactly Shakespeare," she commented, scanning the fractal patterns that apparently translated into something the aliens might comprehend. So that's what their language was based upon. Repetitions and sequences and mathematical exponents. No wonder Ransom had never found it.

"A small olive branch," Chakotay quietly offered, "is still an olive branch."

Janeway handed the PADD to Kim. "Run this through your translation matrix."

"Set your weapons down," Chakotay suggested.

When Janeway didn't countermand, Paris looked up in question. "Commander?"

Chakotay held out a passive hand. "Somebody's got to start trusting somebody around here."

"Belay that order," Janeway roughly said. When he turned to her, she added, "I appreciate your optimism, but in this case . . . weapons."

She'd cut him down again, this time in front of everyone. Trust? Not this time. Would she ever trust again? Even the two of them weren't sure they trusted each other completely right now. The line was drawing itself right between them.

Around her, everyone drew a weapon, even Chakotay, and charged their phasers with waiting power.

"Ready to transmit," Kim said.

Janeway glanced at Tuvok. "Drop shields. Bridge only."

As if that would make any difference for the lower decks.

Tuvok worked with one hand, his phaser ready in the other.

The alien tone began almost instantly as the shields went down. Janeway braced to fire at anyone who was threatening. If the aliens didn't like the sound the ship was now sending, then it was all over. They'd be like Ransom, fighting day in and day out, for years. This would be *Voyager*'s equinox.

No one spoke, no one shouted. No one warned, "Here they come" or "There they are." Glowing with angry incandescence, the first alien globe appeared on the upper port side. Agitated, an alien broke through, its cranial membrane parted and bladed, its teeth bared, claws grasping. Racing from its scalpel cut in the spatial plane, it veered toward Harry Kim, the nearest crewman to the globe portal.

Somehow, whether by self-control or sheer shock, Kim managed to hold himself back from firing right away. The clicking and spinning of the universal translator matched all their heartbeats.

Just before Janeway would've fired to defend Kim, the alien stopped in midair. Its head changed, turning bulbous and softer. It seemed confused, opening and closing its knuckly fingers, kneading its palms with two-inch claws. Obviously a predator, she noted in a silly instant of detachment.

As if they didn't know that.

But it had stopped. It was hovering.

She began to reach out her hand in what she hoped was a universal gesture, but suddenly the creature reversed itself, flashing its tail, and disappeared back inside the globe, which collapsed almost immediately, taking the warning tone with it.

Well, there's hospitality.

At least it was quiet now.

"Raise shields," Janeway remembered to order.

Everyone turned to Kim and waited as he fidgeted at his controls. "If they understood our message," he said, "they haven't responded."

The ship shook briefly, a shudder like a sailboat taking a blunt wave. Another attack.

"There's your response," Janeway told them, letting

herself sound as harsh as she felt. "Activate your deflector pulse."

"Shields are holding at sixty-two percent," Tuvok said.

"That should buy us another few minutes of peace and quiet. I suggest we make the most of it. Focus your efforts on repairing the warp drive. We've got to find the *Equinox*."

Shoulder slumped, Chakotay picked up the PADD with the apparently useless fractals. "If it's all the same to you, I'd like to take another stab at this message. If we reword—"

"They're not listening, Chakotay. We should be tracking Ransom, not tinkering with adverbs."

Get out—off the bridge, before this all starts again. She pushed away from the command center and headed for her ready room, feeling a few gashes in her spirit that needed licking.

When she got in there, the door didn't close behind her right away.

He had followed her in.

"Want your first officer's advice?" he asked. Somehow he managed to keep from putting emphasis on any of those key words.

"Allow me." Janeway turned to face him. " 'Our deflector is losing power, and when it fails we'll be defenseless. It's *Voyager* we should be worrying about, not the *Equinox*.' "

"You'd make a great first officer," he said. "It's advice worth taking."

"Maybe so. But we have a crew member trapped on that ship."

"Is this really about Seven?" Chakotay asked, risking opening the can of worms. "Or is it about him? Ransom?"

"I don't know what you're talking about," Janeway said, and she knew—they both knew—she was lying.

"You've been known to hold a grudge," he said. "This man betrayed Starfleet. He broke the Prime Directive, dishonored everything you believe in, and threw *Voyager* to the wolves."

She could've gotten a great I-told-you-so. He seemed to have changed his tune, or at least a few notes of it. Or perhaps he was baiting her again to see what the past hours' events had done to her.

"Borg, Hirogen, Malon," she ticked off. "We've run into our share of bad guys. Ransom's no different."

"Yes, he is. You said it yourself. He's *human*. I don't blame you for being angry, but you can't compromise the safety of this ship to satisfy some personal vendetta."

"I appreciate your candor," she said in a warning tone. "Now let me be as blunt. You're right, I am angry. I'm damned angry. He's a Starfleet captain and he's decided to abandon everything this uniform stands for. He's out there right now, torturing and murdering innocent life forms just to get home a little quicker. I'm not going to stand for it. I'm going to hunt him down no matter how long it takes, no matter what the cost. If you want to call that a vendetta, then go right ahead."

On the saw-toothed challenge, Chakotay began to turn and leave, then changed his mind. Perhaps the cloying understanding of near-death held him here, and the fact that they were a long way from out of this. Janeway deplored the fact that he really was doing his job, trying to see if his captain were dividing her causes in a time when they needed full concentration on survival.

"Ransom wasn't an engineer or a warrior, Kathryn," Chakotay reminded. "He was a man who worked on high-flown theories, not hard physics. He thought in terms of leaps of probability. The reality of time and distance was more real to him because his ship would take twice as long to get home—not seventy years, but a hundred and fifty. They had *no* chance of getting home in their lifetimes, Captain. The Prime Directive? It feels pretty far away when one of those aliens hits you and sucks the life out of you. Take it from me—"

"I felt it too, remember?" Putting distance between them, she went behind her desk but remained standing.

"And it worries me what it might've done to you," he admitted. "Seems to me you're holding a different measuring stick up to Ransom than we've ever held to ourselves. We've stopped entire wars that would've happened if we hadn't accidentally been here. There are those who will argue that we were wrong, that we had no business tampering with destiny, even if the destiny was ugly. Do regulations condemn any and all interferences? Or just the interference that goes sour? What kind of rule is that? 'Don't interfere, unless it all turns out well'?"

"We stopped that warhead to save—"

"To save the ship," Chakotay said forcefully, "not to stop a planetary catastrophe. That's my point. If our ship hadn't been in danger, would you have argued it wasn't our business to get between the business of two planets? Maybe that civilization's next Stalin is alive and well now because we stopped a disaster from happening. Ransom saved his ship his way, and we saved our ship our way. Yes, I know, this can drive a person crazy. Morality—what a problem!"

He flopped his arms uncharacteristically and the new skin on his cheeks flushed.

"Maybe you'd better leave," Janeway invited. "This isn't helping."

Raising his voice just a little, Chakotay moved to meet her as she stepped across the back of the desk. "It'll help if I understand your underlying motivations."

Janeway fumed, trying to isolate herself, trying not to think of him at all, but only of her own ground-glass responsibility. "It's my duty to make the call on Ransom and take him into custody. What I hope or understand doesn't matter anymore. I'm forced into the role of prosecutor. I represent the law here. Our law. His law."

At this, she visibly fought to control herself, to retain some of her old evenhandedness beneath the weight of her prosecutorial mantle.

"I understand his reasons, Chakotay. They're reasons, not excuses. Sometimes we have to step back and say that holding back is part of what our training and our obligation and our oaths are about, and we *will* hold ourselves to the ethics even though we die trying."

As Chakotay watched, hard-eyed, Janeway retreated deeper and deeper into the sanctuary of protocol, the only place she felt safe. Her struggle showed in her face, a leathery mask of deep suffering.

"I have to keep us on the side of regulations," she said, "and interpret them strictly, even though I understand their elastic application in practice. That's not my job here now. My job is to uphold the strict interpretation, and also what I believe is right."

Chakotay braced his legs. "I'm just cautioning you, Captain, which is *my* duty. In my opinion, you're forcing yourself to defend a line you've never visited. We're a long way from home, just like Ransom. How desperate will we have to be before the laws of civilization break down under the laws of survival? Do you think we can never be that desperate? Don't forget . . . I know what it's like to have my ship overwhelmed completely."

In a move that surprised him, she shot up from her chair and met him in that challenging stance, with the desk between them and the gulf widening.

"Be careful, Commander," she warned. Her voice was a shredded wreck. "Don't you talk to me about lines and edges. I represent a standard of behavior that we certainly *will* uphold on this ship, in this quadrant, with anybody we encounter, and we're going to hold Rudolph Ransom and every single one of his crew accountable. Is that clear enough?"

Caught by the intrigue of moral turmoil, Chakotay leaned forward with his fists on the desk. "You've seen bad types before in this quadrant, Captain. Why are you so worked up about Rudolph Ransom and his crew?"

"Because they're humans! They're not just other 'bad types'!"

"So? Are you so race-conscious that they're any worse than Klingons or Borg or any other thousand races who might spawn a bad egg? Somehow we have to hold humans to a higher standard? Or are you afraid," he roared, "of how it reflects on you?"

"What's that supposed to mean?"

"It means you know the same survival instinct might get a grip on you someday, and you have to crucify Ransom in order to beat off your own inner ghosts. I think you have to make the law of civilization win or you might break down like he did. You can't let him get away with this because you see too much of yourself in him, the same dark side that every commander has to possess in order to command effectively. Are you over-reacting because you don't like the image Ransom lays on humans or are you afraid of what *you* might become?"

Itching in her stained and torn uniform, throbbing with muscle strains, bruises, and a pounding headache, Janeway slammed the desk chair out of her way so hard that it struck the viewport rail. "Chakotay, that's damned well enough!"

His lips drew back with conviction and his black eyes blazed as he turned for the door. "Aye, Captain, but remember while you're on this witch hunt . . . the witch is in the mirror."

CHAPTER

12

"WHY'D WE STOP?"

"This planet has a pathogenic atmosphere. It'll keep us from being detected while we make repairs."

Ransom responded as Max Burke came back onto the bridge and saw that they were in orbit around a peaceful looking planet that was entirely fern-green except for the poles, which were silvery.

Noah Lessing looked up from his station. "We also found a few deuterium deposits."

"Take an away team," Ransom told him. "See if you can localize the ore."

Burke squared with Lessing as the latter stood up. "You won't be protected from the aliens. Arm yourselves with phaser rifles. At the first sign of trouble, we'll beam you back."

"Aye, sir."

When he left, Ransom took his place in front of Burke and asked, "How're things going with the codes? Has that girl decided to talk?"

"No, she's decided not to. And with a Borg, that's a permanent fix. Their doctor is dissecting her Borg mechanics. He seems to be enjoying himself. Last time I was in there, he was actually singing."

"Singing?" Ransom chuckled. "You mean, like music?"

"You know . . . 'De ocular node's connected to de sensory node, de sensory node's connected to de cortical node . . . de cortical node's con—' "

"Max! Stop while we're both sane. *Our* doctor never sings, does he?"

"No, he's not half as much fun as this guy."

"Let's go down there," Ransom said, leading the way. "I want to talk to her."

Burke kept up with him easily as they hurried through the ship. "It won't do any good. Janeway's got her completely brainwashed. Seven doesn't know how to be logical anymore. She's just completely loyal."

Ransom shrugged. "A captain could do worse in a crew member, Borg or not."

Smiling, Burke shook his head. "I wish you'd make up your mind if you're going to hate Janeway or not, so I know what to do!"

"I don't hate her. Hell, I hardly know her. She's just the obstacle I have to get past right now, Max. How that happens is up to her. I'll do what I have to, whatever it takes to get us home. If she gets in the way, I'll run over her." He held up a hand as they approached the research lab. "Don't talk about it in front of Seven. Let's see if we can move her."

They strode in to an admittedly disconcerting sight—The Doctor had Seven strapped to a table, and he was dissecting her brain by going through her Borg eye socket.

The Doctor was finishing a sentence: "—being unfettered by ethical subroutines has made me far more efficient."

As they approached, Ransom and Burke both winced at the condition of Seven on the table. The eyepiece she normally wore now lay on the table's glossy surface. They could see the Borg circuitry in her head, twice as disturbing because this head now turned to look at them with its one human eye.

"Status," Ransom asked, pushing down the insides of his stomach.

"I'm going to extract her cortical array," The Doctor said. "It contains an index of her memory engrams. But once I've removed it, her higher brain functions—cognitive skills, language—will be severely damaged."

"Is there another option?"

"If I had several weeks, but you said time was of the essence."

This wasn't good. Did everything have to be a trial?

He moved to Seven. Please let her be sensible as well as loyal.

"Tell me the codes," he ordered.

"No," she said.

"Janeway was right about one thing. You are unique . . . it would be a shame to lose you."

Seven regarded him icily. "Your compassion is irrelevant."

Ransom leaned forward a little. "Do you think this is easy for me? The sight of you on that table . . . but you're leaving me no choice!"

"No choice," she repeated. "You say that frequently. You destroy life forms to attain your goals, then claim they left you no choice. Does that logic comfort you?"

His hands started to shake. What she didn't know was that he was beyond comfort. "The codes."

"You will have to destroy me to obtain them."

Agonized by her stubbornness, Ransom also admired her stalwart sense of purpose. He understood it, too. Die if you must, for something worth dying to protect. She spoke of choices—this was one of those.

He nodded to The Doctor, who picked up a medical tool and began working again on the young girl's exposed circuitry.

As Ransom stiffly led Burke out of the room, he heard the bizarre sound of The Doctor beginning to sing. " 'The reticular node's connected to the occipital node' . . ."

In *Voyager*'s sickbay, awful things were happening. Ugly, unfortunate things. Captain Janeway paused as she came in the entry vestibule, held in place by the argument going on in the medlab. Neelix's voice . . . and The Doctor's.

"I heard about this but I just couldn't believe it, just *couldn't* believe the rumor that our own doctor was committing some kind of vivisection experiments!"

"This isn't vivisection. This is an autopsy."

"Is that what you call it? This alien deserves a decent burial! Or a cremation . . . or something other than this!"

"Don't you have some pots to clean?"

"The captain won't allow this!"

"It's a medical emergency. Sickbay is my jurisdiction."

Her stomach tightening at the mention of herself, the captain, knowing how that changed the tenor of almost any conversation on board, moved slowly forward and peeked into the medlab.

The doctor was picking up a laser scalpel. On the diagnostic table before him, an alien body lay spread grotesquely, its tail hanging over the edge of the table. The creature was partially dissected already, but Neelix had The Doctor by the arm and was holding him back from continuing, the two engaged now in a primal dance of defiance.

"I can't let you!" Neelix swore.

"Remove your hand," The Doctor threatened, "unless you want it amputated."

"You wouldn't dare!"

As they struggled for control of the laser scalpel, a terrible guilt swarmed over Janeway and she stepped into the room. "Please state the nature of the medical emergency," she said, trying to be wry.

As they halted their actions and stared at her, she saw that her attempt at lightening the moment had failed.

"Captain!" Neelix's face was flushed nearly orange.

"He took these remains from the biolab without authorization!"

"I'm working on a way to counteract the alien toxins," The Doctor flatly explained. "Which means I'll have to dissect a few corpses."

Neelix swung to face him. "What if we find a way to communicate with these beings? We may need to return their dead intact! As a gesture of goodwill!"

"Fine!" The Doctor's arms stiffened at his sides. "Take it away. Give it a proper burial. And while you're at it, make room for some of *Voyager*'s crew."

Suddenly, cold down to her feet, Janeway felt the insurmountable problem shift from their shoulders to hers. The arguments had been posed and now had to be arbitrated. That was her role, her burden.

She looked at the dead alien, the animalistic face, the teeth, claws, sharklike body, and tried to empathize with it as a fellow intelligent being...but she couldn't find the link she needed to decide more in its favor than in her own living shipmates' favor. A delayed image of Chakotay's crinkled-cardboard wounds and his nearly fatal experience haunted her suddenly. What if she could find an antidote by dissecting these bodies? What if she could help her own at the others' expense?

"Proceed, Doctor," she said, her voice a box of gravel.

The Doctor's icy expression took her by surprise. "I'll need two more."

Neelix's eyes crossed to her, filled with anguish and disappointment. He said nothing. Absolutely nothing.

"They're already dead," she argued, more with herself than him.

He still said nothing. Instead, the ultimate hurt, he turned and walked out of sickbay. Neelix, speechless?

"Rumor has it," The Doctor began as Janeway started to leave and now turned back, "that we've lost track of the *Equinox.*"

"For now," she told him. "But we'll find them."

"Please inform me the moment you do," he said.

Janeway parted her lips to ask him why a medical program would make such a request—and make it sound like an order—when he seemed to realize he'd made some kind of faux pas and immediately said, "In case there's an armed conflict. I'll want to prepare for more casualties."

Something about the way he spoke, the way he glanced at her but didn't really look at her . . . Janeway gave in to her own troubles and decided his explanation made sense.

As long as there was a reason.

"Come in."

Captain Janeway sat at her ready-room desk, studying a desktop monitor that showed several points of repair and adjustment going on all over the ship that needed her diligent surveillance. Beside her was a PADD that disturbed her very much. How close was she coming to that "line" both Ransom and Chakotay talked about? She could barely feel her legs, she was so tense.

Chakotay strode in, looking remarkably normal for what they'd all been through, except for the dirt on his uniform and the expression on his face.

"You wanted to see me?"

Careful of her tone, Janeway picked up the PADD. "It's not like you to submit recommendations in writing."

He stood before her desk and clasped his hands behind his back. "The last time we spoke, you weren't exactly receptive."

"I'm afraid I'm not going to be very receptive this time either," she warned. "It's an interesting idea, but the Ankari are fifty light-years in the wrong direction."

He nodded. "I understand that. But they're the ones who introduced Ransom to these life forms. It stands to reason that they might be able to communicate with them. Tell them to call off their attacks."

Lowering her voice, Janeway tried not to sound abrasive this time. "Our first priority is to find Ransom." When he was silent about that—no longer challenging her decision, though he still obviously disapproved— Janeway snatched the angle away from the philosophical problem. "Still no sign of nucleogenic particles?"

"Not yet."

"Then he couldn't have gotten far. Without his 'enhanced' drive, his ship's only capable of warp six." She tapped her monitor and brought up a file, then gestured to it. "I've been studying his service record. He's had his share of run-ins with hostile aliens. It seems that when he's being pursued, he tends to hide. At Epsilon Four, he ran into a Klingon Bird of Prey, and played cat-and-mouse for three days in a nebula before the Klingons finally gave up." She got up then and started pacing to get her back and thighs to relax. "Two years later, he eluded a Romulan warbird by taking his vessel into the atmosphere of a gas giant."

Chakotay remained silent. No opinions. No observations. Could he be that hurt?

She looked at him. "Go to astrometrics. Start looking for the kind of place you'd hide if your ship were damaged."

Argue with me, would you, please?

He stood still for a moment, then unclasped his hands. They fell to his sides. "Yes, ma'am."

As he left the office, Janeway closed her eyes. The breath sank out of her as if she were a pitcher being poured. He had his orders . . . that wasn't the way she'd hoped things would go between them.

Feeling a hundred years old, she moved to the viewport and gazed out at the nearest star system, a foggy blur on the edge of a stellar dust cloud. Blue, mostly.

Was he right? Was Ransom? How long before she had to admit they weren't going to make it back to Earth? Not this way, dogging along under conventional power. They couldn't go on being a little isolated island of Federation law, all by and for themselves. Ransom had realized that right away, and she had condemned him for it. Was he right? Could they never possibly succeed under conventional power?

It's not fair, but he's still accountable. It's a reason, not an excuse. Because I haven't walked in his shoes, I can't judge him? Yes, I can.

At what cost, Chakotay? We have to live with each other, all of us in this floating fortress. What cost for us?

As she gazed out the viewport at the stars, the mindless stars, she saw her own sorrowful reflection in the port window. Hair mussed, dirty, frayed. Fierce lines bracketed her mouth. Her eyes were undescribable.

The witch in the mirror was one unhappy lady.

Tranquility base . . . the alien coastline. Ivory sand, lapping crystal-colored water, wide-winged birds.

Ransom breathed deeply, conning himself that he was breathing the cool windborne air of the shoreline instead of the stuffy recirculated stuff of a half-crippled ship. This was a good place, wide and free. Sprawling with life. Birds, bugs, lizards . . . not like the Skeleton Coast.

What . . .

In his mind he worked to focus the vision of the beach. On a distant dune, frilled with rushes and patterned with the tracks of sand crabs, stood a human figure, a woman. Willowy and windblown, she gazed at him with the sun streaking her long blond hair. She stood in a haze of warm air. He couldn't see her face, but she was looking at him. Haunting him, watching him—

Even through the blur of distance and haze, her eyes asked questions of him that burrowed to the depths of his soul. She stood on the dune, her legs braced, as sea water lapped at the crabs walking below on the white sand. Watching, watching.

He pulled the synaptic stimulator from behind his ear. Her eyes were still on him in his mind.

Around him now, his dismal ready room was a sudden comfort, a place he understood, with the right kinds of surprises. The mind, that was something else.

Curiously looking at his synaptic stimulator, he summoned his sense of immediacy and went out onto the bridge, where he held the device before Marla Gilmore at the engineering auxiliary station.

"How was the beach?" Gilmore asked.

"Do these programs have people in them?"

She looked up. "No. Just landscapes. Why?"

He paused, thinking of describing what he had seen. "Forget it," was his decision. "How's the away team doing?"

Hills and wilderness. A scent of pine, and something else that couldn't be likened to anything on Earth. He'd smelled something like that on Omicron-Indii once, though. Nutty, but perfumed.

"Stay down."

"Aye, aye."

Chakotay motioned to the security team behind him and Tom Paris to keep back a few steps. His tricorder was reading life forms—human. His victory was soured by the fact that his relationship with his captain was strained right now and his heart wasn't in this capture.

There were trees here, plenty of them, billions of them, trillions. Every one had a fern growing out of its lower trunk, so the land was unaccountably lush and spongy with fungus and moss. The planet was an utter wilderness, no settlements or advanced life forms at all, give or take the occasional large arthropod. As far as Chakotay could tell, the largest land animals on this continent were a kind of feral pig-type semi-predator that could be easily scared off with a sharp shout. Unless they wanted to have a luau for Neelix to cook, they didn't need to stick around here very long.

"Shh," he warned, and motioned Paris to duck. Paris nodded, and crouched to wait, as ordered.

Chakotay shifted forward, following the signal on his tricorder, and now voices could be heard in the gully below.

Carefully, he reached out one hand and parted the chartreuse fronds before him.

There, below, were Noah Lessing and another *Equinox* crewman whom Chakotay did not know.

Lessing was saying, "I'm reading a vein of ore. Azimuth one seventeen, thirty meters. It could run pretty deep. We might need to use phasers to excavate it." Lessing paused then, and smiled as he surveyed the velvety moss at the gully floor. "McKinley Park . . . I used to take my sister there when we were kids. This looks just like it."

Glancing as Paris, moving very carefully, came to his side, Chakotay strained to listen.

"Let's see," Lessing went on, "as I recall there was a family of ground squirrels who lived over there . . . and there was a patch of poison ivy right next to it. When I was ten, I walked right through it. Swelled up like a

Rigelian bloodworm. When we get back to Earth, the first thing I'm going to do is see if that—"

Chakotay came to his feet as Lessing and the crewman climbed the embankment to within twenty paces of him and Paris. Paris also stood up, and both of them aimed their phaser rifles at the two grimy-looking sojourners.

It turned out to be a mistake to expect them to come quietly. For an instant even Chakotay forgot that these men, all of *Equinox*'s crew, lived a life of sudden necessary action and had learned a long time ago not to hesitate.

The crewman instantly grabbed for his holstered phaser. Only the swung butt of Paris' rifle aborted the deadly move. The crewman smashed into the ferns, his jaw badly bruised.

This gave Lessing an instant to dive for cover, firing as he went. A phaser bolt scored the bushes next to Chakotay, forcing him to crank sideways into a palmetto, lacerating his left hand. Angry now, he brought his rifle around and fired wide, winging Lessing in the shoulder as the other man tried to dodge behind a tree. Lessing slumped to the ferns.

When Chakotay got to him, Lessing was already coming around. Dazed and defeated, Lessing blinked up at Chakotay and everything the *Starship Voyager* meant to his kind of pioneer.

Gripped by empathy and admiration for the level of survivalism these crew members demonstrated, Chakotay glanced at Paris, who was just taking the other crewman into custody.

Now this part was over. The hard part was just starting.

He tapped his badge. "Four to beam up."

Ransom paced his bridge. In his mind were lush forests with his crew exploring. Space, thousands of light-years long between here and home. Green tails and claws, fissure globes, and the woman on the dune still watching him from the ivory sand in the back of his mind. He knew who she was. She was the souls of those animals come to challenge him. She was Kathryn Janeway in a dream package, leering at him from behind a book. He'd beaten everything else. He'd beat her eventually. He'd return to the beach and drown her.

"Captain," Gilmore said, as if she knew she was interrupting. "We're receiving a subspace transmission."

Whipping around, Ransom felt all his internal alerts snap on. "From who?"

"I can't tell."

His console showed nothing. "I don't see a ship out there. Open a channel."

Gilmore worked her controls, but nothing came over subspace. Wait—there was something—wrong channel, though . . .

"Doctor to Equinox! *Respond!"*

"We can hear you," Ransom answered.

"Voyager's found you! They've —tered orbit!"

For a moment Ransom didn't comprehend how he could know, then remembered that the *Voyager*'s doctor was trapped on his ship and the *Equinox* doctor was on the starship. On the starship! Extreme close range!

"They polarized their hull to mask their approach! I believe they've . . . —mbush . . . team . . . the —net!"

"Get him back!"

"I can't."

"Ransom to away team! Prepare to beam back to the ship!"

"They're not down there." Gilmore's voice cracked.

Ransom dropped into his chair, his face stiff with grim determination, and struck the alert controls. "All hands to battle stations!"

"I've got them, Rudy," Gilmore said. "Thirty thousand kilometers—closing fast. They're firing!"

The ship rocked hard. Ransom rushed to the helm himself to steady the course. For a moment he couldn't make himself key-in a new vector, sensing that he was leaving crewmen down on that planet. She had said they weren't there anymore, hadn't she?

"Direct hit," Gilmore reported. "Minor damage."

"Return fire."

"They targeted our power core."

"Marla, come down here! Take the controls. Get some crew up here."

She fired the ship's phasers from up there, then stumbled down toward the helm, but Max Burke erupted from the lift, shot to the upper deck, and took over the tactical and science stations for her. Gilmore dropped into the helm and keyed the weapons consoles from there.

"They can't find the shield grid generator, I'll bet," Burke said with great satisfaction. "They're trying to divert more power to their sensors." He glanced with a tricky glinting smile at Ransom. "She won't be able to do it. We've damaged their deflectors. If they go down, the aliens can break through. That'll distract her."

Ransom nodded, but couldn't muster a smile. Which "she" was he talking about?

"They're targeting our weapons arrays," Gilmore reported.

"Hello again," Burke muttered to his console. "It's B'Elanna. She's trying to bypass our security protocols."

"Stop her," Ransom authorized.

"Max!" Torres' voice came directly through the workstation where Burke was standing. *"Listen to me!"*

"Back for round two, BLT?"

Ransom almost interfered, but decided to let Burke handle that woman. The captain had his own woman problems. One at a time.

"I wish you didn't have to be one of them," Burke told the engineer over there.

"Max! Please!"

His shoulders set tightly, Burke cut her off just as a buffeting jolt slammed the ship three degrees to starboard.

"Weapons are down!" Gilmore cried.

"Janeway to Ransom. Surrender your vessel."

Ignoring the call, Ransom scanned Gilmore's helm. "We still have thrusters, don't we?"

"Aye, sir!"

"Lay in a course through the planet's atmosphere. Sixty degrees vector!"

"That's close . . ."

"We're a science ship. We can go closer than she can."

"Crossing into the ionosphere . . . vector ninety . . . eighty . . . seventy . . . vector sixty degrees—"

"Hold that vector. I want to scratch *Voyager*'s belly with those trees."

"She's following us," Burke reported. "They're starting to tremble. I can actually see it. Rudy, they're firing!"

"Shields are heating up, sir," Gilmore warned. "Friction reaching tolerance levels."

"What about *Voyager?*" Ransom pulled out of his chair and used the navigation monitor to access what Burke was seeing. "Her shields are weakening. Thirty-one percent . . . twenty-nine . . . hold course, Marla. We can take it. She can't. That starship was never built to get this close."

Burke yelped with victory. "Their inertial dampers just fell! She'll have to bear off now. Why isn't she bearing off? Is she crazy?"

"She hates me," Ransom commented. "That does terrible things to a person. Look at her . . . She thinks she's angry because I've broken the rules of behavior, but it's really her own fear she's fighting. But look at her. In her panic to remain civilized, she's becoming uncivilized herself." His face began to glaze with sweat as the temperature in the ship rose. He gazed into the monitor, at the sight of *Voyager* shuddering as the two ships streaked through the dangerous thermospheric breath of the planet. "It's like a policeman in a fervor to catch a criminal . . . he starts breaking the law himself, beating people to get answers, trampling the rights of others, shooting into the dark . . . She's torn up inside. She's terrified of not holding on. Just look at her . . . risking her ship and all her crew's lives, just to have the last word."

As he watched, his ship firing regularly now, throwing spears of phaser power back at the rattling starship, which, by the way, had stopped firing and was now concentrating on not turning into a giant rotisserie, the starship suddenly heaved upward and veered off the pursuit track.

"They're retreating," Gilmore shuddered. She made no effort to hide her relief.

"Take us up," Ransom ordered.

Burke kept his eyes on his controls. "They took heavy damage. Shields, propulsion . . ."

"Get us out of here, Marla."

As the ship whined out of the atmosphere, fighting the planet's gravity every inch of the way, Ransom found a moment to climb to the upper deck and clap Burke on the arm. "Good work. It's a good thing you knew that woman well enough to predict what she would do."

"Just battle tactics," Burke said with a shrug. "The battlefield of the heart."

"I'm sorry, Max."

"No, it's okay. A ten-year-old scar is pretty thick."

"What's our condition?"

"Most systems show green."

"Marla, go to warp speed." Ransom moved on a sore

knee—when had he hurt his knee? —back to the lower deck as the ship cleared the solar system and blasted into hyperlight. He gazed at the aft monitors, showing open space and the sun and its planets they had just left.

"Sorry, Captain," he uttered, "and welcome to the Coast."

CHAPTER

13

"THEY'VE GONE TO WARP."

The defeat in Tom Paris' words, his posture, his expression, brought everyone to a sullen point.

Janeway quickly acted to give them something to do besides repair damage. "Match their course and speed."

"We can't," Harry Kim told her unceremoniously. "Not until we restore primary systems."

"Time?"

"We'll need a few hours."

A few . . . several . . . some . . . damn.

"At least we didn't come away empty handed. I'll be in the cargo bay. Tuvok, you have the conn."

"Aye, Captain."

His tone had returned to normal. So much better than the strained urging he had been giving her while they pursued the *Equinox* through the deadly atmosphere. She still heard his voice as the ship shook and the dampers fell off-line and she continued to pursue the demon before her—*Captain . . . Captain!*

Before she even realized where she was, the big cargo-bay loading doors brushed open before her. She turned to the side deck, where crewman Lessing sat with his hands bound in Starfleet security manacles. His friendly face was scratched, and he was tensely defiant.

Chakotay stood off to one side, dirty and also scratched. Must be some rough foliage down there.

"I want Ransom's tactical status," Janeway demanded, squaring away over Lessing. "I want it now, Mr. Lessing."

She hoped her tone communicated the facts—that Ransom had been officially relieved of duty, that Lessing no longer took orders from him legally, and that Janeway was the law enforcement here. The wrong answer would transfer Lessing from a straying but loyal crewman to a criminal conspirator himself.

"Or what?" he responded. "You'll hit me?"

Eyes burning, Janeway leaned in close. "No, crewman. I'll drop the shields around this room, and let your little friends pay you a visit."

"That would be murder." He didn't think she'd do it.

"You could also call it poetic justice," Janeway said. If Ransom could call his actions survival, then she could call hers anything she wanted.

Lessing eyed Chakotay, standing a few feet away. "I

suppose the plan is that you're going to come to my rescue right now?"

Chakotay shifted uneasily, and resentfully. "There's no plan as far as I know. The captain's on her own."

Hard-cut, Janeway demanded again, "Ransom's status. Now."

"No way in hell," Lessing said.

Janeway straightened. "We all make our own hell, Mr. Lessing. I hope you enjoy yours. The comm is active. We'll be outside if you have a change of heart."

As Lessing's expression moved through several incarnations, Janeway stalked out of the cargo bay with Chakotay following her. She was glad he followed. Could be trouble if he didn't.

In the corridor, the nearest wall panel was ten feet from the bay door. She went straight to it, activated it, and started pushing buttons.

Chakotay came to her side. He said nothing at first, probably expecting her to be activating the gravity control or changing the pressure in there to make Lessing believe something was going on.

What he didn't know and now realized, something *was* going on.

"What are you doing?" he challenged, noticing the sequence she was activating.

"Weren't you listening?" she shot back. On the small monitor, she called up a picture of Lessing sitting in the cargo bay, shackled, shuddering in his chair. Inside, the alien tone began to wail.

"Bridge to captain," Tuvok called through the

comm, *"we've lost shields in section twenty-nine alpha."*

"I know. Stand by."

Beside her, Chakotay shifted, tense and disbelieving. "Don't do this."

"He'll break."

The alien tone now screamed through the cargo bay, growing louder and louder by the second.

"Captain, a fissure is opening in that section!"

"Understood."

"He's a loyal officer!" Chakotay protested. "He's not going to betray his captain. Put up the shields!"

"He'll break."

"Captain!"

"As you were!"

In sheer defiance, Chakotay put his hands to the panel and punched a code.

"LEVEL NINE AUTHORIZATION REQUIRED," the computer responded, on critical mode.

Failed, Chakotay slammed his fist into the wall. "Damn it, Kathryn!"

"You're panicking," she insisted. "He's going to talk!"

His forehead beaded, Chakotay drew his phaser, threw her one last furious glare, and plunged through the bay doors with his weapon high.

In the cargo bay, Noah Lessing sat crushed into his chair with terror, helplessly shackled as an electric globe opened over his head.

Chakotay fired, collapsing the fissure as it opened. The tone continued to whine as other fissures tried to open around them. As Janeway watched, deliberately not interfering, Chakotay dragged Lessing out of the bay and into the corridor. As the doors swept shut, he pressed Lessing up against the bulkhead, crushing one fist and his phaser to the shaken crewman's bare neck.

"Okay," Chakotay broiled, "you've demonstrated your loyalty to your captain. Fine. Now let's talk about the Ankari!"

Having proven she was probably crazy, Kathryn Janeway watched the ghastly scene with cold appraisal. Was Chakotay just doing his job? Or had he reached his own equinox?

By separate paths, they had both reached the line.

The briefing room. Normally a place of calm discussion, reports, facts, and options. Today, something else.

Everyone knew, by now, about the break in allegiance between the captain and the first officer. Janeway sat at the head of the glossy table, ceding the moment to Chakotay, who seemed to want it. She sat in silent awareness that the final decision, no matter how the day wrangled itself out, would be hers. They all knew that. She owed it to them to let all the arguments vent themselves, to allow every possibility to be explored. Then, she would decide and they would follow her orders. They were all uneasy. The only change in that course was an unthinkable and irrevocable course for them to take—mutiny.

Despite her conviction, she was ice-blooded and embarrassed. Chakotay had held himself back from the edge—she hadn't. Like Ransom, she had convinced herself she was right. He did what he did for survival, she did what she did for civilization.

Now her crew doubted her. None of them met her eyes. That was Chakotay's fault.

Tuvok, Paris, Torres, and The Doctor sat at the table, all heads of critical shipboard functions during battle stations. Chakotay was leading the conversation under the pall of his captain's stony glare.

"It's there," he was asking. "How do we find it?"

B'Elanna Torres, still stinging from her failure to stop Max Burke from using her own tricks against her, asked, "If there's an Ankari vessel less than two light-years from here, why haven't we detected it?"

"Apparently they use a unique form of propulsion that makes them hard to find."

Paris leaned on an elbow. "You think they'll be willing to help us?"

"It's worth a try," Chakotay hoped. "Mr. Lessing has kindly agreed to show us how to adjust the sensors. Once you find the Ankari ship, set a course."

"Aye, sir," Paris said, dubious.

The Doctor then asked, "Did our prisoner disclose any other information?"

"I'm afraid not," Chakotay said, irritated. "The rest of you continue repairs. Dismissed."

They all stood up. All, including Chakotay.

Janeway let them all get to the door, except Chakotay.

"Commander," she called, low-toned.

He stopped as if he'd expected that, and turned. They were alone now.

"All right," Janeway told him, "we're going to try it your way. But I want to make one thing clear—"

"Our priority is to get Ransom," he said. "If there's one thing you've made clear, it's that."

This was bad, very bad. Janeway didn't like it. She thought she might, the sense of power, the ultimate decision, the fact that by law they all had to do as she decided. Such things worked well enough with a crew, but for her and Chakotay, the arm's-length friction hurt more and more with every passing hour.

She softened, hoping her eyes communicated that. "We've had our disagreements, Chakotay," she said, using his name as a branch between them. "But you've never openly opposed me."

His lips pressed flat. "You almost killed that man today."

"It was a calculated risk. I took it."

"It was a bad call."

"I'll note your objection in my log." She tried to make it sound like a joke, but when it clunked to the deck she knew she'd made a mistake.

Anger rose in Chakotay's distinctive eyes. His jaw suddenly set. "I don't give a damn about your log! This isn't about rules and regulations! It's about right and wrong, and I'm warning you . . . I won't let you cross the line again!"

In that electrical moment Janeway came to her feet to meet his glare at the same level. By standing she made them equals, not a captain and an officer, but two commanders with different methods of handling the same situation.

Different methods . . .

"Then you leave me no choice," she said. "You're hereby relieved of duty until further notice."

That shocked him.

In fact, it shocked her too. What had she just said? What was she protecting? Her right to use her judgment while pursuing another captain for using his? This was getting out of hand.

"What's happened to you, Kathryn?"

His voice was quilted with disappointment, worry, even fear. How could she explain anything more than already had been said between them? How could she make him understand that she had to hold the barrier high if they were to remain civilized?

She gazed at him. "I was about to ask you the same question."

"Captain, we have a contact," Tom Paris called from the bridge, saving them from yet another chance at maybe working this out. That was fast—of course, two light-years was practically in their weapons locker.

They left the ready room, but not exactly together.

The ship was tracking another vessel, an oddly shaped nugget running at high impulse, trying to avoid the starship—and there wasn't a chance of that anymore. So they'd been shadowed all this time by the perpetrators of this whole situation.

"They're not responding," Tuvok said immediately as Janeway came into her command chair.

"Tractor beam," Janeway ordered.

Tuvok looked up. "Captain, the Ankari ship has done nothing to warrant—"

"*Do it!*"

She was getting sick of this! Questions!

"We're being hailed," Kim said.

"On screen."

On the main viewer, a swollen-up excuse for a humanoid with a head like a pus-filled boil eyed—Were those eyes?—the *Voyager* bridge.

"*Starfleet?*"

"Yes," Janeway said instantly.

"*Leave us alone. There's nothing of value on our ship.*"

"We need your guidance. Your 'spirits of good fortune' are attacking us."

"*Of course they are! You've been killing them!*"

Janeway sat up a little at the glimmer that she might have been right all along. "We're not the ones responsible."

"*Equinox.*"

"That's right. Can you communicate with the aliens?"

Probably a bad choice of words. To them, she was an alien.

"*Release my ship.*"

"I can't do that. Not until you agree to talk to them."

The Ankari paused. He might've been consulting someone else. Janeway couldn't tell.

"*I will summon them. But you must talk to them. You must convince them.*"

The challenge—yes, that's what it was—left Janeway numb and uncertain. Did she have the right words?

These aliens lived on a completely different astral plane, developed under the most foreign of circumstances. Would they have a culture? A civilization? Would they look at her as an individual? She hadn't yet looked at them that way.

The cargo bay again. Now this was a place of conflict for Kathryn Janeway, a place forever stained with her encounter with Chakotay. As she came in, with Tuvok at her side, to meet the two Ankari representatives and their funny summoning device, the absence of Chakotay at her other side was a burning wound. She wanted him back. How would it look if she disobeyed her own order?

"I'm Captain Janeway," she introduced without asking their names. "This is Commander Tuvok. I'm sorry we don't have time to get to know each other. Summon the spirits, please."

Luckily, she'd remembered to throw in the "please" at the last minute. After all, despite the fact that she had an iron grip on their vessel, they were basically doing her a favor.

She glanced at Tuvok, who nodded once. The cargo bay was completely sealed off from the rest of the ship. If they died here, they would be the only ones.

"Bay shields down," Janeway ordered.

She didn't grasp her weapon, but kept her wrist pressed against it just in case. Her heart thudded in her chest. Her legs felt prickly, as if they were going numb. She recognized the feeling.

Tuvok worked a remote control for the outer shields. Almost immediately, the alien warning tone began to whine in the air. Fissures opened above. Two . . . three . . . some of them closed, but others opened, as if the spirits couldn't quite make up their minds whether they were attacking or not.

Get it over with. Kill us or talk. I've got fences to mend down here in humanland.

There was one—an alien, whipping about with its greenish tail curling and swashing. But it didn't attack. Janeway couldn't imagine what was different, unless the Ankari had primed the situation by explaining to them that this was a confab.

"They say," the Ankari captain began, "they want the humans to die."

Conveniently not human himself, Tuvok seemed to take this almost as a joke. "A difficult place to start a negotiation."

Janeway turned to the Ankari. "Will they understand me?"

The big swollen head bobbed. Probably a nod.

Stepping out into the middle of the cargo bay, where there was no chance of cover whatsoever, Janeway raised her voice. "We didn't do this to you. We're trying to stop the humans who did."

Three spirits now flashed in and out of the fissures, agitated. Funny how body language could be the same between astral planes of existence.

"They don't believe you would harm your own kind," the Ankari translated.

"We have rules of behavior," Janeway called. "The *Equinox* has broken those rules by killing your species. It's our duty to stop them."

The Ankari waited, listening to the enhanced shrieks and howls from the stirred-up spirits.

" 'Give us the *Equinox*' . . . 'Give us the *Equinox*,' " he chanted. "They insist on destroying the ones who are responsible."

Tuvok, perhaps sensing Janeway's own level of agitation, was driven to speak up. "We will punish them according to our own rules. They will be imprisoned. They will lose their freedom."

Shrieks bellowing now at a perfect level of rage, the spirits lashed about, unsatisfied. This was only serving to make them angrier. Now what? If they were mad before, they were completely insane now. Could she coax them back from that before they stepped up their level of attacks?

"All right!" she acceded. "If you stop your attacks, I'll deliver the *Equinox to you!*"

Tuvok swung into her periphery. "Captain, you would be violating countless protocols," he warned.

"To hell with protocols!" she roared. There had been enough loss already, professionally, personally, culturally. There wouldn't be any more, not another inch.

"Starfleet Command will hold you accountable," he told her sternly, ridiculous as that was.

"We're a long way from Starfleet Command," she bit off.

That sounded familiar . . .

Tuvok stopped short of grasping her arm as Chakotay might, but he did it with his voice. "Captain—"

She turned to him abruptly. "I've already confined my first officer to quarters. Would you like to join him?" When he didn't answer, she turned back to the Ankari. "Well?"

The Ankari eyed the spirits for several more seconds, listening to the whine and wail.

Finally the sound dropped away to a high-pitched buzz.

"They agree," he said.

CHAPTER

14

"WE'RE GOING TO NEED MORE FUEL. WE'VE ONLY got enough left to jump another five hundred light-years."

"Fuel . . . is that a euphemism for what we're using now? You mean we need to kill more life forms."

"Several more."

Sitting in his command chair, eaten up by the words he had just slapped Max's face with, Rudy Ransom was as hollowed out as he had ever been. This was like that first day after the first week, his mind crackling with grief and responsibility for the lost thirty-nine. The dead. His dead.

The count was starting to weigh on him again. He'd beaten it off until now. Janeway had brought it back.

She'd really pursued him, really fired on him. He hadn't thought she would.

Could she believe so much that he had committed crimes? Was he a mass murderer? She had no more reason to be sure of that than he did to be sure he wasn't. No one had communicated with those green whiplashes yet. He'd tried. He'd definitely tried.

Fired upon, by another Starfleet captain. The searing aftermath was hard to take, harder than the fight itself. He felt glued to his seat.

Burke hovered over him, waiting for orders. Poor Max expected him to give the order to summon more "fuel." The first officer's expression was less than helpful, carrying no sympathy at all, and in fact he seemed irritated that Ransom was lapsing into these inner questions.

Yes, of course. Max could see that something was happening to him. They'd always thought alike.

"Rudy, are you okay?" Burke ultimately urged.

Ransom blinked. "It's getting to me, Max."

Burke's eyes crimped. "Aw . . . don't do this. Not now. Not when we've come so far."

Pushing out of his chair, Ransom killed the conversation, just as he had killed everything else around him, including his own conscience. Burke's cold-hearted anguish drilled horridly into Ransom's soul. Look what he'd turned his innocent crew into. Innocent Max, who'd started out so charmed and idealistic about their new mission to deep space. Innocent Marla—who wouldn't hurt an alligator if it were chewing her leg off—up there with her weapons trained behind them in the direction of a fellow Starfleet captain and her ship and the laws they all stood for.

The woman on the dune . . . she was still watching him from the far side of his mind.

"I'll be in the lab," he said. He gave no order for more fuel.

When he walked into the lab four minutes later, the first thing he heard was the damned distorted *Voyager* doctor singing some asinine tune while hunched over the table.

On the table lay the limp body of the beautiful woman. Ransom's skin crawled as he came around, saw closely the exposed Borg circuitry, the brain cavity, and The Doctor's probe. As The Doctor cheerily dug into the depths of the skull, Seven's groggy voice joined him in the last line of the song, something about darlings and loss and romance and forlorn hope.

The mockery of life and music gutted Ransom as he watched the grim scene.

"How much longer?" he demanded.

Aberrantly happy with himself, The Doctor kept working. "Another hour. Maybe less."

He kept humming the ridiculous tune. On the table, Seven kept responding in a distorted mechanical harmony.

"Her auditory processor," The Doctor said proudly. "We used to practice duets together. In fact, I taught her this song."

He kept singing, and Seven kept responding every time the probe touched her circuitry.

Ransom didn't even register the words they were singing. The sound, the sight, were too horrible to digest. She wasn't singing. She was *reacting* to a probe. Mechanical, cold, dead. She was making the words, the notes, but there was no life in them. They had taken it from her, what little she had managed to keep for herself. They had taken even more from her than the Borg had. At least they had left her alive. The lives of the aliens, the life of this girl . . . after that, who else's life? Captain Janeway? Her crew?

"Enough!" he roared.

The singing stopped.

The Doctor looked up. "Why the long face, Captain? You're about to get your crew home." He noticed then that Ransom was gazing sorrowfully down at Seven, and added, "She tried to stand in your way. You had no choice."

"No choice . . ." Ransom stepped back. "Thank you, Doctor."

The two words hammered the inside of his skull.

"When all this is over," The Doctor said, "perhaps you'll allow me to teach you my repertoire. I'm going to need a new partner."

The twisting of hopes almost choked Ransom. Had he poisoned everyone on board? Even the hologram?

His quarters were cool, even a little chilly. He barely remembered walking here. He saw no corridors before him, but only the dissected skull of the beautiful girl, the latest head on his belt.

The synaptic stimulator to waited in mechanical patience on his bedstand. He picked it up.

Moments later, he stood again upon the shoreline

vista, watching the shore birds float and the reeds wave. Down and down the shoreline, ice-white sand glittered. The wet sand, the dry sand, the dune . . . There she was.

He moved toward her.

Closer . . . closer. She was coming to him now, her face obscured by blowing blond hair, like some advertisement for a travel agency.

This was no incorporated automaton, no decisionless android programmed or brainwashed.

Ransom moved to her. She pulled her hair from her face.

Beautiful . . . beautiful . . . alive.

"You," he said. "What are you doing here?"

His voice echoed strangely, again and again, over the water.

You you you you you doing here here here here

"Hiding," Seven of Nine told him, her voice no longer gravelly. "Like you."

"I'm not hiding," he protested.

A wave lashed the shoreline. Seven glanced at it, appreciating the lovely peace. "It's beautiful. I can see why this brings you comfort."

"I don't know what you're talking about," he told her.

"But it isn't real," she said, as if he hadn't spoken at all.

Ransom smirked, then got angry. "You're not real. Leave me alone."

"It's not too late to stop," she told him passively.

"I don't have a choice!"

"Find another way."

"There *is* no other way!"

"Stop trying to hide!"

"I told you!" Ransom backed off two paces. "I'm not hiding! Get away from me!"

But he couldn't move, couldn't leave, even though this was his mind, his dream.

She stood before him, her face losing its sculpted appeal. *"End this!"*

"No!" Ransom screamed.

Was he screaming in protest? Or because her face had changed now to the skull-split head of one of the spirit aliens—

He put both hands to his head, driven to madness by the corruption of the girl.

The image winked out.

Sweating, panting, rattled, he was sitting in his quarters holding the synaptic stimulator in one clammy hand. Yes, of course he was still here . . . it was only a dream. It was fake. His innards were eating themselves out.

The line was outside of his grasp. He couldn't reach it, pull back to it . . . upon his shoulders, the Starfleet uniform began to grow heavy.

"Bridge to Ransom. Rudy?"

Max's voice, calling to the captain, his leader.

Ransom sat, shaking.

"Bridge to Ransom."

He knocked his combadge, almost scraping it off his chest. "Go ahead . . ."

"You'd better get up here."

His chest heaved, even hurt. "On my way."

When he got to the bridge, his uniform was now cloying with sweat, cold sweat. Burke, Gilmore, and Thompson manned the bridge by themselves. Ransom noticed instantly that Burke was worried.

"*Voyager*'s approaching at high warp," Burke said while he worked his station, hunched in his chair over a lower monitor. "There's a class-two nebula less than a light-year from here. Janeway's sensors won't be able to track us once we're inside. I think we should—"

"No." Ransom moved stiffly to his command center. "Full stop. Open a channel."

Burke straightened. "Change of tactics?"

As first officer, he had a right to know.

Unfortunately, there would be nothing invigorating in this set of orders.

"You could say that," Ransom told him. "It's time we find another way home."

Burke came out of his chair. "Another way!"

"We're going to cooperate with Janeway. If she's willing."

Gilmore and Thompson now turned also to stare at him. He understood—he was the only one among them who had never flinched, never broken, not for a moment.

"Rudy," Burke began, "with all due respect, have you lost your mind?"

"Just the opposite."

As Burke stared in unshielded amazement, an alarm rang on Gilmore's board.

"They're within range," she reported, her voice shaking. "They're charging weapons!"

Ransom ignored Burke's glare. "Hail them."

"Belay that order!" Burke snapped. "Raise shields!"

"You're relieved of duty, Commander," Ransom said. He'd actually been ready for that. Burke probably really did think his captain was losing his grip. He was trying to help him hold on to it.

Suddenly glazed with sweat, Burke drew his phaser and pointed it at Ransom. On stun? Or something else? "I'm taking command. Anyone who isn't with me, speak up now!"

No one said anything. Obviously anguised to a breaking point, Burke grabbed Ransom's phaser. "Take him to the brig!"

Apparently Gilmore also thought the captain was cracking. For what she probably thought was for his own good, she drew her own phaser and moved toward him.

"I'm sorry," she said. *But come with me.* Ransom went.

"What's the status of our weapons?" Burke was asking.

"Full complement of torpedoes," Thompson said. "Minimal phasers."

"Open a secured channel to their sickbay. Stand by weapons."

"I'm here." That was The Doctor.

"We're going to need your help, Doctor. See if you can find *Voyager*'s current shield frequency."

"What's their range?" Burke asked.

"Eight hundred kilometers."

"Arm torpedoes. Fire!"

"Direct hit, her port shields. They're holding. They're firing on us!"

"Brace for incoming!"

The lift doors breathed open. Without even looking, Ransom stepped out, following the backs of Gilmore's legs. The ship shook under them, causing his arms to flare, and he looked up.

"This isn't the brig," he pointed out. Instead, they were in the engine room.

"I know," she said. "I'm with you, sir. Let's find a way to end this."

She lowered her phaser.

Slightly reinvigorated by that, Ransom felt his heart divide between his crew, some loyal to him, others loyal to the other him. How could he fault any of them?

It'll be all right, Max. We'll all clear our heads.

He moved to a station. "We'll need to access transporter control."

"I'll do it."

Ransom touched his combadge. "Doctor, this is the captain."

"Yes?"

"How's Seven?"

"I'm about to detach her cerebral cortex implants—"

"Don't do it. I want you to put her back the way she was. We don't need the information anymore."

"You have the data you need from her? After all my work?"

"Yes, I don't need it anymore," Ransom fibbed. "I want you to reestablish her integrity. How long will it take?"

"Well . . . a matter of minutes. She was much harder to take apart than she will be to . . ."

"I want her as good as new, right away."

"You're an interesting man, Captain."

"Do the work. I'll explain later."

He didn't wait for a confirmation. He hoped The Doctor thought Ransom still had the bridge and didn't call to check with Burke or anyone else. As the seconds ticked off, he held his breath for Seven's recovery.

"We're dropping out of warp," Gilmore said, off her monitors. "The port nacelle's venting plasma *Voyager*'s still in hot pursuit."

Ransom checked the nearest monitor. "Tap into the bridge comm. I want to eavesdrop."

She worked a panel. Almost instantly, the voices of all the familiar players began to boil through the engineering speakers.

"Doctor to Equinox! I've got their shield frequency! I'm transmitting it to you now!"

"They'll try to remodulate. Keep monitoring."

"Aye, sir!"

"Slow to one quarter impulse. Launch another torpedo."

At her station, Gilmore followed the drama. "We're launching another one . . . *Voyager*'s put full power to her forward shields. Direct hit . . . deck four. They've got a hull breach."

"Bet she's wondering how we broke through her

shields," Ransom commented. "She thinks that doctor is her doctor."

"They're moving out of range. I'm reading a remodulation of their shields. Rudy, Max is taking a pursuit course."

"Oh, Max, why . . ." Ransom's groan rattled in his throat.

"*Voyager*'s lost impulse power. There goes their weapons array . . . They're rotating their deflector frequency every few seconds, trying to get them to stay up."

"This can't go on," Ransom muttered. "Hail them from down here, Marla. Find Janeway for me."

"Go ahead. I think I've got them."

Ransom drew a cleansing breath, then leaned toward the comm. "Captain, I'm prepared to surrender the *Equinox,* but I'm no longer in command. Max decided to stage a little mutiny. I think I can stop him. I've isolated transporter control . . . I can beam all of us to *Voyager*. You might want to have some guards standing by. Not everyone here's going to be happy to see you."

Janeway was silent. Probably shocked. Why? That a man could change so suddenly?

Wasn't all that sudden.

"*Proceed,*" Janeway spoke, keeping her tone even. "*Bridge to security.*"

"Thank you for not gloating," Ransom said lightly.

"*I have no right to gloat, Captain. None at all.*"

"I know what you mean, believe it or not. Marla, wide-range transporter beam."

"Ready, sir."

"Begin with the bridge crew."

As she worked, Ransom continued to listen to the bridge activity.

"Someone's trying to beam us off! Force fields!"

Gilmore worked furiously. "They're deflecting the targeting scanners."

So much for getting the bridge crew off. The rest of the crew wouldn't be able to pull such a trick, not from the other parts of the ship.

"Then beam the others to *Voyager,*" Ransom decided. "Yourself included. I'll deal with Max."

As Gilmore did as she was told, Ransom moved to another station. "Computer, give me access to the shield grid."

It worked. The computer was still functioning under the assumption that he was in command.

"Marla," he called at the last second, "here."

He tossed her a remote computer cartridge, especially encoded.

"That's Captain Janeway's doctor, with his ethical subroutines restored. When you get to *Voyager,* tell her the doctor over there is ours. Have her upload him back into their system. Her own EMH will be able to take back his sickbay."

As the transporter beam began to hum, Marla's sad eyes embraced him. "Rudy . . ."

Typically, once his decision was made, he never gave it another thought. He waved a hand to her and offered a fatherly grin. "Go. It's all right. I'll be right over."

* * *

"The Doctor's not transmitting anymore!"

Thompson's call of panic sent a jolt of desperation through Max Burke. They had to get through this and get Rudy back here on his bridge where he belonged, without the guilt put on him by that calculating woman over there.

"Burke to Doctor! Report!"

The Doctor's voice came, but the words were all wrong. *"I'm afraid your physician's no longer on call."*

Burke felt his stomach constrict. Everything was falling apart.

"Max, this is the captain. I've just dropped the shield grid, everywhere except the bridge and my current location. Vital systems are exposed. I suggest you beam to Voyager *while you still can."*

Slamming his hands to his thighs, Burke shuddered with anger and disappointment. This was maddening. Rudy was poisoned.

Fissures!

They began opening all over the bridge!

Beneath them, the ship trembled with a violent power drain.

"The core's overloading!" Thompson called from the engineering station, over the whine of entry tones. "We've got to get out of here!"

"Where!" Burke roared. *"Voyager's* brig?"

"It's better than being vaporized!"

"We've still got a working shuttle!"

Thompson abandoned his station and whirled to face him. "The shuttle bay's two decks down!"

Burke snatched up a phaser rifle and fired into two of the opening fissures.

"Sir," Thompson fitfully began, "the aliens—"

"We'll make it!"

Everyone on the bridge now rushed for the lift, drawing phasers as they ran. Thompson, Burke noticed, joined them at the last minute. What choice did he have?

They burst out of the lift two decks down, firing freely the instant the doors opened, and continued firing freely as fissures broke before them, behind them, and at their sides.

Fight! Keep fighting! Never give up! Rudy had taught them well. If only that damned Janeway had butted out!

"That way!" he called, and angled down the port corridor, around the corner—

Screams broke behind him—human screams. He recognized the tenor and didn't turn to see his shipmates die. When the alien tone broke, he whirled and fired at the sound, collapsing two more fissures. More screams.

A gurgling gush at his left side . . . that was Thompson. Gone now.

Was anyone left?

He kept shooting, wildly now, frantically. The whole corridor was hidden now behind opening fissures. There was nothing to stop the aliens. Not even nominal, struggling shields.

When he turned to run forward again, he came face to face with his past and future. A green bony skull, fanged lips, claws out of a children's story.

He squeezed the trigger, but his phaser rifle sputtered and would not fire. Drained.

Energy coiled around him, an envelope of icy fingers, shriveling his skin instantly. He felt his bones dry up and his skin sink as he was driven to the deck. His eyes squeezed tight and there was air rushing through his skull.

Rudy . . . we made it. Look over there . . . you did it. We're home . . .

Janeway stood on her bridge, unchallenged, perhaps vindicated in the crew's minds, though not in her own. She summoned all her self-control to avoid calling Chakotay back to the bridge until this played itself out. She wanted him here, but that would send the wrong signal. She didn't like this win. It was corrupt.

"There's only one life sign left," Harry Kim sadly reported. "It's Ransom."

Only one. *I know the meaning of that.*

She worked the nearest console. "Captain?"

Rudy Ransom's calm face appeared on the screen, scored with dirt and lined with sudden age. His voice played through the starship's comm system like the narrator speaking over events playing out on a screen.

"Things didn't work out exactly as I planned. But you've got everyone worth getting."

Her chest caved in at his words—he meant everyone that could serve *Voyager.* The message was crushing. Burke. That strong, loyal young man. And Ransom himself—

"We're beaming you out of there," Janeway attempted, feeling a deep need to exercise a little charity, if a little late.

He shook his head mildly. *"No. This ship is about to explode. I've got to put some distance between us. I've accessed helm control."*

"You can set the autonavigation and then transport to *Voyager*."

"No time."

Nausea joined the crushing feeling in her gut. There was plenty of time. The screen cut out.

On the *Equinox*, Ransom took hold of a small device and put it behind his ear, then turned some kind of control on it. He spoke over the comm link. *"You've got a fine crew, Captain. Promise me you'll get them home."*

Janeway's voice barely made it over the link. "I promise."

The sound of the alien tone began to break in *Equinox*'s engine room. Fissures opening, the warp core winding up to overload . . .

On *Voyager* Janeway indulged in a silent moan. This wasn't what she had ever had in mind.

As they watched, the *Equinox* raced away from the starship, rushing in a swept arc through the cloud of some past cataclysm. It dragged interstellar matter with it for a few thousand miles, farther and farther, smaller and smaller, until it was only a point of light in the deep distance.

Booooooooommmmmm

A wash of light broke, as if a child's finger had

drawn chalkdust across a blackboard. The tail of dust turned to sparkles. Warp residue.

Ransom had, in the end, confirmed Chakotay's guess that he wasn't out for himself. Even at the last action, he was protecting his crew, if only to free them from having to follow him anymore. He had, with this single decisive action, commended his surviving crew to Janeway's command with his blessing.

I wonder how long he was ready to die.

Surrounded by her somber crew, Kathryn Janeway watched the sad repercussion of a day gone bad.

Quick and crisp. If she could write her own farewell, this would do.

"Hang on, Captain," she murmured.

No one else heard. No one else was listening.

CHAPTER
15

"THE ALIENS FROM THE FISSURES, IT SEEMS, CAPTAIN, have returned to their realm now that *Equinox* is gone. What are your orders?"

As he asked his question, Tuvok stood with Tom Paris, Harry Kim, and B'Elanna Torres at his sides, the scene looking incomplete. They were all reserved in their captain's presence. They hadn't quite forgiven her. Understandable, since she wasn't even close to forgiving herself.

"Secure from general quarters," she said, her throat dust-dry. "Put a team on the shields and get the integrity back up. Damage control should work around the clock, all watches. Make sure The Doctor's program is secure too, no lingering ghosts of the other doctor. Let's not take chances. Have him check Seven thoroughly and make sure she's back to normal. Convene a

247

meeting of the *Equinox* officers and all *Voyager* officers and department heads in the briefing room in thirty minutes. Have all other crewmen and the deckhands of the *Equinox* crew watch on monitors. Attendance is required. I want this all resolved in the next hour. It's over and I want it to feel over."

"Aye, Captain."

"The rest of you, take your posts. If anyone wants to speak to me privately, I'll be in my quarters this evening. Consider the invitation open. I'd like to hear what you think."

That alone seemed to relieve Tom Paris. His expression relaxed just to hear her invite them to tell her off. He met B'Elanna's eyes, and Janeway could tell that they were back on track. Quietly, they both moved to their posts. Harry Kim openly smiled at her as he, too, moved back to his console.

As Tuvok turned to fulfill those orders, Janeway stepped to the upper deck.

"Tuvok . . ."

He turned. "Yes?"

"Reinstate Mr. Chakotay to his post with my compliments. He can supervise the repair teams. Have the ship's log read that he acted in the best interest of the ship and crew."

"We will all be gratified, Captain. Thank you."

"Don't thank me. I don't want to be thanked."

Tuvok lowered his head once in a passive nod. "Understood."

And he really did.

* * *

"There. Good as new."

The sickbay was a reassuring place for Seven of Nine, especially as she heard The Doctor's words telling her she was whole and well again. Somehow that gave her a curious sensation in the middle of her body that did not compute in her mind.

"I'd like you to regenerate for the next few hours," The Doctor completed. "It'll help stabilize your cortical array."

"Understood." Seven stood up and allowed him to make a final adjustment to her eyepiece, but the work was done. All balance was restored. All sensations functioning.

Why, then, was The Doctor hesitating over her? He was no longer working, but only standing and looking at her in that curious searching way humans sometimes had . . . and he was not even human.

"Regarding the . . ." he paused, selecting words carefully, "unpleasantness aboard the *Equinox* . . . I hope you don't think less of me."

"Your program was altered," she told him.

Yet he still seemed troubled. Why? Nothing was his fault. His program—

"It's quite disconcerting," he went on, "to know that all somebody has to do is flick a switch to turn me into Mr. Hyde."

His face showed a burden that Seven found deeply troubling. She resisted the reaction and took instant refuge in hardware. "Perhaps you should enhance your program with security protocols," she suggested. "It will prevent such tampering in the future."

"Good thinking."

"When I'm done regenerating, I'll assist you."

"Thanks."

She went to the door, then surprised herself by pausing, much as he had a moment ago. "You were off-key."

The Doctor tilted his head. "I beg your pardon?"

"Third verse," she reminded, "second measure."

His pride flashed. "That's impossible!"

"Your vocal modulations deviated by point three zero decihertz," Seven confirmed inarguably. "I can help you with that, as well."

Was it working? Her attempt at . . . was it teasing?

"Really," The Doctor roughly said, with a tinge of challenge. "Holodeck two, tomorrow, sixteen hundred hours. Just you, and me, and a tuning fork."

Seven felt the sides of her mouth draw outward without her meaning them to.

"I look forward to it," she said.

Thirty-five minutes later, Kathryn Janeway paced uneasily before all her officers, and all the *Equinox*'s officers in the briefing room aboard the steadily improving *Voyager.* Already damages were being repaired. There was more light in the room now. Debris had been cleared away, though the carpet was still filthy and the table scratched. They were stood down from Red Alert.

A few paces away, Chakotay stood silent, though he no longer averted his eyes from her. She hoped he had seen the recording of what had happened to Ransom, that it was the other captain who made the ultimate choice to die. She didn't want him thinking any worse of her than he already did.

As the two crews settled and stopped fidgeting, Janeway surveyed the *Equinox* officers with a controlled expression. She didn't want them to think she approved of their behavior, but she also didn't want them to think she hated them or that they would be vilified here. Another thin line.

"You're all welcome aboard," she began. "I want you to know that Captain Ransom's death was at his own hand. We gave him every opportunity to beam aboard. We all wanted to save him. Whatever you may think, I respect him very much for his strength and conviction. In the end, he commended you to this ship and asked me to get you home. I have my own way of doing that. You'll have to live with it."

She paused a moment, clasped her hands behind her back, and gazed briefly at the carpet before looking up again.

"The last time we welcomed you aboard, you took advantage of our trust. You betrayed this crew. I won't make that mistake again."

As the words hung, the other crew looked nervous. Would they indeed spend thirty years in her brig?

She just wanted them to think about it for a moment.

"Noah Lessing," she began then, "Marla Gilmore, James Morrow, Angela Tassoni, Brian Sofin . . . you're hereby stripped of rank. You'll be expected to serve as crewmen on this vessel. Your privileges will be limited and you'll work under close supervision for as long as

I deem fit. This time, you'll have to earn our trust. Dismissed."

She nodded to Tuvok, who motioned the complement out of the room. As they all filed out, Janeway moved to Chakotay. The two of them stood looking at each other for as many seconds as it took to empty the room. A long silence.

The door swept closed.

"Repairs?" she asked.

He offered a nominal shrug. "Coming along."

"How's the crew?"

"A lot of frayed nerves. Neelix is organizing a potluck to help boost morale."

She managed a little smile at the idea. "Will I see you there?"

"I'm replicating the salad."

"I'll bring the croutons."

The clouds broke when he smiled at her. What a relief!

As she led the way out onto the bridge, where they both had plenty of work to do, Janeway felt her shoulder muscles suddenly break too. He was walking beside her now, close enough to make a difference.

The bridge around them was a cluttered mess, but more lights came on as they stepped down through a sprinkle of debris to the command deck.

"You know," she said, "you may have had a good reason to stage a little mutiny of your own."

He gazed at her, wondering if she meant he might have been justified to do it.

"The thought occurred to me," he said, "but that would've been crossing the line."

The chord of understanding rang and rang. He made a small gesture—toward the command chair. Inviting her back into his sphere of trust? She really wanted to be there.

As she turned toward the chair, a glint of metal caught her attention, beneath the shavings and dust. She bent down, and retrieved the ship's commission plaque.

U.S.S. VOYAGER
UNITED FEDERATION OF PLANETS
Starfleet Registry NCC-74656
Intrepid Class
Kathryn Janeway, Master and Commander

With the side of her hand, she scraped dust from the brushed metal plaque.

"All these years . . . all these battles," she murmured. "This thing's never fallen down before."

Chakotay came to her side again, and they both thought of the man who had driven them apart and who had sacrificed himself so they might come together again. "Let's put it back up where it belongs."

Janeway stood up and looked at him warmly. He'd said "let's." They did it together.

When the plague was back in place, hanging on a dirty bulkhead as proudly as ever, they retreated to the command center. Chakotay seemed content, if reserved, and started to leave to pursue his many duties.

"Wait." As his foot touched the bridge step, Janeway reached out with one hand and grasped his wrist, both to hold him here and also to provide a bond they both very much needed. With the other hand, she tapped her chair controls and began to record a message.

"Captain's log, *U.S.S. Voyager,* Stardate 53105.2. Captain Kathryn Janeway recording. We have incorporated the *Equinox* survivors into our crew. This log entry is an official tribute to Captain Rudolph Ransom, commander of the Starfleet Science Vessel *Equinox,* and to his officers and crew who did not survive their voyage. Captain Ransom and his ship's entire complement faced difficult decisions in the Delta Quadrant, but throughout their ordeal they comported themselves with courage and determination. Let the record read, hereafter, that they died in the line of duty. Captain Janeway . . . out."

Look for STAR TREK Fiction from Pocket Books

Star Trek®: The Original Series

Star Trek: The Next Generation®

Star Trek: Deep Space Nine®

Star Trek®: Voyager™

Flashback • Diane Carey
The Black Shore • Greg Cox
Mosaic • Jeri Taylor
Pathways • Jeri Taylor

#1 *Caretaker* • L. A. Graf
#2 *The Escape* • Dean W. Smith & Kristine K. Rusch
#3 *Ragnarok* • Nathan Archer
#4 *Violations* • Susan Wright
#5 *Incident at Arbuk* • John Gregory Betancourt
#6 *The Murdered Sun* • Christie Golden
#7 *Ghost of a Chance* • Mark A. Garland & Charles G.
     McGraw
#8 *Cybersong* • S. N. Lewitt
#9 *Invasion #4: The Final Fury* • Daffyd ab Hugh
#10 *Bless the Beasts* • Karen Haber
#11 *The Garden* • Melissa Scott
#12 *Chrysalis* • David Niall Wilson
#13 *The Black Shore* • Greg Cox
#14 *Marooned* • Christie Golden
#15 *Echoes* • Dean W. Smith & Kristine K. Rusch
#16 *Seven of Nine* • Christie Golden
#17 *Death of a Neutron Star* • Eric Kotani
#18 *Battle Lines* • Dave Galanter & Greg Brodeur

Star Trek®: New Frontier

#1 *House of Cards* • Peter David
#2 *Into the Void* • Peter David
#3 *The Two-Front War* • Peter David
#4 *End Game* • Peter David
#5 *Martyr* • Peter David
#6 *Fire on High* • Peter David

Star Trek®: Day of Honor

Book One: *Ancient Blood* • Diane Carey
Book Two: *Armageddon Sky* • L. A. Graf
Book Three: *Her Klingon Soul* • Michael Jan Friedman
Book Four: *Treaty's Law* • Dean W. Smith & Kristine K. Rusch
The Television Episode • Michael Jan Friedman

Star Trek®: The Captain's Table

Book One: *War Dragons* • L. A. Graf
Book Two: *Dujonian's Hoard* • Michael Jan Friedman
Book Three: *The Mist* • Dean W. Smith & Kristine K. Rusch
Book Four: *Fire Ship* • Diane Carey
Book Five: *Once Burned* • Peter David
Book Six: *Where Sea Meets Sky* • Jerry Oltion

Star Trek®: The Dominion War

Book 1: *Behind Enemy Lines* • John Vornholt
Book 2: *Call to Arms . . .* • Diane Carey
Book 3: *Tunnel Through the Stars* • John Vornholt
Book 4: *. . . Sacrifice of Angels* • Diane Carey

1252.01

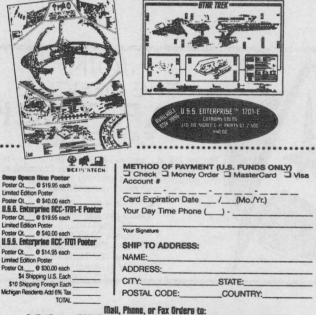

OUR FIRST SERIAL NOVEL!

Presenting, one chapter per month . . .

The very beginning of the Starfleet Adventure . . .

STAR TREK
STARFLEET: YEAR ONE

A Novel in Twelve Parts

by
Michael Jan Friedman

Chapter Three

Chapter Three

President Lydia Littlejohn sat on her window sill and watched the sun melt into the mists over San Francisco Bay. She rubbed her tired eyes. Littlejohn had always believed that if Earth could win her war with the Romulans, everything after that would come easy.

As it turned out, she had been wrong.

"They should have responded by now," said Admiral Walker, a bushy-browed lion of a man in his early sixties. As usual, he was pacing the length of the president's office. "The bastards are having second thoughts."

Clarisse Dumont, a diminutive, pinch-faced woman a bit older than the admiral, shook her head. "As usual, you're jumping to conclusions. If you knew the Romulans better," she said, brushing lint off the sleeve of her woolen sweater, "you would understand they're just taking their time. They *like* to take their time."

Walker shot her an incredulous look. "*I* don't know the Romulans?" he harrumphed. "I've only been directing our forces against them for the last four and a half years."

"As I've pointed out several times before," Dumont told him with undisguised contempt, "fighting the Romulans and *knowing* the Romulans are two vastly different things."

"And how would you know that," asked the admiral, "considering you've never knocked heads with them? Never traded laser shots? Hell, you've never even seen one of their birdships."

"I've never seen a quark either," the woman countered sharply, "but I have no doubt that it exists."

Walker grunted. "You don't have to remind me about your credentials, Ms. Dumont. But a Nobel Prize in particle physics doesn't make you an expert on alien behavior."

"That's true," said Littlejohn, interceding in her colleagues' discussion for perhaps the tenth time in the last few hours. "But in addition to being one of Earth's foremost scientists, Admiral, Clarisse is also one of our foremost linguists. And without her help, we would never have gotten this far in our negotiations."

Walker's nostrils flared. "I don't dispute the value of her contribution, Madame President. I just don't see why she feels compelled to dispute the value of *mine*."

Littlejohn sighed. "We're all on edge, Ed. We haven't slept much in the last two days and we're afraid that if we say the wrong thing, these talks are going to fall apart. So if Clarisse seems a little cranky, I think we can find it in our heart to forgive her."

Dumont shot a look at her. "Cranky, Madame President? Why, I've never been cranky in my entire—"

"President Littlejohn?" said a voice.

Littlejohn recognized it as that of Stuckey, one of the communications specialists who had been coordinating their dialogue with the Romulans from an office lower in the building. The president licked her lips. "Have we received a response?" she asked hopefully.

"We have indeed," said Stuckey. "Shall I put it through, ma'am?"

"By all means," the president told him.

A moment later, her office was filled with the fluid, strangely melodious voice of a high-ranking Romulan official—not the individual actually in charge of Romulan society, but someone empowered to speak for him.

Littlejohn was able to recognize a word of the alien's speech here or there. After all, they had been negotiating the same items for days. But for the most part, it was gibberish to her.

The message went on for what seemed like a long time— longer than usual, certainly. Also, she thought, the words were expressed in an emotional context she didn't believe she had heard before. It sounded more contentious to her, more belligerent.

Oh no, the president told herself. Not another step backward. Not when it seemed as if we were getting somewhere.

Then the message was over. Dumont plunked herself down in a chair and massaged the bridge of her bony nose.

"What did they say?" the admiral demanded. "For the love of sanity, woman, don't leave us hanging here!"

Dumont looked up at him. Then she turned to Littlejohn.

"What they said," she began, "was they accept our terms. The neutral zone, the termination of their claim to the Algeron system . . . the whole ball of wax."

The president didn't believe it. "If they were going to give in across the board, why didn't they concede anything before this? Why did they seem so bloody uncooperative?"

The older woman smiled knowingly. "As I said," she explained, "the Romulans like to take their time."

Commander Bryce Shumar stood outside the turbolift doors and surveyed his base's operations center.

The place looked a lot better than it had a couple of weeks earlier. Shumar and his staff had patched up the various systems and corresponding consoles and brought them back on line. Even the weapons launchers were working again, though he didn't expect to have to use them.

Not with the war over . . .

Of course, the commander reflected, it had been easier to repair their machines than their people. He had lost eight good men and women to the Romulans, and four more of his officers might never be the same.

But they had won the war. They had beaten back the alien aggressor.

Shumar understood now where the *Nimitz* had been while his base was under attack. The ship, like half a dozen others, had quickly and secretly been moved up to the front—all so the enemy wouldn't notice that a flight wing had slipped away and made the jump into Romulan space.

The commander couldn't help applauding what that wing had accomplished. But at the same time, he resented having been left so vulnerable. He resented the deaths of the eight people who had given their lives for him.

"Sir?" said Kelly, who was again ensconced at her security console.

He glanced at her. "Yes?"

"Commander Applegate has beamed aboard and is on his way up," the security officer reported.

Shumar nodded. "Thanks."

He would have met the man in the transporter room, but Applegate insisted that they rendezvous at Ops. Apparently, the new base commander got a little queasy when he transported.

Abruptly, Shumar heard the lift beep and saw its doors slide open. A tall, fair-haired fellow in an Earth Command uniform stepped out of the compartment and nodded to him.

"Good to meet you in person," Applegate said, extending his hand.

Shumar shook it. "Same here." He indicated Ops with a gesture. "As you can see, we cleaned up the place for you."

Applegate nodded appraisingly. "If not for the burn marks," he observed, "one would never be able to tell that this facility was the focus of a pitched space battle."

Shumar winced. People who used the pronoun "one" had always bothered him. However, he wouldn't have to get along with Applegate for more than a half hour or so. That was when the *Manticore* was scheduled to leave . . . with the *former* commander of Earth Base Fourteen securely aboard.

"Well," said the new man, "I shouldn't have too much trouble here." He smiled thinly. "Running a peacetime base shouldn't be nearly as difficult as running it during wartime."

"For your sake," Shumar told him, "I hope that's true."

"Well," said Applegate, "you probably have a few things to take care of before you go. Don't let me keep you."

Shumar nodded, though he had already packed and said his good-byes. "Thanks. I'll check in with you before I take off . . . to see if you have any last-minute questions, that sort of thing."

"Outstanding," responded his successor.

The commander winced again. He didn't care much for people who used the word "outstanding" either.

Making his way to Kelly, he leaned over and pretended to check her monitors. "He's not half as bad in person as he was onscreen."

"You're lying," she replied. "I know you."

"You'll be all right," Shumar assured her.

"I won't," she insisted. She looked at him. "Promise me something."

He shrugged. "What?"

"That when you get your hands on another ship, you'll take me along."

The commander chuckled softly. "What would I do with a security officer on a research vessel?"

Kelly scowled at him. "I can do a lot more than run a security console and you know it. In fact, I was third in my high school class in biogenetics. So what do you say?"

Shumar sighed. "It doesn't pay very well."

"Neither does Earth Command, in case you haven't noticed." She glanced at Applegate. "Tell you what, I'll work for free. Just promise me."

"You would do better to hook up with Captain Cobaryn," he said. "Mapping expeditions can be a lot more exciting."

Kelly rolled her eyes. "Let's make a deal. You won't mention Captain Cobaryn and I won't mention Captain Dane."

The commander's stomach churned at the mere mention of the man's name. In his opinion, the galaxy wouldn't have lost anything if Dane had perished in the battle for the base.

"I agree," he said.

"Now promise," Kelly told him. "Say you'll take me with you first chance you get."

Shumar nodded. "All right. I promise."

"Thanks," said the security officer. "Now get out of here. Some of us still have work to do."

He smiled. "Take care, Kelly."

Patting her on the shoulder, he started for the turbolift. But he wasn't halfway there before he heard Ibañez calling him back.

"Commander?" said the communications officer.

"Yes?" responded Applegate, who had wandered in among the consoles.

Shumar looked at him and their eyes met. Then, as one, they turned to Ibañez for clarification.

"Sorry," the comm officer told Applegate. "I meant Commander Shumar."

The blond man smiled politely. "Of course." And he resumed his tour of the operations center.

Shumar made his way over to Ibañez. "What is it?" he asked.

"Commander," the man told him, "there's a subspace message from Earth. It looks like you've got new orders."

The commander felt his brow furrow. "That's not possible. My resignation was approved. After today, I'm no longer in the service."

Ibañez shrugged helplessly. "There's no mistake, sir. You're to report to the president's office."

Shumar looked at him. "The president . . . of *Earth?*"

"That's right," said the comm officer. He pointed to his

screen. "When you get there, you're to meet with someone named Clarisse Dumont. Unfortunately, this doesn't say what she wants with you."

The commander grunted. He knew Clarisse Dumont. For a short while, they had served on the same university faculty. Of course, that was before she had won the Nobel Prize for particle physics.

But what did she have to do with Earth Command? And why was she summoning him to the president's office, of all places?

"Do me a favor," Ibañez told him. "The suspense is killing me. When you get to Earth and you meet with this woman, give us a call and let us know what it's all about?"

Shumar nodded. "I'll do that," he said numbly, making another promise he wasn't sure he could keep.

Ambassador Doreen Barstowe shaded her eyes.

To the east, under a thin, ocher-colored sky that ran to a dark, mountainous horizon, a cleverly designed configuration of variously colored shrubs moved restlessly with the wind. With its twists and turns and sheer variety, it was the most impressive example of a Vulcan maze garden that the ambassador had ever seen.

Barstowe turned back to the thin, elderly Vulcan who had shown her to this part of Sammak's estate, and stood with her now on the landing behind his house. "Are you certain he's out there?" she wondered.

The attendant, who had identified himself as Sonadh, regarded the woman as if he had better things to do than escort an alien around his master's grounds.

"Sammak told me that he would be working in his garden," Sonadh assured her. "As for certainty . . . it is said that such a state can only be achieved through investigation." He lifted his wrinkled chin. "Would you like me to conduct one for you?"

Barstowe smiled at the hint of sarcasm in the suggestion. "No. Thank you anyway. I'll take a look around myself, if that's all right."

"It is indeed," the Vulcan told her. Then he turned and walked back into the embrace of his master's domicile, a sprawling, white structure whose size alone was evidence of Sammak's prominence.

The ambassador gazed out at the profusion of color again. If

Sammak was out there, she told herself, she would find him soon enough—and no doubt derive pleasure from the finding. She descended several white stone steps to the level of the ground and began her search at the only place possible—the maze's remarkably unobtrusive entrance.

The shrubs that bordered the initial passageway were a majestic golden orange, Barstowe found, lighter than the sky above them. But soon they gave way to an ethereal silver, a sprightly green, and a soft, pale yellow. It was immediately after that, in a corridor of deep, startling crimson, that she caught sight of a humanoid figure in white garb.

Sammak, she thought. No question about it. She could tell by the curling gray of his hair. The Vulcan was kneeling, pruning back a branch that had grown out too far.

He didn't turn to acknowledge his guest. Instead, he spoke a single word of recognition: "Ambassador."

Barstowe responded with the same economy. "Sammak."

Finally, he glanced at her. "I trust you are in good health."

"I am," she told him. "And you?"

"I have no complaints," the Vulcan responded.

The human touched the crimson shrubbery, which was made up of slim, pointed leaves. "I don't recall seeing this color the last time I was out here," she said. "Is it a seasonal effect?"

Sammak looked pleased. "It is," he confirmed. "In the colder months, these tuula leaves turn pink with small brown spots." He assessed them for a moment, brushing the underside of one with his forefinger. "But I have come to prefer them this way."

"So do I," Barstowe told him.

The Vulcan regarded her. "It has been a long time since last we saw each other. More than three years."

"Travel has been limited," the ambassador noted. "None of us in the diplomatic corps get around as much as we would like."

Sammak's brow creased ever so slightly. "But I do not imagine you have come to Vulcan simply to compliment me on my tuula bushes."

Barstowe smiled. "That's true. In fact, I came to give you some news. It seems the Romulans are suing for peace."

Sammak was known to be a great believer in the teachings of Surak, an individual who prided himself on his ability to master his emotions. Yet even he couldn't conceal a look of surprise . . . and approval as well, she thought.

"Peace," said the Vulcan, savoring the word.

"That's right. The Romulans were staggered by their defeat at Cheron," the ambassador explained. "If the war goes on much longer, their homeworlds will be threatened."

Sammak looked at her. "Poetic justice?"

Barstowe shrugged. "One might say that."

A few years earlier, the Romulans had pushed their offensive all the way into Earth's solar system. If not for the courage and determination of Earth's forces, the war might have ended then and there.

For a moment, the Vulcan seemed to mull over the information she had given him. "I am pleased, of course," he said at last. "As you know, Ambassador, I spoke against my world's decision to remain neutral in the conflict."

Barstowe nodded. "I recall your speech. It was quite stirring."

Sammak grunted. "For all the good it did. Clearly, neutrality was an illogical stance. If the Romulans had succeeded against Earth, they would have come after Vulcan in time as well."

"We of Earth always believed so," said the ambassador. "Together, my people and yours might have pushed the Romulans back in three years instead of five or six. And if we could have secured the aid of some of the other neutral worlds, it might only have been a matter of months."

The Vulcan sighed. "It is useless to engage in conjecture. The past is the past. Surak taught us to look to the future."

Barstowe saw her chance. She took it.

"I'm glad you hold that conviction," she told Sammak. "You see, my superiors have a revolutionary idea—one that can radically change the face of this quadrant for the better."

The Vulcan returned his attention to her, his dark eyes narrowing. "And the nature of this idea . . .?"

The human met his gaze. "I'm talking about a union of worlds," she said. "A federation designed to offer its members mutual protection against aggressor species like the Romulans . . . and maybe even facilitate an exchange of ideas into the bargain."

Sammak took some time to ponder the notion. "A federation," he repeated. He shrugged. "It is, as you say, a revolutionary concept."

"But one whose time has come," said Barstowe. "As we speak, similar conversations are taking place between Earth's ambassadors and people of vision on a dozen worlds from Sol to

Rigel—worlds like Andor, Dopterius, Arbaza, Dedderai, and Vobilin."

The Vulcan cocked an eyebrow. "I am impressed."

Barstowe smiled again. "That's a start. But what I really want—what I *need*—is your support, my friend. You see, I would like very much to present this idea to T'pau . . . and I'm sure my arguments would be more persuasive if I didn't have to present them alone."

Sammak considered the proposition for a moment. Then he nodded. "I will accompany you to T'pau's court, Ambassador. And as you suggest, we will plead your case together."

The human inclined her head. "Thank you, my friend."

Her host shook his head. "No, Ambassador. For giving me an opportunity to improve my people's lot, it is I who should thank you."

"Have it your way," Barstowe told him. "Who am I to argue with someone as eloquent as Sammak of Vulcan?"

When Admiral Walker entered the room, forty-six faces turned in his direction and forty-six hands came up to salute him.

He knew every one of them by name. Redfern, Hagedorn, McTigue, Santorini . . . Beschta, Barrios, Jones, Woo . . .

"At ease," the admiral said, advancing with echoing footfalls to the exact center of the soaring gold and black conference facility.

Earth Command's surviving captains relaxed, but not much. After all, they were men and women who had learned to thrive on discipline. That was why they were still alive when so many of their comrades were dead.

All around Walker, curved observation ports conformed to the shape of Command Base's titanium-reinforced outer hull, each one displaying bits and pieces of the visible galaxy. Only a couple of weeks ago, Earth's forces had seen the enemy abandon the last of the closer pieces.

As for those that were farther away . . . well, the admiral thought, that was the subject of this blasted meeting, now wasn't it?

"I know you've all got people you want to see and no one deserves to see them more than you do," he told the assemblage, his voice bounding from bulkhead to bulkhead. "With that in mind, I'll try to make this brief."

Forty-six pairs of eyes attended him, waiting for him to begin. Walker took a breath and did what his duty demanded of him.

"I have just come from a meeting with President Littlejohn—a very important meeting, I might add." The admiral scanned his officers' faces. "She tells me there's a change on the horizon—one that may keep us from being caught with our pants down the next time an invader comes knocking."

The prospect met with nods and grunts of approval. No surprise there, Walker mused. These were the men and women who had borne the brunt of Earth's miserable lack of readiness for five long, hard war years. No one could be happier to see some improvements made.

That is, if they were the *right* improvements.

"This change," he told them, "is manifesting itself as something called The United Federation of Planets. It's an organization that's going to include Earth and her allies. So far, we've got eight official takers. Several more are expected to follow over the course of the next few weeks."

The captains exchanged glances. They seemed impressed but also a little skeptical. The admiral didn't blame them. Nothing of this magnitude had ever been seriously contemplated.

"And that's not all," he said. "This Federation will enjoy the services of something tentatively called a 'star fleet'—an entity that draws on the resources of not just Earth, but all member worlds."

"You mean we'll be flying alongside Tellarites?" asked Stiles.

"And Dopterians?" added Beschta, obviously finding the notion a little difficult to swallow.

"Right now," Walker declared, cutting through the buzz, "the plan is for all fleet vessels to include mixed crews. In other words, we'll be working shoulder to shoulder with all Federation species."

The officers' skepticism seemed to increase. Hagedorn raised his hand and the admiral pointed to him. "Yes, Captain?"

"These fleet vessels, sir . . . where will they come from?"

"A good question," said Walker. "For the time being, we'll be pressing our Christophers into service. However, I expect we'll start building a new breed of ships before too long."

Hagedorn nodded thoughtfully. "And will our crews simply

be expanded, sir? Or will we be losing some of our human crewmen to make room for the aliens who'll be joining us?"

The admiral cleared his throat. "Actually," he told his officers with unconcealed distaste, "it hasn't been decided yet who will be asked to command these vessels."

The skepticism he had seen in his audience escalated into outright disbelief. But then, Walker himself hadn't believed it when the president apprised him of the situation.

"Sir," Beschta rumbled, "this is an outrage! We are the only ones with experience in such matters. How can an alien be expected to come out of nowhere and take command of a military vessel?"

The admiral scowled. This was the part of his presidential briefing that he had liked the least. "I truly regret having to impart this information," he told the men and women standing around him, "but there's some opposition to the idea of a purely military-style fleet . . ."

Bryce Shumar gazed at the small, wrinkled woman standing on the other side of the briefing room. "A star fleet," he repeated.

"That's right," said Clarisse Dumont. "An entity that will draw on the talents of each and every Federation member world . . . and eventually, over a period of several years, replace Earth Command and every other indigenous military organization."

"That's very interesting," the commander told her. And it was, of course—especially the notion of a united federation of worlds. "But what has it got to do with me?"

Dumont frowned, accentuating the lines in her face. "There's a lot about this star fleet that's not settled yet, Mr. Shumar . . . a lot of contention over what kind of fleet it's going to be."

The commander folded his arms across his chest, his interest piqued. "What kind of contention?"

The woman shrugged. "If people like Admiral Ed Walker have their way, the fleet will be a strictly military organization, dedicated to patrolling our part of the galaxy and defending member planets against real or perceived aggression. But to my mind, that would be a waste of an unprecedented scientific opportunity."

Her eyes lit up. "Think of it, Mr. Shumar. Think of the possibilities with regard to research and exploration. We could seek out undiscovered life-forms, unearth previously unknown civilizations. We could go where no Earthman has ever gone before."

It was unprecedented, all right. "I'm listening."

"If we're going to make that point," Dumont told him, "if we're going to establish the vision of a research fleet as something worth pursuing, we're going to need scientists in the center seats of our vessels. Scientists like you, Mr. Shumar."

He looked at her. "You're asking me to apply for a captaincy? After I spent years on a remote Earth base, watching out for Romulans and longing for the day I could return to my work?"

"I'm sure your work is important," the woman conceded. "But this is more important. This may be the most important thing you ever do."

Shumar wished he could tell her she was crazy. But he couldn't. He saw the same possibilities she did, heaven help him.

Dumont fixed him on the spit of her gaze. "Will you do it? Will you help me mold the future?"

He frowned, hating the idea of putting off his research yet again. But, really, what choice did he have?

"Yes," said Shumar. "I'll do it."

Dumont nodded. "Good. And keep in mind, you'll be receiving the support of some of the most powerful people on Earth—men and women who see this opportunity the same way we do. With even a little luck, we'll turn this star fleet into the kind of organization we can all be proud of."

Shumar figured that it was worth the sacrifice. He just wished it were someone else who had been called on to make it.

Hiro Matsura stared out a curved observation port and longed to get back among the stars.

The last two days on Command Base had been increasingly tedious for him—and he wasn't the only one who felt that way. The other Christopher captains were antsy as well. He could tell by the way they stood, the way they ate, the way they talked. They wanted out of this place.

"Touch of cabin fever?" asked a feminine voice.

Matsura turned and saw Amanda McTigue joining him at the observation port. "More than a touch," he admitted.

McTigue grunted, frowning a bit beneath her crown of plaited blond hair. "We'll be out of here before you know it," she told him. "That is, most of us. The ones they end up picking for this new fleet of theirs . . . who knows what'll happen to *them*."

"Yeah," said Matsura. "Who knows."

He knew there wasn't a chance in hell that he had been selected by the Fleet Commission. After all, he'd heard there were only six spots open, and three of them had reportedly been earmarked for non-military personnel.

Hagedorn was dead certain to get one spot, and Stiles and Beschta were the front runners for the other two. There were a couple of space jockeys deserving of the honor in Eagle and Viper squadrons as well, but Matsura's money was on his wing-mates.

After all, they were the best. They had proven that over and over again. And Hagedorn, Stiles, and Beschta were the best of the best.

Suddenly, the door slid open and Admiral Walker entered the room. Matsura and McTigue everyone else in the room faced Walker and straightened, their hands at their sides. As always, Beschta thrust his rounded, stubbly chin out with an air of invincibility.

"Good morning, Admiral," said a dozen captains at once, their voices echoing in the chamber.

"Morning," Walker replied flatly, as if the word left a sour taste in his mouth. "At ease, people."

As Matsura relaxed, he noticed that the admiral didn't look happy. But then, when had Big Ed Walker *ever* looked happy?

"I've received a list of the Star Fleet Commission's selections," the admiral announced. He took in everyone present with a glance. "As I expected, three of you have been chosen to command vessels."

Here it comes, Matsura thought. He turned to Beschta, Hagedorn and Stiles, who were standing together in the front rank of the group, and prepared to congratulate them on their appointments.

Walker turned to Hagedorn. "Congratulations, Captain. You've been appointed a captain in Star Fleet."

Matsura's wing leader nodded, expressionless as always. He seemed to accept the assignment like any other.

"Sir," was his only response.

Next, the admiral turned his gaze on Stiles. "Congratulations," he remarked. "You've been selected as well."

Stiles' smile said he had only gotten what he deserved. "Thank you, sir," he told Admiral Walker.

"You're quite welcome," the admiral replied.

Beschta, Matsura thought, rooting silently for his friend and mentor. *Say the word. Beschta.*

For a moment, Walker's gaze fell on the big man and Matsura believed he had gotten his wish. Then the admiral turned away from Beschta and searched the crowd for someone else.

Damn, thought Matsura. It's not fair.

He was still thinking that when Walker's gaze fell on him— and stayed there. "Congratulations," said the admiral, staring at the young man across what seemed like an impossible distance. "You're our third and final representative. Do us proud, Captain."

Matsura felt his heart start to pound against his ribs. Had he heard Walker right? No . . . it was impossible, he told himself.

"Me, sir?" he blurted.

The admiral nodded, his blue eyes piercingly sharp beneath his bushy, white brows. "That's right, Captain Matsura. *You.*"

Matsura tried to absorb the implications of what he had just heard. "I . . . I don't . . . I mean, thank you, sir."

"Don't mention it," said the admiral.

The other captains in the room looked at one another, confused and maybe even a little angry. No doubt, they were asking themselves the same question Matsura was: why *him?* Why, out of all of the brave men and women standing in that room, had Hiro Matsura been tapped for the Federation's new fleet?

Out of the corner of his eye, he saw Beschta's reaction. The big man looked embarrassed, as if he had suddenly realized he had come to the meeting without his pants. Then he turned to Matsura.

His expression didn't change. But without warning, he brought his hands together with explosive results. The report echoed throughout the chamber. Then Beschta did it a second time. And a third.

By then, some of the other captains had joined in. With each successive clap, their number grew, encompassing the disappointed as well as the admiring. Before long, everyone but Admiral Walker was applauding, making a thunderous sound that Matsura could feel as well as hear.

The admiral nodded approvingly. Then, as the noise began to

die down, he said, "Dismissed." And with that, he turned and left the chamber.

Matsura was dazed. He couldn't bring himself to believe what had happened. However, the sadness in Beschta's eyes told him it was true.

The younger man made his way through the crowd until he stood in front of his hulking mentor. For a moment, neither of them spoke. Then Beschta shrugged his massive shoulders.

"It's no big deal," he growled. But the bitterness in his voice belied his dismissal of the matter.

Matsura shook his head. "It isn't right," he said.

Anger flared in Beschta's eyes. "It doesn't have to be right. It is what it is. Make the most of it, Hiro—or I'll be the first to tear you out of the center seat and pound you into the deck. You hear me?"

Matsura could see the pain through the big man's act. "It should have been you," he insisted.

Beschta lowered his face closer to his protege's. "Don't ever let me hear you say that again," he grated. *"Ever."*

The younger man swallowed, afraid of what his friend might do. "Okay," he conceded. Suddenly, an idea came to him. "Why don't you sign on with me as my exec? That way, I know I'll come back in one piece."

The big man's eyes narrowed in thought for a moment. Then he waved away the idea. "I've got better things to do than be your first officer," he rumbled proudly. "There's still an Earth Command, isn't there? There are still ships that need flying?"

"Of course," Matsura assured him.

"Then that's what I'll do," said Beschta. He managed a lopsided smile. "If your fancy Star Fleet gives you a day off sometime, come look for me. I'll be the one flying circles around all the others."

Matsura grinned. "I'll do that," he answered.

But he knew as well as the big man did that Earth Command wouldn't be what it had been in the past. After all, there weren't any more Romulans for them to fight. And whenever a threat reared its head, Star Fleet would be the first wave of defense against it.

Beschta nodded his big, jowly face. "Good. And as the admiral told you . . . make us proud."

Matsura sighed. "I'll do that, too," he said.